MW00940330

SARAH'S
Love

WILLIAM B. STOCK

outskirts
press

Sarah's Love
All Rights Reserved.
Copyright © 2022 William B. Stock
v3.0

This is a work of fiction. Names, characters, businesses, places, events, lo-
cales, and incidents are either the products of the author's imagination or used
in a fictitious manner. Any resemblance to actual persons, living or dead, or
actual events is purely coincidental.

The opinions expressed in this manuscript are solely the opinions of the author
and do not represent the opinions or thoughts of the publisher. The author has
represented and warranted full ownership and/or legal right to publish all the
materials in this book.

This book may not be reproduced, transmitted, or stored in whole or in part by
any means, including graphic, electronic, or mechanical without the express
written consent of the publisher except in the case of brief quotations embodied
in critical articles and reviews.

Outskirts Press, Inc.
http://www.outskirtspress.com

Paperback ISBN: 978-1-9772-4552-6

Cover Photo © 2022 www.gettyimages.com. All rights reserved - used with
permission.

Outskirts Press and the "OP" logo are trademarks belonging to Outskirts
Press, Inc.

PRINTED IN THE UNITED STATES OF AMERICA

Dedicated to my father, Julius Stock,
who gave me my love of words.

CHAPTER I

Harry Goldsmith and Napoleon had a great deal in common. Napoleon was an outsider, a Corsican of humble origins, who came to rule France. Harry rose from a working-class family in Brooklyn to become a commanding force in Manhattan's legal world. Both men were of modest stature, and they compensated for it with military bearing and uniforms, but Harry's uniforms were dark three-piece suits with gold watch chains and spectacles. His close-cropped, curly white hair and practiced gaze with his cold blue eyes heightened the impression of a man in complete control of himself.

But when Sarah Mendes resigned from Goldsmith & Hammer, on a snowy night in late January, Harry's facade crumpled. He was struck dumb, and Sarah's veneer of the all-competent super-woman also fell by the wayside. She resigned while fighting back tears.

Harry was the first to regain his composure. That was why his name was on the door. He handed Sarah a box of tissues from his desk, placed a yellow legal pad in front of himself and uncapped his Mont Blanc fountain pen with the gold tip. "Let's do this properly," he began. "When are you leaving?"

"February 28th. I might be able to stay a bit longer if you really need me, but not much. I'll see that all my files are in order before I go, and I'll brief whomever you assign to take them over."

Harry made a note. "Are you going to be taking any business with you?"

She repressed a sigh. "No, I'm not taking any business with me. I'm not going to be practicing law any more."

"You, not practicing law? I don't believe it." Harry lowered his pen. "Okay. Let's get to the point. Why are you leaving? If it's for more money, we'll beat any offer."

"No, no, it's not for more money. Dear God, you pay me a fortune." She was making nearly a million dollars a year.

"Then why?" He said this softly, putting down his pen and holding his open hands out to her.

Were her eyes tearing up? "It's my marriage. The time I spend at work is taking me away from Allen. We're turning into strangers. I've got to adopt a different life-style that will give us time together."

Harry capped his pen with a sharp snap. "I could

use a drink, Sarah. How about you?" Sarah nodded, and Harry headed to a small bar in an alcove at the back of his office. He had to find some reason to step away from her in order to control his temper.

I should have known Allen was making her do this, Harry thought. Her husband was a loser; he had worked only four months at Goldsmith & Hammer and wouldn't have lasted even half that long if Sarah hadn't made excuses for him time and again. That Sarah married Allen after he had left the firm 'for mutually amicable reasons' (as everyone agreed to politely call it) only made him even more contemptible in Harry's eyes: Allen was a failure who had adhered himself to success like a leech onto the body of a healthy, Olympic swimmer.

Sarah seldom mentioned Allen after he left the firm, but Harry heard second-hand reports that he drifted from job to job, never lasting more than a short time anywhere. When last heard of, Allen was making a few dollars a day filing papers for attorneys and answering calendar calls for them in court. He also took long walks in Central Park and went to movie matinees while his wife worked.

Harry came back into his office holding a brandy snifter in each hand. His face had a look of studied neutrality. "And what is this new lifestyle you have in mind?"

Sarah sipped her brandy and slowly began to regain her composure. "When Allen and I were on our honeymoon, we went to Zueno, that's a little island off the south coast of Puerto Rico."

"I remember," Harry reflected. "You had quite a good time there as I recall. You went back there a little while ago to think things over."

Holding back another sob, Sarah nodded. "We stayed at a little hotel called the El Dorado. It's a converted Victorian house with a beach and a dock. It was up for sale, and I bought it. We signed the papers over the Thanksgiving weekend."

Harry touched his palms together and put his fingertips to his mouth. "Sarah, I do have some comments to make, but first I want to know that you are more in control. Compose yourself. Please take as much time as you need. I'm stepping out of the office to make a few calls, but I'll be back in about five minutes."

The minutes passed, and, when Harry returned, Sarah was calm. She slowly turned the large antique globe in the corner of Harry's office, her eyes glazed. "Yes, it's a big world," Harry said. "Do you really think you'd be happy in such a small part of it?"

"I believe so," Sarah replied.

"Well, Sarah, now that I've collected my thoughts, please be seated. I won't be long."

When Sarah was new to the firm, Harry had spent long hours explaining the law to her. Now, they assumed the role of mentor and pupil for, perhaps, the last time and they both knew it.

"First," Harry began, "if you wanted to work fewer hours for less money, the firm would be happy to come to such an arrangement with you. Would you consider that?"

"I have. I just don't think it would work. As long as I practice law, I'm going to want to work at it hard. I can't bring myself to leave at seven o'clock with a project half-done. So, I've got to walk away from it cold turkey." She took another swallow of Harry's brandy.

"But what do you know about running a hotel?"

"Nearly nothing," Sarah replied. "But what did I know about securities law before I came here? I learned on the job, and I'll do it again. Besides, the owner has agreed to stay on for a few weeks to help us get the hang of things."

But Harry knew what buttons to push. He adopted his most fatherly tone. "Sarah, the Metcalf appeal is due to be heard before the Supreme Court in April. I wanted you to argue it...there!" He pointed at Sarah. "You just smiled for an instant. You're burning to do the appeal. Sarah, you may be able to fool yourself for a short time, but you can't fool me. You don't want to leave the law. You can't leave it."

Sarah was at a loss for words, but only for a moment. "Metcalf?" she asked with real surprise. "You would let me argue it? We stand to make $20 million if we win. I thought you would give the argument to some high-priced Washington firm, or even do it yourself to crown your career."

Harry answered with the sadness of a man confessing his limitations. "Ten years ago, I would've done it, but I'm too busy running the firm to take weeks off to prepare for the argument. And, let's be honest. I'm too old. Give me one minute to answer a question, and I'm on safe ground, but the Supreme Court won't give you that minute."

He pointed at her again, not to accuse but only to acknowledge the truth. "You wrote the brief. You clerked at the Court. Who else deserves the honor more?"

Sarah felt a part of herself starting to swoon, as if she were falling in love against her will. She gripped the arms of her chair and whispered, "You are as persuasive as the day you hired me, but my mind is made up. The answer is no. My resignation is effective on February 28th. Please wish me luck."

Now, Harry began to worry that he might lose control. "Oh Sarah, that I do with all my heart." For a brief moment, they both stopped talking.

"I'll miss you," Sarah said.

Harry recovered first. He asked her if he could drop her off at home. Sarah agreed, and, ten minutes later, they were exiting the lobby of their office building, briefcases in hand, heading out into a New York winter's night and a warm, waiting limousine.

They headed north as Harry and Sarah chatted amiably about various cases and clients, carefully avoiding any mention of the bomb she had just exploded. When the limo reached 57th Street, Harry told the driver to head up Central Park West and then, take the 66th Street transverse to the East

Side.

"Why are we taking the long way?" Sarah asked.

"I have my reasons," Harry said. "You'll see."

At 66th Street, the limousine turned right and headed across Central Park; once past Tavern on the Green, they traveled through a dark, snow-covered forest with not a living soul to be seen. The only illumination came from their car's headlights. Off in the distance, through the bare branches of the trees, they could glimpse the lights of the mountainous apartment buildings on Fifth Avenue.

"You came this way for the view," Sarah said.

"I admit I did," Harry said. "I've always loved New York on a winter's night, especially the contrast between a dark and deserted Central Park and the lights of Fifth Avenue. Every time I take this route home, I feel like a medieval pilgrim traveling through a dark forest to an enchanted realm beyond."

Sarah began to cheer up. "You got to the Upper East Side because you belonged there, Harry. You arrived long ago."

"But you too have arrived Sarah, which is why you will always be welcome back at the firm. Tell me, would you compromise with me and call this adventure of yours a year's leave of absence? I'd like to keep your name on the stationery."

Sarah was quiet for a moment, but then, she held out her hand. "You've got a deal, Harry."

They shook hands, but before he released his grip, he suddenly asked, "and, how about coming back to argue Metcalf? How can you resist writing *fini* to your legal career with an argument before the Supreme Court of the United States?"

Sarah broke into an involuntary smile, and she knew Harry saw it. "All right," she finally said, "but please, no more."

"No more, Sarah, I promise, but anyway, we've arrived at your apartment if I'm not mistaken."

The limousine stopped in front of 610 East 68th Street. Sarah grabbed her briefcase and stepped out onto a curb covered with snow and slush. "Thanks, Harry, I'll see you tomorrow."

"Good night, Sarah," Harry said. Then, after a moment's pause, he added, "and regards to your husband." Then, he leaned over, closed the door and the limousine sped off.

Sarah made only the faintest reply when the doorman wished her good night.

The apartment was dark when she walked in. She cracked open the door of the bedroom and saw her husband in bed, sound asleep. Good, Sarah thought, I just couldn't face Allen tonight. The morning is soon enough. She walked into the center of the living room and kicked her shoes off. She luxuriated in the sensation of the off-white shag rug between her toes.

Suddenly, more than anything in the world, Sarah wanted a hot shower. She dropped her clothes and briefcase on the spot. As she turned to the bathroom, she glimpsed her naked image in the smoky mirror over the green sofa.

Sarah stepped into the shower and turned on the hot water. Suddenly, she began to cry. Goodbye to the apartment on East 68th Street, which served as her fortress from which she would make forays into all the exciting places of the city; farewell to old friends and so long to summer walks through Central Park and Sunday brunches in smart cafes. Triumphs in court and boardroom would come no more. Everything was gone, and the future was a great unknown she would face with a husband whom the world had written off as worthless.

Sarah wept so hard that she sank to the floor of the bathtub where was taking her shower. The warm water dripping down her body seemed both to comfort her and mock her. "And now," she said, "a long farewell to all my greatness. A long farewell to all my greatness."

CHAPTER II

Sarah Leah Mendes: there was a woman. Sarah was her father's daughter. He always taught her to be guided by her head, and she obeyed him. Sarah's beauty and common sense came from her mother as did Sarah's stature. Standing nearly six foot tall, she always caught the eye wherever she went. Sarah moved through life with the grace of a swan and the pride of a Caesar.

Sarah was the daughter of a Jewish family from Antwerp. Her family had lost its diamond business in World War II; her father Maurice, born just after the war, rebuilt the business and turned it into an empire.

As the years passed, her father's business interests brought him to New York so often that he moved his family there when Sarah was twelve. Sarah arrived not knowing a word of English; by the time she was eighteen, she was fluent.

Smart as a whip, Sarah graduated Brandeis with a double major in theatre and political science. Her drama professor, Mr. Miller, urged her to try for a career on the stage, but Sarah knew the risks involved, and she knew that she did not want to gamble with her future; rejecting temptation, she chose the law and was thrilled when Harvard chose her.

As graduation from law school neared, it seemed to Sarah she had all the world before her, and she had the wisdom to be grateful for it. Indeed, it can be argued that the first really upsetting experience Sarah ever had in the law was when she encountered the law firm of Goldsmith & Hammer.

———•((•))•———

Sometime in the mid-1990's a letter arrived at the mid-Manhattan office of Goldsmith & Hammer, attorneys-at-law. The envelope was made of expensive paper with a strong rag content, but, except for the return address, it did not otherwise call attention to itself.

Helen was Harry Goldsmith's secretary. As she went through the morning mail, the letter caught her eye. She picked it up, examined it, and then carried it unopened into Harry's office. Harry looked up from his New York Law Journal as she entered. "What is it, Helen?" he asked.

"I think you'll want to read this for yourself," she replied.

Harry looked at the letter. "Now why is Harvard Law School writing to us?" he wondered aloud. He opened the letter, read it, and smiled.

"What is it?" Helen asked.

Harry looked up with a broad grin. "I'll save that as a surprise," he said as he folded the letter and put it in his desk. "In the meantime, take two hundred dollars out of petty cash. Run over to the liquor store near Grand Central and get a couple of bottles of good champagne and have all the attorneys meet me in the library at noon sharp."

The library was the most beautiful room in Goldsmith & Hammer. Twelve o'clock came, and all the partners and associates were assembled, each with a paper cup in hand. Some of them asked Harry what was going on, but he would only tell them to be patient as he circled the room and poured champagne for everyone.

When everyone's cup had been filled, Harry raised his own and spoke. "I know you're wondering why I called you here. This is why." And he pulled out the letter from his pocket and held it up. "Earlier today, I received this from Harvard."

Adjusting his glasses, Harry began to read:

"Dear Mr. Goldsmith:

Your firm's growing reputation in the field of securities as well as mergers and acquisitions has come to the attention of many of our prospective graduates, and they have asked this office if we could arrange interviews for them with your hiring committee. Therefore, the career placement office wishes to extend to you the opportunity to interview selected graduates of our school in the coming academic year. If you are interested . . . ."

"The rest is pretty standard stuff," Harry said as he looked up. "But here's the important thing: every lawyer, every law firm, wants to know when they have arrived. Some say it's when you have an office on Fifth Avenue; some say it's when you have Fortune 500 clients. I say it's when Harvard Law wants you to interview their graduates. I say this calls for a champagne toast."

There were words of congratulation, scattered applause, and cups raised to the lips.

But Harry's eye caught something amiss. "Max," he asked, "why aren't you drinking?"

Everyone stared at a tall saturnine figure standing in the corner by the tax treatises. He stood over six feet tall and had a big belly; his curly hair was beautifully styled in contrast to a handsome face partially masked by a double chin and flab. His gargantuan body was clothed in a dark Brooks Brothers suit with a button-down Oxford pin-stripe shirt and a burgundy tie with a gold clasp. In his bejeweled hand the plastic cup sat cradled, untouched. That was Max Hammer.

"Why don't I drink, Harry? I'll tell you. When we started this firm, it was a hole in the wall. It was just you, me and a part-time secretary. This firm wasn't built by Harvard or Yale. It was built by a bunch of hard-working guys from places like The Bronx Law School with their brains and sweat. Now that we're successful, Harvard -- out of the goodness of its heart -- is willing to let us hire one of their graduates for $100,000 a year and a limousine ride home each night. I say to hell with them. Let them start their own firm and see if they can get half as far as we have! If you really want a trophy for the firm, I'll be happy to go shoot a moose."

Everyone stared at Max. Finally, Harry broke the silence. "Max," he said, raising his cup again, "I've always valued your opinion, even if I haven't always followed it. Even if we don't hire a Harvard grad, can't you at least drink to the honor of being asked?"

"I'll drink, but only as a favor to you." Max downed his cup in one swallow and turned toward the door. "Now if you'll pardon me, this little meeting has cost us at least twenty-five hundred dollars in billable time, and I've got to start making it up."

That was in September; Goldsmith & Hammer's interview date was set for the middle of January. Harry reserved the honor of interviewing at Harvard for himself, and he cleared his schedule for the appointed day several months in advance.

At the same time, Max marked the approach of the interviews by muttering "Harvard" frequently in

Harry's presence in a tone usually reserved for saying "Tsk, tsk."

On a cold January morning, Harry walked out of his apartment at eight o'clock and promptly tripped on a stray patch of ice. His feet flew out from under him, and he hit the pavement hard. His briefcase fell out of his hand and popped open when it hit the sidewalk. Papers began to scatter in the breeze.

Within a moment, Harry's chauffeur and the doorman were picking him up. "Get my papers," Harry said, wincing from pain. As the doorman chased down the pages, Charlie, Harry's chauffeur, helped him into the back seat of the limo whence he called home and office to explain what had happened. Fifteen minutes later, Harry was being helped into the emergency room at Lenox Hill Hospital.

The doctors called it a small hairline fracture in the ankle. They put Harry's right foot in a cast, gave him crutches and assured him it could have been much worse. By two o'clock, he was in bed in his apartment and his wife Grace was preparing tea for him.

Now Harry had time to worry. The interviews were tomorrow. Who was going to do them? He picked up the phone and called the office.

"Helen, this is Harry. Would you confirm for me that the Harvard interviews are tomorrow?"

"Yes they are. You've cleared your entire day for them."

"Well, Helen," he said, "it is pretty obvious that

I'm not going to be going there. Check the calendar and tell me who is free tomorrow."

"Max Hammer," she replied.

"No, besides him."

"There isn't anyone else."

Harry began to sense things were going wrong and that he had no power to stop them. "I can't believe that only Max is free. What about Brad McDonald? What about Roy Cook?"

"Mr. McDonald will be in Washington all day at the SEC, and Mr. Cook will be in federal court." Her calm tone of voice only added to Harry's growing panic.

"All right," he said grasping at straws, "are there any senior associates available?"

Again, there was a silence, this time longer than the first one. Harry imagined he could hear computer keys tapping and pages being turned. Finally, Helen spoke again. "No, I'm afraid not, Harry. Only Mr. Hammer is free tomorrow."

Harry was silent for a moment. He contemplated postponing the interviews, but then he decided that it would make Goldsmith & Hammer look like an irresponsible, small-time outfit. Sending Max was the lesser of two evils, but only by a hair.

"Let me speak to Max then," Harry said at last.

"Why I'll be happy to do the interviews," Max said after Harry explained the situation. "I'd like to see if these kids are as overrated as I think they are."

Harry fought back a groan, "Now listen Max,

you're not going there to ventilate your inferiority complex about the Ivy League. I just want you to conduct interviews the way you always have and then go home. Dear God, our firm's reputation could be riding on this."

"Okay Harry, you have my word that I'll be on my best behavior."

Would that be good enough? Harry wasn't sure, but now he was past the point of no return. "All right Max, Helen will arrange plane tickets, and she'll give you copies of the resumes Harvard sent us." Then he hung up the phone and tried to put the matter out of his mind.

Max was a creature of habit. He worked until 7:30 that evening, ate dinner at a steakhouse and then went home to an empty apartment. (After his last divorce he decided he preferred such living arrangements.) He read some papers he brought home from the office and, after watching the evening news, he fell asleep.

At eight o'clock the following morning Max sat at his desk, reviewing a draft of a new stock prospectus. Nine o'clock came and went, and he was still engrossed in his work. At ten o'clock Helen appeared at his office door and warned him if he didn't leave for the airport immediately, he'd never catch the Boston shuttle. Horrified, Max looked at his watch, shoved his papers into a briefcase, grabbed his coat and ran out. Helen barely managed to toss Max his plane tickets as he raced past her. He left her holding the envelope with the resumes.

Three hours later, out of breath and angry, Max found himself in the Harvard yard.

Harvard is beautiful when covered in snow, but Max was not interested in aesthetics; he just wanted to get back to New York. He stopped a student and asked where Wagner Hall was. Five minutes later, he was being shown into the office of the placement director. She was a petite woman with gray hair in a bun.

"Good afternoon, Mr. Goldsmith," she said, extending a hand in welcome. "I'm Amy Wolf."

Max offered a pudgy paw in return. "I'm afraid I'm not Harry Goldsmith. He's my partner. I'm Mr. Hammer. He was indisposed so he asked me to cover for him."

"Well, welcome anyway," Amy said, starting to sense that something was amiss. She picked up an envelope from her desk and handed it to him. "Here are extra copies of the resumes of the students you'll be seeing today, as well as sample interview questions you may find useful."

I think you know what you can do with those questions, Max thought to himself. But what he said was, "Thanks. Where do I meet them?"

"Follow me," Amy replied, and a few moments later Max found himself in a small room with a desk and two chairs.

"I'll give you a few moments to get comfortable, then I'll start sending them in."

"Okay," Max replied. "I'm ready for whatever you send me." And indeed, he was. Max opened the envelope she had given him and pulled out a small stack of resumes. They were pinned with a paper clip. He flicked it away with a fingertip. Max did not bother looking at the questions; he had his own in mind.

Suddenly, there was a knock on the door and a young man in a good suit stood before Max. "Hello," he said earnestly. "My name is John Pinkerton."

"Sit down," said Max, indicating the chair on the other side of the desk. He pulled the young man's resume out of the stack and inspected it. "I see you're actually John Pinkerton the Third." He accented the last two words as if they were the punch line of a joke. "Tell me, Mr. Pinkerton, how much money are you looking for?"

The student was taken aback by such a blunt question. After a moment, he said, "I assume you have a pay scale for entry-level associates."

"Actually, we don't," Max replied sweetly. "We generally ask job applicants what they think they're worth, and, if we agree, we hire them." He smiled, raised his eyebrows and, putting his elbows on the desktop, folded his hands under his chin.

Pausing for a long moment, the student finally took a leap into the dark, "Well, according to the New York Law Journal, a firm of your size should be paying an entry-level associate between $110,000 to $115,000 a year, not counting signing bonuses and housing allowances."

"Really?" said Max in a happy voice. "I must tell the partners that. Then his tone of voice changed, and he was suddenly in deadly earnest. "Listen, kid," he growled, "we pay heavily for talent, not for potential. Tell me what you can do that deserves $115,000 a year. We'll worry about signing bonuses later."

John Pinkerton had no ready answer. After a longer pause than the one before, he said, "Well, I've concentrated my course work in bankruptcy and securities regulation."

Max held up a hand and brought it down contemptuously. "I used to teach securities law as an adjunct professor. I know that course work doesn't teach you how to practice law, experience does. Tell me what you know how to do in securities law, and bear in mind I can hire someone with two years experience at the Securities and Exchange Commission for $100,000 and that's without paying a signing bonus."

Then Max lit up a cigar. He favored Phillies Blunts. The student paused yet again, then politely said, "There's no smoking," and pointed to a sign on the wall. Max looked up at the notice; it read 'No Smoking Is Permitted.' He turned back to the student and said, "Sorry, but I disagree with your interpretation. It merely says that it is permitted for me not to smoke. It doesn't prohibit smoking."

"That's ridiculous," the student said, attempting to rally.

"Possibly," Max volleyed back, still smiling, "but it is a legal argument, and sometimes you have to take some far-fetched positions to defend your clients. Tell me, do you think you're capable of making such arguments if someone gives you $115,000 a year?"

Coughing from the smoke and sensing there was no right answer to the question, the student replied, "I don't know."

"Fine," said Max. "When you have answers to my questions, come back and talk to me." Then he added, "You can go now, and send in the next winner on your way out."

Max disposed of two more candidates in rapid succession. During a break in the action, he stood up and stared out the window, puffing away on another cigar.

Then there were footsteps, followed by a knock at the door and the voice of a young woman. "Is this Goldsmith & Hammer?"

Max turned and stared. Max was a man who savored women's beauty, especially since he was never able to persuade a woman to stay with him for any length of time. To him, Sarah Mendes was God's plenty.

"Hello," Max said effusively. "Please take a seat."

But Sarah didn't sit. "You're not allowed to smoke here," she said. "And even if you were, the fumes offend me. Please put out your cigar."

"Sure thing lady," Max said. He opened the

window and threw his cigar out. Several snowflakes flew in before he closed it. "Have a seat," he said with a gesture.

Dear God, Sarah thought, and she sat down cautiously.

Max looked through the papers on his desk, which was now a mess, hunting for her resume. Then he realized he didn't know her name.

She saved him the trouble of asking. "I'm Sarah Mendes. Would you like to see my resume?" Max accepted the copy she handed to him.

He looked at it and said, "Your name is Mendes. *Habla Español*?"

Is he for real? Sarah thought. "No, I'm a French-speaker by birth," she replied. "My family is from Belgium. We are Sephardic Jews. Mendes is a common name in our world."

"Ah, French, the only French I know is '*Voulez-vous coucher avec moi ce soir*'?" Max chuckled at his own cleverness.

Sarah reminded herself what year it was and wondered if it was possible if men like Max still existed. Her uncertainty made her remain seated instead of heading for the door.

"Now I see that you were a theater and political science major at Brandeis," Max said as he scanned her resume. "Tell me, why didn't a pretty girl like you become a model or actress or something? You look too pretty to be a lawyer."

Sarah was so aghast she remained silent. Then,

Max asked another question.

"What will you do when you get married and start a family?" Max asked.

The shock of his words hit hard. "Mr. Hammer, that question is illegal."

"Don't tell me you're one of those stupid feminists," Max said.

"No," Sarah replied, "merely a soon-to-be lawyer who doesn't want to work for someone whose questions break the law and violate my privacy."

Max was getting angry now. "Listen, I'm just trying to give you a sample of the kind of pressures you can expect when you practice law!"

Sarah replied in icy tones. "Mr. Hammer, I'm on the Dean's List, and I'm an editor on the law review. I know how to handle pressure, but you remind me of Fred Flintstone with a law degree, and I don't think I know how to handle a Neanderthal." She rose from her chair. "And another thing," Sarah said, as she touched her cheek, "my face is up here, not on my chest. You haven't made five seconds of eye contact with me since I came in here."

Now, Max was furious. "Lady, don't flatter yourself, I've seen better."

"On a statue, perhaps, in a centerfold, certainly, but on a real woman who would voluntarily have anything to do with you? That I do not believe." Sarah looked at her watch and then asked Max what his hourly billing rate was.

"Four hundred fifty an hour; why the hell do you

want to know?" he replied.

Sarah opened her wallet and dropped forty dollars in front of Max. "What the hell is this?" he demanded.

"I just bought back my introduction to you," Sarah quietly said to him, and then, she turned and headed out the door.

"Now wait a minute ..." Max shouted, only to realize that he had no idea how to complete that sentence. The door slammed, and he could hear her walking away.

Ever the pragmatist, Max looked at his watch and saw that he had completed four interviews in twenty minutes. This gave him more than two hours before he had to leave for the airport to go back to New York, so he dumped his papers on the desk and began to work.

He was deeply immersed in his labors when someone in the room, a woman, cleared her throat. Max looked up to see Amy Wolf. "Mr. Hammer," she said softly, "are you quite finished?"

"Yes, I am," he answered. "Frankly, the quality of your candidates was disappointing to me, except for the Mendes girl. She had a spark."

"I agree with you; she is exceptional," Amy remarked. "She is the only candidate who survived meeting you intact." She held the door open. "Now I have to ask you to leave and never come back, ever."

"Okay, if that's the way you want it." Max said nonchalantly. "It is no skin off my nose." He shoveled his papers into his briefcase and walked out without a backward glance.

Max walked across the Harvard Yard. Then, he hailed a cab and headed off to Logan Airport. When he checked in for his return flight, the clerk at the reservations counter gave Max a message to call his office. (Max hated technology: he never carried a cellphone).

After Max reached Helen at the office, he was told to call Harry at home.

"Hello, Harry," he began. "How are you feeling?"

"Fine, Max, just fine," but there was something strange in the tone of his voice; it was too calm. "Tell me, how did the interviews go?"

"About as I expected," Max replied. "I thought they were all badly overrated. No, I take that back. There was one girl with real fire in her belly. Trouble is, she's one of those nut-job feminists."

"Really," Harry replied in that voice that was calm, too calm. "Was that Ms. Mendes?"

Now Max paused, then he asked Harry how he knew her name.

"You underestimate yourself Max. I got off the phone with Amy Wolf half an hour ago. You've just reduced several of Harvard's finest to shambles. Happy?

"But you are right about the Mendes girl. She's exceptional. In fact, she's going to sue us for sexual harassment. Not only will that black ball us from interviewing in good law schools for the rest of our lives, but the publicity will not help us either."

"Oh, oh," Max said. "What can I do to fix matters?"

"Do?" Harry asked calmly and then screamed out an answer: "You can come back to the office and do your work! That's what you can do! After a great deal of groveling, I've arranged to meet with both Ms. Wolf and Ms. Mendes tomorrow morning at Harvard. Since I can't get on a plane with my crutches, I'm leaving by limo at 4:00 A.M. tomorrow morning."

"Harry," Max said in a low register. "I'm sorry."

Harry's screaming began to wind down. "We'll all be sorry if I can't fix this, and if it means hiring her, just remember that every dime I have to spend to get her over and above our regular starting salary is coming out of your partnership share. Good night. I'll call you after the meeting is over."

Harry had a terrible dream that night. The end of a life's hard work seemed to float in front of his eyes. He sat as a defendant in court. "The next case is Mendes vs. The Law Firm of Goldsmith & Hammer," intoned an angry judge. "Harry Goldsmith will take the stand." He woke up in a cold sweat.

Sarah was also having troubling thoughts. When she entered the Placement Office right after leaving Max, she found Amy Wolf trying to console several angry and confused students. To boost everyone's morale, Sarah announced on the spot that she intended to sue, but within hours she began to have regrets. She sought out Amy before close of business that same day.

I'm worried," Sarah told her. "I'm convinced that man didn't come up here to interview us for jobs. He came here to work out an inferiority complex against Harvard. There are people like that. We played into his hands by getting upset.

"And if I do sue him, I won't be Sarah the Harvard graduate anymore, I'll be 'The Woman Who Sued.'" Sarah made quote marks in the air with her fingers as she spoke the last four words. "I'll be marked as a trouble-maker and no good firm will have me."

"I see your point," Amy said in soft, professional tones.

But Sarah was not easily consoled. "No, you don't, at least not all of it," she explained. "I can forgive and forget a boor -- I've had my share of blind dates -- but this is a man who likes to hurt people. I feel I've got to do something about him. I just don't know what. And the horrible part is that I never wanted to work for that lousy firm in the first place. They're just a hole in the wall. I just signed up for the interview to practice for the really big firms coming up."

Amy took a deep breath before she spoke. "I think the best thing to do is to state your feelings to this Goldsmith man when he gets here. He sounds reasonable. Just don't mention that you're not going to sue until you hear what he says."

Sarah sensed a voice of reason and nodded

agreement. She left the office, promising to re-turn at a quarter to nine the next morning to await Harry's coming. To put everything out of her mind, Sarah studied late into the night in the library.

Dawn saw Harry preparing for battle. He awoke at three and dressed himself in the modern equivalent of a knight's armor. He wore a dark pinstriped suit and a polished black left shoe. (The other foot was in a cast.) He wore a cashmere topcoat, a Homburg on his head, and a white scarf around his neck. His person was trimmed with gold - his eyeglass frames, his wedding ring, his watch, and a chain across his vest. Where a knight would carry a sword at his side, Harry carried a briefcase. He was ready.

Charlie helped him into the limo, and they headed north from still-sleeping New York up to Cambridge, Massachusetts.

Sarah awoke at seven. She put on her jogging suit and circled the campus. Sweating and her heart still racing, she showered and then put on her most se-vere interview suit: a dark dress with a white blouse and a small gold pin on one lapel. After a leisurely breakfast, she headed over to Amy's office to wait for Harry.

Harry tried to sleep during his long car ride up to Massachusetts, but he couldn't, and he could not face the papers in his briefcase either. Instead, he sipped coffee from a thermos his wife had given him while thinking over all the trouble Max's big mouth had caused over the years. Why did he put up with

Max? Harry sighed and concluded a partnership was a lot like marriage. You take the good with the bad.

Once parked in a visitor's lot at Harvard, Harry set off with crutches while Charlie carried his brief-case. They were a team.

Amy was standing at her office window when she spotted them. "Sarah," she said, "come take a look at this."

Sarah was taken aback. "It's got to be him," she said. Then she had an idea. "Let's get our coats on and go meet them."

The two women walked down the front steps of Wagner Hall just as the strange duo got there. "Mr. Goldsmith," said Amy as she held out her hand.

Swinging one crutch to the other arm, Harry shook her hand. "Ms. Wolf, I presume. It is a pleasure to finally meet you."

And then Harry turned to face Sarah, extended his hand, and said, "It's a pleasure to meet you too, Ms. Mendes. 'Sorry it had to be under such circumstances."

Am I supposed to be angry with his man? Sarah thought. I feel like he's a long- lost uncle. But what she said was: "It's a pleasure to meet you, Mr. Goldsmith."

"Call me Harry," he replied with an easy charm, and the ice was broken.

The four of them stood there in the snow for a moment, and then, Harry had an idea. "Is there any place nearby where we could have a leisurely brunch? I could stand a bite and it might make for better conversation."

Amy said that the Hotel Empire off Harvard Square had the best French toast in town. That was good enough for Harry, and off they went.

The Hotel Empire offered an old-world ambiance. The walls had stained wood wainscoting, the tables had cloth napkins, and the waiters wore black vests with bow ties. Once the food began to arrive and the mood turned cheerful, Harry explained how Max wound up conducting the interviews. "If I had known what was going to happen," Harry concluded with a wry chuckle, "I would have crawled up here." Everyone laughed.

Then, Harry turned to Sarah. "Ms. Mendes, now I must ask a most unpleasant question. What exactly did Max say and do when you met him?"

Sarah was now so at ease that she had half-forgotten why they were all there. Assuming now a formal, lawyerly mien, Sarah told Harry everything that had happened. She was careful to include her side of the conversation with Max. Harry listened intently, taking notes on a sheet of paper with a fountain pen.

When she finished, Harry studied the list for a moment. "I fear that this was Max on one of his bad days. He has had a number of them over the years."

He told them of the times Max had talked back to judges and been thrown out of courtrooms or held in contempt. Once Max so badly offended a

federal judge that Max was lead out of the courtroom in handcuffs, and Harry had to race down to
court with a checkbook to pay the contempt fine.
Another time, Max threw a half-eaten sandwich
at the head of an arbitration panel. Max's temper
had cost the firm several clients over the years, but
Harry had usually been able to persuade them to
come back after everyone cooled off.

Sarah listened and was frankly puzzled. "Why do
you put up with Max?" Sarah asked. Wouldn't your
firm be better off without him?"

"Why do I stay partners with Max?" Harry asked
wearily to no one in particular. "Let me answer with
a question: Sarah, how long have your parents been
married?"

"I beg your pardon?" Amy said.

But Sarah answered the question. "Over thirty
years, but what has that got to do with anything?"

"Bear with me for a moment," Harry said. "Is
their marriage a good one?"

"Very, why do you want to know?"

"Just one question more. "Do they ever argue?"

"Of course they do, in French, English and a
smattering of other languages. They can really go at
it."

"Ah," said Harry, raising a finger to make a point,
"they fight, but they stay together. That's the way it
is with Max and me. He has his faults, I've got mine,
but, taken as a whole, our partnership is a good one.
That's why your parents are together and that's why

Max and I remain partners."

Seeing puzzled looks on their faces, Harry tried to explain. "Max and I go back forty years, back to when we were kids in Brooklyn. Neither of our families had much, but Max had a tougher path than anyone else I ever knew. His father died young, and Max had to start working at sixteen. He went to college and law school at night. When he graduated, he got a job with a good firm -- the best break of his life! -- and he gave it up after two years to join me. I had just gone out on my own, and I had nothing to offer but hard work and hope. The rest is history."

Harry spread out his hands. "I'll stand by Max forever," he said. "Wouldn't you?"

Sarah was silent for a moment, and then, she agreed that she probably would.

Harry took a swallow of tea and continued. "So, I am here for two reasons. The first is to offer an apology. Ms. Mendes, on behalf of Max, myself and the entire firm, I deeply regret the way you were treated yesterday. If my words are not enough to make amends, please tell me what will."

All eyes looked at Sarah now.

She hesitated for only a moment. "If it were up to me, I'd be happy to just let it go, but I feel an obligation to all the others that Mr. Hammer has probably done this to in the past and will probably do it to in the future. Let him apologize to me directly, and I'll forget what happened."

Now it was Harry's turn to be silent. Finally, he

said, "I can't fault your reasoning. He will apologize to you at the next partners' meeting, and we'll fly you to New York for it. Is that acceptable?"

"Yes it is. Thank you, Mr. Goldsmith."

But Amy had also been taking notes. "What was your second reason for coming today, Mr. Goldsmith?"

Harry had realized that he was getting off cheaply: words cost nothing. But Harry also began to sense that Sarah was an exceptional woman, and one of the secrets of his success over the years had been his ability to spot budding talent and nurture it. He answered firmly. "Frankly, I wanted to know if Ms. Mendes would still consider working for our firm, provided, of course, the matter with Max is straightened out to her satisfaction."

Everyone looked at Sarah; this was her moment. She daubed her mouth with a linen napkin and then said, "I will consider your firm after Mr. Hammer apologies. But I have one question: how do his subordinates work with Max?"

"Quite well actually," Harry replied. "They have all learned to ignore Max when he has his bad moments, and, once he realizes his antics aren't upsetting anyone, he stops. It's as simple as that."

"It seems to me," Amy interjected, "that further discussions should wait until Sarah visits your firm in New York."

Everyone agreed, and the brunch concluded with pleasant generalities.

After the meal was over, Sarah stood next to Harry on the street as they waited for Charlie to drive round the limo. "I'm sorry you had to come up for such a brief conversation," Sarah said.

"I brought it on myself, Ms. Mendes," Harry replied. "I wanted to keep up appearances, so, instead of postponing the interviews, I sent the wrong man for the job."

"Can't you stay for an hour so I can show you the campus?"

"It's not necessary Ms. Mendes," Harry replied. "Your kind reception was worth the trip. But there is a matter I'd like to put to you now that we're alone. I'd like to know if there are any charities I could make donations to in your name. Really, an apology is only words, I'd like to put something real behind it."

Sarah was pleased. "I can name two off the top of my head: the Harvard AIDS project and the American Friends of the Hebrew University in Jerusalem. I spent my junior year there,"

Harry pulled out his notebook and wrote them down. "I'll send them each $1,000. It will be my pleasure."

Now, Sarah smiled. "Thank you."

Harry put his notebook back in his vest pocket and then, looking over her shoulder, he suddenly raised his hand. "And here's Charlie with the car. You'll be hearing from my secretary Helen to set up the trip. Until then, take care and be well."

The limousine pulled up and Harry got in with

Sarah's help. Sarah was surprised to find herself unconsciously waving good-bye as the car left. After it disappeared into traffic, she turned and headed off to her Family Law class.

CHAPTER III

Things happened fast. When Sarah got back to her dormitory, she found a message from Helen on her answering machine asking her to call Goldsmith & Hammer. When she did, Helen greeted her warmly and read her a series of dates for possible visits to the firm.

Sarah checked her own appointment book, and they agreed on a day three weeks off. Sarah would be flown to New York, and limousines would pick her up at each end of her journey.

When Sarah hung up the phone, she was exhausted; the last few days had been rough. But it was a Friday, and the week was finally coming to an end. She spent the afternoon in her room, studying and sleeping. At four o'clock, she phoned her parents in New York to tell them of the strange events of the last few days.

Her mother was curious as to why Sarah wanted

anything to do with Goldsmith & Hammer. Weren't there saner employers in the world?

Sarah agreed that she was off to a rocky beginning with the firm, but Harry Goldsmith seemed to be a good man. They exchanged words of love in French and hung up.

It was almost sundown on a dreary Friday in winter; the Sabbath was coming. Sarah opened a drawer and took out two candlesticks. She put them on her dresser, put a candle in each one and lit them. Every Friday night, she had seen her mother bring in the Sabbath the same way, and it was something that always comforted her.

Sarah's family had moved to New York when she was twelve. She cried and cried. In order to cheer Sarah up, her parents took her on a whirlwind tour of the city: the Empire State Building, the Central Park Zoo, the Staten Island Ferry and the Statue of Liberty. Nothing worked.

But when Friday night came, Sarah's parents had taken her to the Sephardic synagogue on 73rd Street. There, the familiar melodies lifted Sarah's spirits, and she stopped crying. For the rest of her life, she never forgot the comfort she felt that night.

Sarah put on her tan, cashmere trench coat and walked across the campus to the Harvard Hillel house for Friday night services. The night was cold, and her feet made a crunching sound in the snow as she hurried along. Older now, she went less for reasons of faith (somehow the strain of law school pressures together with the crush of new ideas seemed to push such things out of her mind), but rather to be with friends.

The young rabbi who led the Friday night service spoke warm words for such a cold night. At the end of the service, he made an announcement that took everyone by surprise: two people had gotten engaged. It was a 'mixed marriage' -- the man was in medical school and the woman studied philosophy. The rabbi wished them both "Mazel Tov" (meaning 'good luck') and led the congregation in "Siman Tov," a Hebrew song meaning essentially the same thing.

Other people's engagements and marriages did not bother Sarah very much. She knew her time would come.

At the end of the service, everyone went into the social hall for an oneg Shabbat: tea and cake and good company.

Melissa Klein, a friend of Sarah's, who was one year behind her in law school, was the first to ask Sarah the question: "What's all this about some abusive interviewer you met? Are you really going to sue?"

Sarah had an answer ready. "No, it has all been straightened out, and please don't spread it around. It's really a small matter that I'm tired of talking about."

Sarah did not have a boyfriend; she was just too busy. She did have friends who were men, but she drew a very sharp distinction between the two. One in the latter category, Jason Weckstein, came over to her. She had a foolish reason for liking his company: he was even taller than she was.

"Good Shabbos, Sarah. How have you been? Everyone's talking about . . . ."

She held up her hand. "Don't say it, Jason. I know what you're going to ask about, and I don't want to discuss it any more. Believe me, it's nothing, nothing at all. Tell me, how are your interviews going?"

"Great, he said, "I don't have any definite offers yet, but I've got commitments to visit firms in New York, Chicago, Los Angeles and even Honolulu for follow-up interviews. If nothing else, I'm going to see a lot of America."

"You'll do fine, I'm sure," and she held up her Styrofoam cup of tea in a toast.

Jason sensed long ago that Sarah had only wanted to concentrate on her legal studies. He accepted that and settled for her friendship now while hoping for the future. "Where are you going after this?" he asked.

"Back to my dorm to sleep," she said.

"Can I walk you there? We can get lattes at Starbucks on the way."

Sensing his real purpose, Sarah was gentle in her reply. "No thank you, but let's do it when I have a little more energy."

Jason sighed, doubting whether that time would ever come.

Sarah went back to her dormitory by herself. After a long night's sleep, she spent the rest of the weekend studying and working at the Law Review.

CHAPTER IV

Sarah was getting busier and busier. Between her course work, her work on the Law Review and the job interviews she was getting, she had little time to think about Goldsmith & Hammer and the antics of Max. Gradually, she simply looked upon her upcoming trip to New York City as a chance to see the old home town for a few hours and nothing more.

Sarah began to get tentative offers in the $130,000 to $135,000 range, and she became a formal candidate for clerkships on the Second Circuit and the Supreme Court. Whenever she thought about Goldsmith & Hammer, she began to think that she might be better off just accepting Harry's apology, canceling her trip and letting matters rest.

Still, when the appointed day came, she found herself standing in front of her dormitory at 6:45 a.m., briefcase in hand. A limousine pulled up in the darkness, and the driver asked, "'Are you Miss Mendes?'"

"That's me," she said.

The plane ride to New York was short. When she exited the plane at LaGuardia, she saw Charlie, Harry's chauffeur, waiting for her with a sign that said 'Mendes.' "Hello, Ms. Mendes," he said. "It is a pleasure to see you again."

As the limo crossed the Tri-Boro Bridge into Manhattan, a phone in the back seat rang. Charlie told her to pick it up. It was Harry. "Good morning, Sarah. How was your flight?"

"Very easy," she said. "I'm flattered that you sent your personal chauffeur to pick me up."

"Charlie doesn't work for me exclusively," Harry replied with a chuckle. "We use him to chaperone important guests, and that's what you are. I look forward to seeing you on your arrival."

Sarah leaned back and enjoyed the ride.

Half an hour later, the limousine pulled up in front of 500 Fifth Avenue, a tall stone building overlooking the New York Public Library. "You want the thirtieth floor," Charlie said as she got out.

A few minutes later, Sarah walked up to a set of glass doors with the words 'Goldsmith & Hammer' written on them. Past the doors was a burgundy rug with G&H in a circle. Harry Goldsmith had put a lot of money into decorating this place.

Sarah announced herself to the receptionist and sat down on a particularly comfortable red leather couch, but she did not have long to wait. A well-dressed, older woman entered the waiting area and walked up to Sarah.

"Ms. Mendes?" she asked. "I'm Helen, Mr. Goldsmith's secretary. Would you come with me please?" They walked down a short corridor with windows that gave sweeping views of lower Manhattan. The corner office had "Harry Goldsmith, Esquire' written across the door.

Harry was standing by his antique globe and speaking to a bespectacled middle-aged attorney with red hair. "Ah, Miss Mendes," Harry said as he shook her hand. "It's a real pleasure to welcome you to our firm. Please have a seat and we'll review your schedule. This gentleman here is Roy Cook. He'll be your guide this morning."

Now Roy Cook shook Sarah's hand. "It's a pleasure, Ms. Mendes. Harry has spoken so highly of you."

The three of them sat down, and Helen handed each of them a blue 'G&H' folder. "This is how I've scheduled your day with us," Harry said.

The paper read:

10:00	Arrival
11:00- 10:15	Orientation with Mr. Goldsmith
11:00-12:00	Tour of the Firm with Roy Cook

12:00-1:00	Partnership Meeting
2:00-1:00	Lunch
2:00-4:00	Preparation of Appellate Argument in General Sound v. Magnus with H. Goldsmith and travel to Appellate Division
4:00	Return to office for Hiring Committee meeting

"You've planned a very full day Mr. Goldsmith," Sarah said. But then, she saw the look he gave her and quickly added, "I mean, Harry. But am I going to court with you today?"

"Yes," replied Harry. "I want you to see us in action. There's no better test of an attorney's competence then to see him -- or her -- in court. The General Sound case is a very interesting appeal that should make for a lively argument, but you'll hear more about it later."

He gestured toward Roy. "Roy here is the head of our litigation department. I've asked him to show you around the firm and introduce you to the rest of our senior associates. You'll be introduced to the partners at the meeting, and they'll discuss the nature of their practices."

"I see."

"And no, I haven't forgotten why you came here today. Max will make his peace with you at the partners' meeting. You will then go to lunch as our guest, and then, we'll head down to the Appellate Division for the argument. And now, I turn you over to Roy."

Sarah's first impressions were correct: the firm was physically beautiful. The offices were spacious and well appointed, the conference rooms were large with commanding views of the city. The library was breathtaking.

Roy saw the look on her face. "We have over 20,000 volumes," he said proudly. Harry's wife was a librarian for many years, and she influenced the firm's acquisitions. Firms a lot bigger than ours borrow books from us regularly, and that is a source of pride here. Naturally, we have just about every online legal research tool known to man, and we have a full-time librarian with a law degree."

After the tour of the physical layout, Roy tried to explain the philosophy of the firm, and his enthusiasm was infectious. Harry saw the practice of law as the writing of beautiful music; Max saw it as war. The two different sensibilities created a marvelous tension, which made working at Goldsmith & Hammer an exciting experience. Roy discussed some of the firm's bigger cases and told her tall stories of flying to London to take depositions and of lawsuits involving millions of dollars and cutting-edge legal questions. It was all music to Sarah's ears. Then, Roy introduced her to the lawyers in the tax, real estate and bankruptcy departments. Sarah was impressed; she was starting to like the place.

And not one of the attorneys she met reminded her of Max.

Sitting with Roy in one of the firm's lounges, Sarah tried to organize her thoughts with a cup of tea in hand. "How have Harry and Max gotten along so well if they're so different?"

Roy attempted an answer. "Harry is a visionary; he tends to think in broad concepts. In terms of analyzing the law and guiding the growth of a firm, few can match him. But he's not a street-fighter with a knack for details and the desire to fight, that's Max. If they hadn't become partners, Harry would probably be a law professor somewhere, and Max would be a solo practitioner chasing ambulances. Believe me, it's a match made in heaven."

"And are you happy here?"

"As a clam," Roy replied. "It's a great place to work. But I see it's almost time for the partners' meeting. Let's go."

As they walked back toward Harry's office, Sarah began to feel like a fool. Why was she doing this? Why didn't she drop the whole thing? Why not just keep on walking out the front door and hustle back to Harvard? Still, Sarah walked with Roy Cook back to Harry's office.

Once there, she found herself at ease; as always, Harry had a knack for staging things to best effect.

The six partners, including Max, were all seated in comfortable chairs around a conference table, drinking coffee and tea and eating pastries and fruit from silver trays.

"Sarah," Harry called out as she walked in, greeting her as if she were an intimate friend. He motioned her to a chair. "Do sit down and tell us your impressions of our little firm."

She sat, politely refusing the croissant while accepting the tea. The attorneys made such gentle and pleasing conversation with her that Sarah forgot why she was there in the first place. Finally, Harry gently turned the conversation back to Sarah's all but blunted purpose by saying "Max?" during a lull in the conversation together with a look of mild reprimand directed at his long-time partner.

Max looked at the floor for a moment, pursed his lips and seemed to suck the air out of his cheeks. Finally, he relaxed his face, steeled himself, and looked up at Sarah. He said this in one breath: "Ms. Mendes, during our meeting at Harvard, I made a number of boorish and unprofessional comments. I apologize for them; they will not be repeated."

Without hesitation, Sarah said: "Apology accepted. The matter is now closed." Then she held out a hand to Max. He was startled for a moment, but then, he shook it.

Max clapped his hands together. "Excellent," he said. "Now we can move forward. Sarah, we have some business that we need to discuss in private, so

I'm sending you to lunch with Jonathan Crane and Annette DeKoven, they are two of our senior associates. When you get back, we can head over to the Appellate Division."

Sarah felt only relief. It had all been painless. "Thank you," she said, and she stood up to take her leave.

"They'll meet you in the lobby," Harry said. "I think you know how to find your way there by now." When the door closed behind her, Harry turned to his partners and said, "All right, what do you think?"

Harry is certainly a master of style, Sarah concluded when she met her lunch mates in the lobby. Jonathan Crane and Annette DeKoven looked as if they stepped out of the pages of a fashion magazine for young lawyers. They are the best kind of salespersons, Sarah said to herself; they don't know that they're selling anything.

"Hello," Jonathan said, offering his hand. "Harry told us to take you anywhere you want to go. What are you in the mood for?"

"Just a salad somewhere," Sarah replied.

"You'll have to tell us all about you and Max at Harvard," Annette said with a laugh. "Every associate in the firm has heard a different rumor."

Sarah let out a weary sigh. "I'm afraid I can't talk about it. The matter is resolved and closed." But, when she saw disappointment on their faces, she added: "Of course, nothing prevents you from telling me your Max stories."

Their faces lit up.

The trio adjourned to a smart little restaurant where Sarah ordered a salad Nicoise and mineral water. Once they began to relax over their food, the conversation returned to Goldsmith & Hammer. Sarah took the lead. "When I first met Harry, he told me some stories about Max.'"

"Did he tell you the one about him being led out of a courtroom in handcuffs?" Jonathan asked eagerly. "That's the topper."

"Yes, he did," Sarah said, "and I'm only wondering how anyone can work with him for any length of time."

"He's really easy to get along with if you simply ignore his bluster," Annette offered.

"And don't forget that he is one fine securities lawyer," Jonathan added. "He is simply an unhappy man."

"Jonathan," Sarah asked, "what is your favorite Max story?"

He thought a moment and then chuckled. "I suppose it's the time we had our annual New Year's party. We had a big rush job so some of us couldn't go. Max ordered in pizza and champagne for us, and he paid for it out of his own pocket. So, you see, he does have a touch of the poet about him."

"Believe me," Annette said, "I've worked for him for three years and I regard his misanthropic rantings as a joke. I simply laugh at them privately and go my merry way. I'm very happy here. The people are nice; the money is good, and the work is challenging. Harry has created a small boutique firm with an international clientele. Now, they want to expand the firm into the medium-sized range, so they are really interested in hiring good people who will stay and grow with the firm."

"But doesn't Max have something against people from big-name schools?"

"Sarah," Annette replied, "you've got to understand the kind of hardships Max had growing up."

"Harry told me about them too," Sarah said with some impatience. "It seems that Max wears them on his sleeve as a badge of pride."

"Well, perhaps he does," Annette agreed. "I admit that the firm used to have a policy of not hiring graduates of the top schools, but rumor has it that one day Harry told Max that if the firm didn't at least start hiring Fordham and N.Y.U. graduates, they were going to have a lot of trouble getting big clients."

"I was the first N.Y.U. grad the firm took," Jonathan said with pride. "Max kidded me about it when I first arrived, but then I proved my worth, and he let up."

Stories and myths about Max poured out of Jonathan and Annette. Sarah let them continue, although now she really wasn't interested in hearing them. Sarah was starting to imagine what was once unthinkable; she might want to work at Goldsmith & Hammer. As to Max, she decided he was a good lawyer but a troubled man. Neither would be an insurmountable problem. Sarah gently turned the conversation to other matters: what kind of training did the firm give its new associates? How much responsibility? What were the chances of making partner? Sarah liked the answers she got. She slowly formed the opinion that Goldsmith & Hammer might actually be a good place to work. Of course, she already had several other offers to consider. And then, there was the possibility of clerking for the Supreme Court ....

Back at Goldsmith & Hammer, Sarah was escorted into Harry's office where she found him standing near his desk, looking out over Fifth Avenue. His hands were in his pockets, and he seemed lost in thought.

"You've got quite a view," Sarah said.

"I know," said Harry. "One of the luxuries I allow myself in life is the privilege of sitting back at times and simply observing the world around me. "But," he said with a slight flourish of his right hand, "you didn't come down from Cambridge to listen to me philosophize. You came to see us in action, and, today, we have a very interesting appeal before the First Department."

"The General Sound case, I believe."

"Correct," said Harry. "Now, let me ask you to define some terms. What is the First Department?"

"The First Department is an appellate court in New York State that hears appeals from trial courts in New York County and the Bronx."

"Excellent," said Harry. "Now, assume you have an eighteen-year-old African-American client who has just been convicted of selling marijuana. Legal Aid has just assigned you to do his appeal. How would you explain to him what you're going to do?"

Sarah thought for a moment before she spoke. She liked being tested. "I'd tell him that the lower court made a lot of mistakes and, based on those mistakes, I'm going to ask a higher court to either throw out his conviction or order a new trial."

"Good," Harry said crisply. "Now define summary judgment for a lawyer and then for a layman."

Sarah was thrilled by the rapid-fire exchange. "For a lawyer, I'd say that summary judgment is when a court decides that there are no material issues of fact, so, it decides the case as a matter of law. For a layman, I'd say summary judgment is when a judge says, 'This case is so clear, I'm not going to bother sending it to a jury, I'll decide it myself.'"

"Good, Sarah," Harry said. "Now tell me what you think of this." He pulled out a sheet of paper from his briefcase and handed it to her. On top it read "Rental Agreement" and beneath those words, were long paragraphs that she didn't bother reading. At the bottom, was a blank line for a signature.

"It looks like a contract."

"Agreed," said Harry. "But is it a contract that a court should grant summary judgment on, saying that a man should be held to its terms?"

Sarah held the paper at arm's length and frowned. "I'd say no," she answered at last. "There's no signature. You'd have to prove a man agreed to be bound by it, and that is for a jury to decide."

Harry nodded and took the paper back. "Sarah, I only hope the First Department thinks as clearly as you do. Now, let's go. Charlie is waiting with the car."

Walking next to Harry as they left the building, Sarah had the same feeling she had as a first-year law school student when she would follow her professors across Harvard Yard after a class was over, hoping to pick up stray pearls of wisdom.

Once they were in the car, Harry turned to Sarah and said, "You'll forgive me if I retreat into silence for the trip to court. I find relaxing before an argument is a great way to organize your thoughts."

"I understand you, Harry," Sarah said. "I'll just enjoy the view."

Twenty minutes later, they arrived at the First Department on Madison Avenue and Twenty-Fifth Street. The First Department is a citadel of the law, a small white stone building with Doric columns and steep front steps. The courthouse created the feeling that one is about to enter an inner sanctum. Harry was still unsteady when he was climbing up steps even though he no longer used crutches. Sarah and Charlie wordlessly helped Harry up the steps and through the heavy mahogany doors.

The lobby lacked only a roaring fireplace and footmen to make it feel like an exclusive men's club from the Victorian era. As soon as they reached the officer at the security desk, Harry asked for a calendar of the afternoon's oral arguments. He scrutinized it with a practiced eye. "Let's see," he said, "we are going to be the first case to be heard today, and the judges will be Pappas, Smith, McHugh, Padilla and Stein. Padilla will be the presiding judge. They're a good panel. Now, let me show you the courtroom."

They passed through two large doors with ornate handles to find themselves in one of the most beautiful rooms Sarah had ever seen. Sarah had seen cathedrals in Europe that did not inspire the same sense of awe. Rows of upholstered stained wooden benches were divided by an aisle with thick carpet that led up to a lectern with two lights on it, one red, one white. ("The white light means you have five minutes left," said Harry. "The red one means sit down.") On either side of the lectern were desks for the opposing sides. The ceiling had a small stained-glass dome in its center.

Beyond the lectern was a long, raised desk with five large comfortable chairs behind it, and, just past them was an elaborately carved wooden wall with a door in its center. ("The judges come out of there," explained Harry.) There was a nameplate in front of each chair as well as stacks of legal briefs.

They sat down near the podium and watched as the surrounding seats slowly filled up with attorneys.

"What goes through your head just before a big argument?" Sarah asked softly.

Harry chuckled. "Honestly, I just look upon it all as a day's work. Of course, it takes about twenty years of practice to get to where you don't care enough to worry yourself sick. When I was younger, every time I finished a big argument in court, I'd go to a bar for a drink. But, now that I'm a big shot, I use the private bar in my limo." He chuckled at this last comment as if to say, 'Don't take me seriously.'

Court officers appeared and took seats at a desk near the judges' bench. Suddenly, an almost theatrical voice boomed out "All rise!" as four black-robed men and one woman came out from the door behind the bench. They paused by their respective chairs and then, as if by an unspoken command, they sat down simultaneously.

No sooner had the attorneys taken their seats, when Judge Padilla, who sat in the center of the tribunal, turned to the court officer, and said, "Call the calendar."

"General Sound v. Magnus," boomed the officer.

Harry rose to his feet. Taking great care to conceal his slight limp, he walked slowly but confidently to the lectern. Sarah could see he was very sure of himself. "Harry Goldsmith for the appellant," he said.

"You may proceed," Padilla said.

"May it please the Court, the issue is whether summary judgment can be granted based on an unsigned contract, especially when the person who allegedly agreed to be bound by the unsigned contract denies he ever saw it, and the respondent has produced no proof that he did. Let us look at the facts. Magnus, Inc. is a producer of independent movies ...."

Soft-core porn for cable, Sarah thought. But she was enjoying herself.

"Magnus had rented audio equipment from General Sound, and it was stolen from a production site. General Sound sued. General Sound sued. Magnus claims they always rented equipment on an informal handshake basis; General Sound claims that Magnus agreed to be bound by the terms of the unsigned contract. Why Magnus never signed the contract is something that General Sound does not explain."

Then McHugh spoke up. "But what difference does it make whether or not the contract is valid? Magnus took possession of the equipment, didn't it?"

"It makes all the difference in the world," Harry calmly replied. "If Magnus was not bound by the contract, then, common law applies, and that only requires Magnus to use reasonable care in looking after the equipment. The contract requires them to be strictly liable for the stolen equipment."

"Counselor," Judge Pappas interjected, "can you explain why the lower court found against your client? I've read the opinion twice, and I'm not sure I understand it."

Oh Harry! Sarah thought. You've won already.

He's just called the lower court judge a fool. You're like an athlete taking a victory lap now.

"Frankly, I'm not sure either," Harry replied. "May I respectfully suggest that the burden of defending the lower court's decision should properly fall on my adversary?"

Judge Smith spoke up. "As I read the case law, when someone signs a contract, you know by the signature that they have agreed to its terms. But, when you want to enforce an unsigned contract, you must prove that the parties agreed to be bound to it. Isn't that a question of fact right there?"

"Precisely your Honor, and that is why there can't be summary judgment," Harry said. He made a very slight bow as if in the presence of royalty.

"Have you anything else you wish to add, counselor?" Judge Padilla inquired.

"Only one thing your Honor, I wish to acknowledge the presence here today of Ms. Sarah Mendes, who is the articles editor on the *Harvard Law Review*. Ms. Mendes has come here today to observe this argument, and she was kind enough to help me prepare for it." Then, Harry turned and nodded toward her.

"Welcome, Ms. Mendes," said the judge. Sarah was so startled that she rose from her seat and made a slight curtsy.

"I thank the court for its kind attention," Harry said. Then he scooped up his brief from the lectern and walked back to his seat.

"You were great," Sarah whispered as Harry sat down.

"Thank you," Harry replied softly. "But remember there are two sides to every argument. And here comes the opposition if I am not mistaken."

A young lawyer was advancing toward the podium. Unlike Harry, who had walked at an easy pace, the young lawyer walked quickly with jerky movements.

"He's nervous," Sarah whispered.

"I know," Harry replied.

The young man put his brief on the lectern and began to speak. "May it please the court, my name is Barton O'Neill for the respondent, General Sound. There is a general principle in the law that lower court decisions should not be reversed lightly...."

"What if they are clearly wrong?" Judge Padilla asked.

The young man hesitated and then said, "Well, if they are wrong, they should be reversed."

"Thank you for telling us our job," said Judge Smith. "Now, tell us why this decision should stand. As I see it, you have an obvious question of fact, and, where there's a question of fact, there can't be summary judgment."

There was no answer forthcoming to that question. Finally, Judge Stein spoke and filled the vacuum. "Young man," he said, "do you have any proof that your adversary's client even saw this contract? I don't see any in the record."

The young man paused. It seemed to Sarah that he wanted to find a hole in the earth that he could jump into. He made one more try. "There is an affidavit in the record by the president of General Sound which states that Magnus entered into the contract."

"But what does that mean? Nothing," Stein shot back from the bench. "Deciding whether someone entered into a contract is what a court does. The affidavit says nothing about how Magnus allegedly agreed to the contract."

The young man scanned the panel from left to right and then right to left, looking for a sympathetic face. He found none. Finally, he said, "May it please the court, I waive further argument and rest on the brief."

"Have a seat, counselor," Judge Padilla said. As the young man turned and walked down the aisle, Sarah saw he was flushed.

Harry stood up and stuck out his hand to the young lawyer. "Good job," he said. Then, Harry motioned to Sarah that it was time to leave. They silently walked out of the chamber.

"Well, what did you think?" Harry asked once they were in the lobby.

"It was very exciting, but I didn't like watching what the judges did to your adversary."

"Neither did I," Harry said. "But, I knew something like this was going to happen. Their brief was very weak. Their whole case was a loser, and no partner wants to go down in flames, so they sent a new associate to handle the argument. That way, when he loses, they've got someone they can blame. I would never do that."

I'm glad you said that, Sarah thought to herself.

Harry paused. "But, let me say this," and he turned to look right at her face. "If you come to work for us, this is the kind of thing we'll have you doing as soon as you're ready."

Sarah looked at him silently. "Thank you, Harry," she said at last.

As Sarah walked into Goldsmith & Hammer for the third time that day, she was beginning to feel as if she already belonged there. But Sarah also realized quietly that she was on an emotional roller coaster. Now was a time to be especially level-headed.

Harry asked her to wait in his office. After five minutes, Sarah was escorted into the same conference room where she had earlier accepted Max's apology. Waiting for her were Harry, Roy Cook and Brad McDonald. Brad headed the real estate department; she had met him earlier that day. The three men sat in leather chairs at a circular table. Harry welcomed her into the room and invited her to sit down there.

"We now come to the end of an eventful day, Sarah," Harry said. "You have made a very strong impression on us, and we would like to make you an offer of employment. Would you consider one?"

"Yes, I would," Sarah said, carefully modulating

her voice so as not to give a hint of her inner thoughts.

"Good," Harry replied, and he handed her an envelope with her name on it. "Here are the terms, take them out and let's review them. Brad is the actual head of the hiring committee so I'll defer to him."

"Okay, Sarah," Brad began. "Your starting salary with us will be $110,000 a year. In addition, there will be a one-time housing allowance of $10,000 and a signing bonus of the same amount. When you are admitted to the bar in New York State, your base salary will increase to $120,000."

"Your offer is certainly competitive for firms of this size." This was Sarah's gentle way of saying that she had already been offered more money from bigger firms. But she had a surprise coming; the hiring committee was prepared for this.

"You will be on a five-year partnership track with the firm," Brad said. "And we are aware that you are being considered for a clerkship with the Supreme Court. If you are accepted, we will count those two years toward your partnership."

Three years to a partnership when other firms demanded eight? Suddenly, Sarah was very interested, but she remained quiet on the surface.

Roy picked up a sheet of paper and began to read. "Now let's discuss your benefits. You will have three weeks of vacation and six personal days annually for the first three years. In your fourth year your vacation will increase to four weeks. Every seven years you will be entitled to a paid three-month sabbatical, which you can spend any way you wish, except that if you practice law, you must have our permission. There is a 401k, and we contribute two percent of your salary, and our health benefits are excellent. Now, Harry will discuss your working conditions."

Harry leaned back in his chair, acting like a man who knows he is offering a good deal. "In your first year, you will be expected to work an unusually heavy schedule because you will be rotated every few months among the major practice areas of this firm: tax, bankruptcy, litigation, real estate and securities law. At the end of the year, we will sit down and decide whether you and our firm are a good match, and, if so, what area of our practice best suits you. Of course, you will have your own secretary and a paralegal."

Harry paused and leaned forward in his chair. "By the way, you know that Max heads the securities department. Would you have any difficulty working under him?"

"Under him, yes," Sarah said, and Harry frowned. But then she quickly added, "but, working with him, I think that would be a great experience." Everyone laughed.

"Touché, Sarah," Harry said. "We would ask you to give us your decision by mid-April. You should know about the Supreme Court by then. Is that acceptable?" Sarah nodded. "Good, and now, on behalf of the firm, I thank you for your visit. Charlie is waiting with the car downstairs to take you back to the airport. Whatever you choose, Sarah, you will always have our best wishes."

She put the envelope in her briefcase, shook hands all around, took her leave, and left them with thanks and compliments.

"Will we ever see her again?" Roy wondered.

"I couldn't read her," Brad said. "She held her cards too close."

As always, Harry had the last word. "Gentlemen," he said as he touched his fingertips together, "place your bets."

Night had fallen in New York. The streets were wet from a light misty rain, but Sarah virtually danced with joy up to the waiting limousine. Charlie held the door for her, but before getting in she looked up Fifth Avenue. The skyscrapers shone with light while the street was filled with people, hurrying toward their lives. Success, power, excitement: everything she ever thought she wanted, seemed near enough to touch, to taste.

But though she was young, she was still wise enough to know that these things were not hers, not now, not yet.

She got into the car and headed back to Cambridge.

CHAPTER V

Sarah slowly began to realize that law school would soon come to an end. It was now mid-March; there were only seven more weeks of classes, and then, there would be finals. After that, she would head back to New York and take a cram course for the July bar exam. Then, it would be off to Europe and Israel as a graduation present. Europe was where she was born and where she still had family. She also had family in Israel, but her memories of that country were more complex.

One night, after Sarah came back to her dormitory from working at the Law Review, she decided to pamper herself. There would be no more studying tonight; instead, she would sit mute in class the next day. She took a leisurely bubble bath and put on some woolen pajamas and brewed herself some herbal tea. Then, settling down in a comfortable chair, she allowed herself the rare luxury of letting her mind drift off ....

———◆———

The Gulf War had broken out when Sarah was a freshman at Brandeis. Her immediate reaction was to want to take a leave of absence and go to Israel to do volunteer work. Her parents, who wrote the checks in her life, were delighted at Sarah's idealism, and horrified at where it was leading her. They flatly refused. A compromise was finally reached; Sarah would finish her school year and then, do volunteer work in Israel that summer.

Sarah signed up with a program administered by the Israeli army and flew off two days after her last final. While on the plane, she reviewed her many memories of Israel: the cosmopolitan tempo of Tel Aviv, the calm peaceful eternity of Jerusalem sitting high on a hill, the mountains of the north and the deserts of the south. But this trip was different than all the others; this time she had something to accomplish and a goal to meet.

When Sarah arrived at Ben-Gurion airport after a twelve-hour plane flight, she was met by a sergeant major with a clipboard. His name was Moti Avrech, and he would be supervising the volunteers. Sarah and the other volunteers were guided to a table loaded with refreshments. A sign said, 'Welcome Volunteers.' Sarah was given a nametag, and she began to introduce herself. She was so excited to be back.

Moti herded them onto the bus, and then, made announcements over a microphone. "Shalom and welcome to Israel on behalf of the Israeli Army. By a show of hands, how many people have been on this program before?" Several people raised their hands. "Good, then you know it is standard security procedure that we do not tell volunteers where they will be going until we are actually on the bus. I can tell you now that we are going to a tank base called Apiron near Ashdot. Enjoy the ride, and we'll talk more when we get there."

When they arrived at Aprion, Sarah thought the tank base looked like a dilapidated factory complex painted in military green, set in a desert with a bare dusting of eucalyptus trees and grass. But there were green rolling hills to the north and a warm wind would blow in from the sea, and it felt like a caress on the cheek. Sarah had never thought much about tanks before this trip. She knew them as little toys her brother had played with. Now, they were every-where: American M-60s; British Centurions; Russian T-55s and Israeli Merkavot. The first time she saw a tank drive by without its turret, it reminded her of a turtle without its shell. She laughed.

Sarah was assigned a room in a barracks with one woman from New Zealand and another from England. The quartermaster issued Sarah a drab green uniform and army boots. That afternoon, the sergeant major gave out assignments: Sarah was assigned to paint tanks three days a week and to help prepare lunch for 150 people the rest of the time.

One morning while eating breakfast in the dining hall, Sarah looked up from her yogurt and salad to see a tall young man with brown eyes and curly hair standing in front of her. He was holding a tray heaping with scrambled eggs, humus and tehina, ground chick-peas. "Bonjour," he said, "they tell me you speak French."

"Oui," replied Sarah.

"May I join you?" he asked. "I've only been in Israel for a few months, and I miss speaking French."

"Please do," Sarah replied. "I don't get to speak French very often either." He sat down with his food tray, and they continued the conversation.

"Oh, why is that?" he asked.

"I was born in Belgium, but my family moved to New York when I was twelve."

"I am from Paris originally," he said. "But, my parents took me to visit New York once. It was such an exciting city."

"It can be," Sarah said. "But don't you think we should introduce ourselves? My name is Sarah."

He returned her smile. "I'm Victor. Tell me, what brings you to Israel?"

"I came as a volunteer for the summer."

"I've made aliyah," Victor said, announcing he had moved to Israel permanently. "I decided to get my army duty over with at once. Then, I want to go to the university."

Sarah admired anyone with more courage than she had. "What has the army got you doing?"

Victor grimaced slightly. "They've made me an apprentice tank mechanic. They told me I didn't speak Hebrew well enough to serve in a combat unit." When she told him her own assignment, he offered his sympathies.

Finally, Victor finished his breakfast with a gulp of coffee. "I've got to go now. Perhaps I'll see you in the motor pool."

They met there the next day, which was Sarah's day to help paint the tanks. Working on tanks is a messy job. First, you must scrape off rust with sandpaper, then, you apply a primer with a brush. Finally, paint is applied with either a bigger brush or a spray gun. Old work clothes and a mask and goggles come with the territory.

Sarah was sitting on the hood of a tank, painting its cannon barrel when she felt someone tap her on her leg. It was Victor. She jumped off the tank to speak to him face-to-face. She was covered with paint, and he reeked of grease and oil. "We're a mess," she said. They both laughed.

But then, Victor suddenly said, "You look so lovely in your uniform. Even covered with paint."

"Thank you," Sarah said, thinking to herself how handsome Victor was.

"Sarah, would you like to go into Ashdot this afternoon to see a movie?" Victor asked. "I can get a pass."

"All right," Sarah said. "I'm done for the day at 3:30. I can meet you in front of the mess hall."

"I'll be there," Victor said.

They enjoyed themselves in Ashdot. Later, on the way back to the base, Victor explained that he had been accepted by the Sorbonne when he graduated high school, but he turned it down because he had his heart set on aliyah. His parents, both attorneys, promptly disowned him, and he went to work in a factory to earn the money he needed.

That sounds like my father, Sarah privately remarked.

The intimacies of a common language in a foreign land drew them together, and Sarah found herself more and more attracted to Victor.

A few weeks after their first date, Victor told Sarah that he had a 72-hour pass. Would she care to spend it with him? Sarah was agreeable, and she suggested they head south through the desert to Eilat and go snorkeling in the Red Sea. Victor had another idea; he suggested they go north to the nature preserve known as the Banyos, and then, spend the night in Haifa on the coast. After Victor told her the Banyos was the closest thing Israel had to a wilderness, Sarah was sold on the idea.

At 6:30 the next morning, Sarah and Victor hitched a ride on a flatbed tractor-trailer that was heading north to the Golan Heights to pick up disabled tanks. They rode with it as far as Afula; then

Victor and Sarah took another bus that let them off at a parking lot on a lonely stretch of road. At the far end of the lot was a wooden gate that opened onto a path leading into the woods.

They wandered by a stream and came to some Roman ruins where they ate their lunch. Sarah thought that the woods were beautiful, but that the loveliness of the nature was marred by all the litter others had left.

"Be patient," Victor said calmly after she told him her thoughts. "I can show you a place that is untouched."

After they finished eating, they walked further along the path, pausing every few steps to embrace and kiss. Then, suddenly, Victor led her off the trail and took her deeper into the woods. "Come with me," he said.

Within a few minutes, Victor and Sarah came to a small clearing with a pond fed by a waterfall. It seemed to have been untouched since the beginning of the world. "It's as beautiful as the Garden of Eden," Sarah said after catching her breath.

"And so are you," Victor said as he slowly drew his finger from her left ear to the corner of her mouth. "That's why I brought you here. Come, let's go into the water."

Sarah demurely rolled up her pants legs and took off her boots. Victor stripped naked. "Victor, what do you think you're doing?" Sarah demanded.

Victor walked over to her, smiled, and began to

unbutton her blouse. She raised her hands to stop him, but then, she paused, and she began to feel a rising sensation. More and more, in the past days, she had felt drawn to Victor, a desire to be at one with him.

Sarah gently took his hands in hers, kissed them and then, with a devilish smile, she got undressed.

Victor looked at her with awe. For a moment he couldn't speak. At last, he said, "you're so beautiful."

She opened her arms, and he came over to her.

Hand in hand, they stepped into the pond. When they reached deep water, they began to embrace and kiss. Her body shuddered, and her breathing became labored.

Then, Victor led her by the hand to a near-by bed of yellow flowers upon which he had placed their clothes. Then, they danced a dance as old as time.

Some people are blessed in their youth to feel a love for another that becomes intermingled with a larger purpose. When Sarah joined together with Victor, she felt at one with the land and the people.

She felt so warm.

She felt so holy.

She felt so happy.

When Sarah and Victor left the Banyos hand in hand, she felt as if her face glowed. Upon reaching the highway, they flagged down a bus and arrived in the port city of Haifa just before nightfall. They spent the night at a youth hostel in Carmel, a suburb perched high on a hill overlooking the harbor.

The next morning, the lovers awoke at dawn to see the sun rise in the east and light up the blue Mediterranean that lay before them. "I love you," Victor said.

For some reason, despite all that she felt for him, Sarah could not bring herself to answer with the word 'love.' Instead, she said, "and you're wonderful." Either Victor did not catch Sarah's precise choice of words, or, perhaps, he did and decided to not to make anything of it.

They took the coastal train running from Haifa to Tel Aviv, their eyes fixed on the sea instead of the urban sprawl that lay on the other side. From Tel Aviv, they took a bus back the base. When Sarah reported back to the sergeant-major, he gave her an odd look and asked her whether she had enjoyed her brief excursion. She said yes and nothing else.

In the next ten days, Victor and Sarah spent every possible moment together. She loved being with Victor. However, she also found herself wanting to push him away. She could not understand herself.

Sarah began to see Victor in two ways: was he a handsome, young idealist or someone who had run away from adult responsibilities to play soldier in a foreign land? If it were the latter, then what did that make her? Victor said that he loved her, and that, before he met her, he had been so lonely in Israel. But then, how did he know about that pond and when it would be deserted? Had he taken other women there?

Finally, decisions could not be put off any longer. "Sarah, I would like you to stay in Israel with me," Victor said.

Sarah was unsure if this was what she really wanted to do, but now she felt trapped. "All right," Sarah said, "I'll call my parents and tell them."

There is a seven-hour time difference between Israel and New York. At seven o'clock in the evening, Sarah made a collect international phone call from the base.

Sarah's father answered the phone in his library. He was overjoyed to hear his daughter's voice. "Sarah, we've missed you. What flight are you taking home?"

"Papa, that's what I wanted to discuss with you and mama," Sarah said reluctantly. "I've met this soldier . . . ."

However, her father had lived more years than Sarah. He cut her off in mid-sentence. "Sarah, you're not thinking of staying, are you?"

Silence. Then, "please, can I explain?"

He cut her off again. "Sarah, you're only nineteen. If you don't come back home, I'll fly over and bring you back." His voice, usually so calm, was now getting angry. "You have worked too hard to throw everything away on a romance."

His last words were cruel, but before Sarah could reply, her mother picked up the living room phone and said, "Maurice, let me talk to Sarah alone."

After getting her husband off the line, Rachel began to calmly speak with Sarah.

"Sarah, I only heard part of the conversation. Have you met a man?" Rachel asked.

Sarah was silent for a long moment, then she said yes.

"And are you in love with him?" Her mother's sweetness and evenness of tone were almost as upsetting as her father's anger.

"I'm not sure," Sarah answered. "I think I am."

Sarah braced herself for a tirade and a direct order that she imagined she would disobey. Sarah was going to cite love as her reason, but there was a surprise waiting for her.

"Sarah," Rachel said, "if you really want to stay in Israel, I'll persuade your father to let you, but I don't think you should. You are simply too young to commit yourself to a man. You just turned nineteen. At your age, your horizons should be opening, not narrowing."

Sarah was quiet. "I see," she finally said.

"Come back to America. Tell your boyfriend that we threatened to cut you off if you didn't. We've already promised you that you can spend your junior year abroad, and you can go back to Israel then. If you really feel love for each other, a year's separation should be easy to bear. True love can survive time and separation; infatuation can't."

She knew her mother was right. Sarah sighed as a lover and obeyed as a daughter. She said goodbye to her mother, and then turned to face Victor who had been standing only a few feet away. Before

Sarah could say a word, Victor spoke. "You're going home."

"Yes, I am, Victor. I have no choice. I can't survive without my parents' support. But they promised me I could spend my junior year in Israel. A year isn't a long time."

"It will be for us," Victor said, and he held out his arms. She ran to him, but, as he held her, Sarah was secretly glad he could not see the relief on her face.

Their relationship became a mere friendship for the rest of her time on the base. Sarah explained to Victor that it was to ease their parting, but she was not sure if this was the truth. Her departure was abrupt: an army bus came to take Sarah and the other volunteers back to the airport. When Sarah waved goodbye to Victor as the bus drove off, she felt as if some harsh ordeal was over; she realized she was happy to be going back to New York.

Twenty-four hours later, Sarah sat quietly in the living room of her parents' apartment, gazing mindlessly out over Central Park. She did not hear her mother enter the room. "Are you thinking of him, Sarah?"

Her mother's soft words brought Sarah out of a private world. "Yes, I guess I was still with him."

She sat next to Sarah and caressed her daughter's hair. "I know. It will hurt for a while."

"But, mother, you knew just what to say. If you had ordered me to come home, I probably would have stayed to defy you and papa just to show my independence."

"And what do you think would've happened then?"

"Oh, you know what would've happened mother," Sarah said with the testiness of someone forced to acknowledge an unpleasant truth. "I would have come back a few weeks later, ashamed and embarrassed. But, what I want to know, mother," and here Sarah looked at her half in anger and half in wonderment, "is how you knew exactly what to say at such a tense moment with no warning?"

"Why Sarah," her mother said, "can't you believe I was every young once and in love? Or infatuated? I suspect you're a romantic when it comes to love Sarah, and that you always will be. Come, let's go out for lunch, and then, I think you could use a walk in the Park. Let's get some fresh air."

Sarah and Victor wrote to each other briefly, but that soon came to an end. Sarah could never remember who it was that wrote last.

———⊶◈⊷———

Sarah jolted back to full consciousness. She was sitting in her dorm holding her cup of tea. All this happened six years ago. Was she really going to slacken off in her last few weeks at Harvard Law School? What was she thinking? She drank her herbal tea, which had turned cold, and got out her books.

CHAPTER VI

As the season for job interviews progressed, Sarah became jaded. First, she would meet with a recruiter on campus, who would be duly impressed with her credentials. Then, she would be invited to visit the firm. She would jet off to Washington, Chicago and New York regularly to be wined-and-dined by firms with hundreds of lawyers. A night in a top hotel was thrown in for good measure. Offers in the six figures would typically follow.

She was not impressed. Sarah surprised herself by comparing these gilded firms to Goldsmith & Hammer. Only Harry had dared to show Sarah what his firm could do; all the others relied on their prestige and the size of their hiring bonuses. Compared to the integrity she found in Harry, the other offers made her feel as if she would merely an impressive trophy to be added to a collection.

But Sarah's heart was not really in any of these interviews, not even with Goldsmith & Hammer. Her goal was to clerk at the Supreme Court of the United States. In the first few weeks of her senior year, one of Sarah's professors, who had clerked for the legendary Justice Douglas, offered to put in a good word for her if she applied. Sarah prepared the necessary application forms and then waited. In fact, just days before her disastrous interview with Max Hammer, the professor tipped her off that Justice Bradford was interested and that she would be called for an interview in a few weeks.

On a quiet Wednesday afternoon in late March, Sarah happened to be in her dorm room when the phone rang.

"Is this Sarah Mendes?" a woman asked in a stern voice.

"Yes, can I help you?"

The reply was no-nonsense. "This is Justice Bradford's chambers in Washington. He has read your application for a clerkship. Can you come to Washington next Wednesday so he can meet with you?"

Wednesday was top-heavy with classes, but Sarah knew what she was expected to answer. "I'll be there. What time should I arrive?"

"Nine o'clock. Bring a photo identification to the side entrance on Maryland Avenue, and security will let you in. We look forward to seeing you." Then, she hung up.

Sarah was excited, but her practical sense told her that she had to prepare for the interview as if she were an athlete competing in the Olympics. She knew it couldn't be done alone. Later that day, Sarah pulled Melissa aside as they were leaving their federal tax class.

"Melissa, can you join me for a cup of tea? Something is up."

"Of course, Sarah. What's going on?"

Sarah looked around to make certain no one was listening. She spoke in a whisper. "I've heard from the Supreme Court. Justice Bradford wants to interview me next week."

"Sarah...," Melissa started to say, but Sarah silenced her by saying that this was not a time to celebrate, but to plan. Ten minutes later, they were seated at a Starbucks, nursing cups of exotic teas.

"This is how I see matters," Sarah explained, barely able to contain her enthusiasm. "Bradford has been on the bench ten years. He has written a lot of opinions. Between now and next week, I think I can read about twenty of them really well."

"But Sarah," Melissa asked incredulously, "you already study harder than anyone I know. Where will you find time to do that?"

"I'm not finished," Sarah said. "I'm also going to skim a study of Justice Bradford, and I'll swim ten laps every day."

Melissa was getting tired just listening to her. "You do what you think you have to do, Sarah. If it were me, just the honor of getting this far would be enough. I'd prepare by getting extra sleep each night. But, if you need my help, you've got it."

"Thank you, Melissa," Sarah said. "I'll try to take it easy."

"I don't believe you know how, Sarah," Melissa said. "But I hope you'll try."

Sarah finished her tea and said good-bye. She stopped off at a stationery store to buy a notebook that she labeled 'Bradford Interview.' Then, she headed over to the library. Sarah consulted with the law librarians, and they helped her find several articles on Bradford. She copied them and then marked off his most important cases with a highlighter. On a second reading, Sarah made an 'X' by the ones that seemed important. Later that night, she downloaded the cases onto her laptop. Just before the library closed, she checked out a book on Bradford.

Sarah then went back to her room and set to work. Sarah pored over the material as if she were possessed, and Melissa was not so sure she wasn't. Melissa visited Sarah every night, partly to offer support and partly to stare at her in awe.

Tuesday arrived. In the late afternoon, Sarah packed her overnight bag and grabbed her briefcase -- how could a lawyer go on an interview without one? -- and took a cab to Logan Airport to get the Washington shuttle. For luck, she also packed a copy of the *Harvard Law Review* listing her as an editor.

Once in Washington, Sarah decided to borrow an

idea from Harry. She got into a taxi at the Washington airport and asked the driver to take her to the Hilton Hotel. Then she handed him a list of sights and said, "Please drive by these places on your way."

The driver handed the list back to her. "I can't do that, miss. Washington is a zoned city for cabs. I must charge you a set fee from where you get in to where you get off. There can't be any side trips."

"There can be," Sarah said. She handed him twenty dollars, and off they drove.

Darkness had fallen, and downtown Washington was filled with light. The Capitol dome, the Washington Monument, and the White House, they all shone as bright as day. New York, at night, gives off the impression of being filled with life; downtown Washington is a city of power during the day with life being lived somewhere else at night. Sarah's taxi drove past beautiful building after beautiful building, and she could only think of all the decisions made in them that affected so many lives.

When they approached the Lincoln Memorial, Sarah asked the driver to pull up for a moment and keep the motor running. She jumped out of the cab and quickly walked up the steps of that beautiful Greek temple of a building. Inside, against one wall, sat a statue of Abraham Lincoln many times larger than life. Sarah approached it reverently and silently asked herself what her motives were in coming there so late at night. The answer was simple: she once saw a movie with Jimmy Stewart where he came to the statue for inspiration in a moment of crisis.

But that was just a movie. Lincoln was a very practical politician who pursued power and glory, but he also had dreams of a better world. Perhaps she could be the same. Sarah was prepared to stand there and ponder, forgetting for the moment that there was a taxi waiting outside, but then, there was noise behind her. She turned and saw a troop of Boy Scouts entering the chamber. "Are we disturbing you, miss?" asked the scout leader.

"No," Sarah replied. "I was just leaving," and she returned to her taxi and headed for her hotel.

Sarah selected the Hilton for the most pragmatic of reasons: it was near the Supreme Court building, and it had a beauty salon if a last-minute need arose. She had dinner in the hotel's restaurant and fell asleep watching a movie on television.

She slept well that night and woke up at sunrise. Switching to a running suit, she did a few laps around the block and then showered and had a light breakfast, reviewing her notes as she ate.

It was 8:15 by Sarah's watch when she left the hotel. She checked out of her room and left her bag with the front desk. That brought her to 8:35. Sarah hailed a taxi. "Supreme Court, please," she said, and they drove off.

Ten minutes later, Sarah arrived in front of the Supreme Court. While the Appellate Division in Manhattan is a little jewel box of a courthouse in the style of a Grecian temple, the Supreme Court is huge, and it reminded Sarah of the ruins of ancient Rome magically restored to grandeur. She was starting to feel a little intimidated.

At first, Sarah thought about marching boldly up the marble steps to the main entrance, but now was not the time to break the rules. She reported to the small entrance on the Maryland Avenue side as instructed. It was 8:55.

"You're expected," said the guard, after Sarah introduced herself. After her briefcase was X-rayed and she went through the metal detector, the guard directed her down a long corridor flanked with the portraits of some of the Supreme Court's most distinguished jurists. Directly ahead, she could see the large statue of Justice John Marshall. But, before she reached it, the guard led her off down a side hallway to a small elevator bank. She didn't have long to wait. Out of an elevator stepped a young woman who walked right up to Sarah and spoke bluntly.

"Ms. Mendes, I presume?"

"Yes, that's me."

"I'm Janet Meadows. I'm the law clerk you may be replacing."

As they shook hands like two Amazon warriors, Sarah quickly looked over Janet's clothes and hair. Sarah concluded she had dressed a little too conservatively, not too much, just a little. Still, there was nothing she could do about it now. Sarah said, "You must be sorry to be leaving."

"I am," Janet replied. "It has been a great two

years, but now I've got to go out into the real world as the judge calls it. But there is a problem with your interview today...."

Sarah looked at her sharply. "Is it still on?"

"Oh yes," Janet said. "However, last night the Court received an emergency petition to stay an execution. The justices are going to meet on it in thirty minutes, and, after that, the judge has a full day scheduled. So, I can't give you an orientation tour right now. Your interview starts in two minutes. Follow me."

A ride in an elevator, a brisk walk down a corridor hung with more oil paintings of distinguished jurists, and Sarah found herself being led into Justice Bradford's office. As he rose from his desk to greet her, Sarah thought that he looked like the popular image of a judge from the 1950's. Tall, with combed-back white hair and blue eyes hidden behind thick glasses, he wore a bow tie, and suspenders held up his trousers. Bradford had a slight belly, but other than that, he still had the physique of a man who had played football for Yale.

"So, you're the little lady who has accomplished so much," Bradford said as he shook her hand. "Do sit down, Ms. Mendes." And he gestured her to a waiting chair.

Little lady? Sarah thought. Don't tell me he's another Max Hammer. But she politely said, "Thank you, your Honor."

"Is there anything I can get you, Judge?" Janet

asked.

"A cup of tea for me, Janet. Ms. Mendes, would you care for anything?"

"No, thank you, your Honor," she replied.

Relaxing in his ox-blood-colored leather chair, Bradford picked up her resume from his desk and said, "Pardon me." Then he began to read it. Sarah used the few moments to take the measure of the man from his surroundings. Two walls were dominated with shelves of books. On a third wall were diplomas, awards, photos of the great men the judge had met in his life as well as a football trophy in a glass case. The fourth wall, which was behind the judge's desk, had a huge window with a magnificent view of Washington. There was only one thing on the judge's desk; it was a thick legal document whose front page had marginal comments in red, but, since it was upside-down, she couldn't make out anything else.

Bradford put her resume down. "You're an editor on the *Harvard Law Review*. That's better than I did. I only checked citations and footnotes."

"Perhaps you were saving your energies to become valedictorian?" Sarah suggested.

"You've made a study of me then," Bradford said.

"What would you think of me if I hadn't?" Sarah volleyed back.

"I see your point," Bradford said with a smile that was all courtesy. "Tell me, have you studied my decisions?"

"Some," Sarah replied.

A knock at the door interrupted them. Janet walked in, left the tea on the corner of the judge's desk, and hurried out. Bradford took the cup and saucer in his hands, leaned back in his chair, and began to sip slowly.

"Speaking of decisions, may I ask why you want a clerkship at this court?"

"Because there is nothing higher that a new lawyer can aspire to," she replied.

The judge seemed perplexed. "Don't you have idealistic reasons, like wanting to help the evolving state of American law?"

"Yes, I do, your Honor," Sarah replied. "But, frankly, I assumed that every applicant talks about her idealism in her interview while keeping her personal agenda quiet. I thought it might be more honest if I reversed the process."

The judge nodded appreciatively. "May I ask you a personal question, Ms. Mendes?"

"If you wish."

"When I graduated Yale, I had a chance to go to Paris for a year to study at the Sorbonne. My family urged me to go to law school first, and they assured me that Paris would still be there waiting for me after I took the bar. But then, there was pressure to get on with my career, and I sealed my fate by falling in love and getting married. I never did get back to Paris as a young man."

Sarah was puzzled. "Pardon me your Honor, but

what is your question?"

"My point, Ms. Mendes, is that you simply don't strike me as being a grind at heart, but that's what you've been doing for years. You'll be buried in paper for two years if you come here as a clerk. You don't need this Court on your resume; you can write your ticket anywhere. Don't you want to live a little?"

Sarah could not think of a quick reply, but she finally explained that, while she appreciated his concern, her personal life was private, and she was happy with the choices she had made.

The judge now looked like a man who had to perform an unpleasant duty.

"Well, here's a question for you," he said, and he pointed to the legal document in front of him. "This is a last-ditch argument to keep a man from being executed. How do you think I'm going to vote?"

Challenged, Sarah felt her body bracing for a fight. She answered calmly, "I can't answer that without knowing all the facts."

"Well, what do you know about my voting record on capital punishment?"

Sarah had the answer. "You have consistently held that capital punishment is constitutional, but, you have virtually never voted to permit an execution. You insist on reviewing the entire record in any case involving capital punishment, and, if there is a 't' that hasn't been properly crossed, you'll vote for a new trial."

Bradford leaned across his desk. "And what do

you think of capital punishment?"

"Are you asking me what the law is?" she asked.

"No," Bradford replied. "I want to know what you would do about capital punishment if you ruled the world."

Sarah was quiet for a moment. She knew he was waiting for an answer. "I would abolish it," Sarah replied at last. "But I don't live in a world where my word is law, and I don't expect to. One of my jobs as a clerk would be to research what the law is and advise you of my findings. I would offer my personal opinion only if you asked for it."

"May I assume then that you disagree with my opinion in <u>Wilkins v. Virginia</u>?"

Reluctantly, Sarah said that she did.

"I see. Tell me some other decisions of mine you don't agree with."

Sarah had walked into a trap. She found herself forced to discuss case after case where she disagreed with the judge. While she spoke, Bradford sat back in his chair, drinking his tea. Occasionally, he would ask a question, and, upon getting an answer, he would smile and return to silence until his next query.

Sarah's throat was starting to feel dry and raspy when there was a knock on the door. Janet poked her head in and said, "Judge, they're waiting for you in the conference room."

He looked at his watch and said, "Oh my! Ms. Mendes, it has been a real pleasure. You'll be hearing from my staff." And then, he shook her hand and quickly hurried out.

From my staff? Sarah thought. That means I'm not going to get it. Her heart sank.

Janet stayed in the room and asked Sarah whether she would like to take her tour of the building now. Part of Sarah wanted to just make a hasty retreat, but her better instincts made her accept.

Back to Cambridge then. Later that evening, Sarah found herself at a bistro nursing a good wine with Melissa and Jason.

"And I thought he'd be impressed that I had read so many decisions of his, but it turns out he expected it. It was like taking a final exam in Constitutional Law. Finally, he asked me how was my French, and, I thought, at last I can shine. I told him I was a native speaker, but he just reached into his desk and handed me a legal publication of the European Economic Union. Then, he asked me to translate on sight. He had me on a speakerphone with someone at the State Department who evaluated me. It was a nightmare."

"It sounds rough," Jason said. "But I still think you probably did better than you give yourself credit for."

"I think so, too," Melissa said. "But tell us what the tour was like."

"Oh, it was as wonderful as you might expect. On the top floor, they have a gymnasium where the justices and the law clerks play basketball sometimes.

They call it the 'Highest Court in the Land.' Then they've got a library with about a quarter of a million books, and, if they really want something obscure, they can get it sent over from the Library of Congress by an underground conveyor belt."

"Dear God," Jason said.

"But something funny happened in the library. Bradford's secretary introduced me to one of the senior librarians there. He gave me a detailed tour of the collection. He also began to ask me a lot of questions about how I'd research various topics. "

"That's significant," Melissa said. "It sounds like they were still interviewing you after Bradford was finished with you."

"I thought of that," Sarah said, and she finished her wine in one sip. "If they were, then, I know I made a few mistakes. As for the rest of the building, just think of the most beautiful set of offices and conference rooms any law firm could have and double it, and then throw in magnificent views of Washington, D.C. and the most advanced equipment anywhere, and you've got it. I just don't know if I'll ever visit the inner sanctum again."

"So, what are you going to do now?" Melissa asked She was already knew what the answer would be.

"I'm going back to my room and review the tapes of the lectures I missed today," Sarah said.

And she did just that.

For a few days, Sarah could only think of the

Supreme Court interview. She might yet clerk for Justice Bradford at the Supreme Court and shoot right to the top of the legal world, or, if she didn't get it, she would have to be content with a hell of a lot of money and power at some prestigious firm. All was well.

A week after she met with Justice Bradford, Sarah found herself walking across the campus with Melissa. The night was warm, and the quadrangle seemed to be full of life. The scent of spring was in the air. Gym bags were slung over their shoulders, and some good time on the racquetball court was all they had in mind.

"I'm really worried about my Suretyships and Mortgages final," Melissa confessed. "It is so confusing. How did you approach it, Sarah?"

Silence.

"Sarah, everything okay?"

Sarah started as if suddenly called out of a deep reverie. "Oh, I'm sorry. Lost in thought."

"Anything good?"

"No, no, nothing. What were you saying?"

——————•((•))•——————

Sarah's thoughts had slipped four years into the past, back to another warm spring night when she felt young and powerful. It was the Brandeis Dramatic Society's production of *Hamlet*, and she was Ophelia. After the curtain fell at the intermission, her ears rang with applause. As she ran backstage to refresh her makeup, the director, Jack Miller, motioned to her.

"Sarah," he said. "Don't vanish when the play is over. Someone wants to meet you."

She was too busy to be intrigued. "Well, who is it?"

"It would take too long to explain," Miller said with the look of a man concealing a pleasant surprise. "This is not an introduction to be rushed. I'll meet you backstage after the last curtain call."

"Okay," she said. "Gotta go." Sarah turned and headed off into the dark bowels of the theater. Is it someone who wants my phone number? she wondered. I don't need a boyfriend right now. Who else could it be?

The play was the thing for two more acts. When she took her last bow, a few roses sailed over the footlights to land at her feet. She picked them up and held them together as a bouquet, casting them into the dustbin with a flourish after the curtain fell.

"Ah, Sarah, there you are," she heard Miller say. She turned to face him and saw at his side a dapper older man, shorter than herself, with a broad smile and a shining pate. Everything about him seemed to say: I am sure of myself. Miller was tall with brown hair, but, somehow, he seemed smaller than this man.

"Sarah," Miller said, "have you ever heard of the

Georgetown Shakespeare Theater?"

"You mean the one in Washington?" Sarah asked. "Who hasn't?"

"Well," Miller said, "this is Hilton Gould, the artistic director. He has seen your performance, and he'd like to talk to you."

Gould smiled and held out an elegantly manicured hand. "It's a real pleasure to meet you, Ms. Mendes. I've seldom encountered a young American actress who could speak Shakespearean verse so well. Did I say something funny?"

Sarah had chuckled at an awkward moment. "I'm sorry. I thought it was funny that you called me an American actress. I just got my citizenship. I didn't know any English when we moved to New York when I was twelve."

The man was unfazed. "And where were you from originally?"

"Belgium."

"I see," he said. Then, speaking in French, he complimented her. "C'est un grand plaisir, mademoiselle, je vous faire la connaissance. "

"Merci, bien," Sarah replied.

An hour later, she was back in street clothes and sitting across from Gould in the Rathskeller, where you could always get a good pot of tea at any hour of the day or night. Miller was there too. He said little.

"The master's program has been a great success," Gould said. "We get applications from all over the country. The secret is that we concentrate on classical theater: a course in reciting blank verse, a course in movement. We even have a course in sword-fighting."

His enthusiasm was infectious, but Sarah's practical nature asserted itself. "It sounds interesting, but I've got two parents who are literally from the old world. They'll give me a blank check for Harvard Law School and a blank stare if I try to do anything else."

But Gould was unfazed. He never lost his confident air. "They'll probably think I'm trying to get you to run away with the circus, but I've talked with a lot of parents of would-be actors in my life, and I have a good track record of persuading them to give their children a *wanderjahr*, a year of adventure, to find themselves. Even if you don't choose a career in the arts, I can promise you a year you'll never forget."

Sarah was thinking. She picked up her tea cup and softly blew away the rising vapor. "But what about money?"

Gould didn't miss a beat. "We have scholarships available. You have to audition before a committee, but if you can repeat your performance tonight, I'm sure it won't be a problem. And by the way, some of our graduates have wound up in law school, but I can assure you they're the happiest attorneys you've ever met. They spent a year living out their dreams."

He leaned back with the satisfaction of a salesman who knew he'd made the perfect pitch.

Sarah was silent again. As the seconds ticked

away, things became awkward. Finally, Miller gently asked, "Sarah?"

She spoke at last. "My parents are coming up for the matinee tomorrow. Would you be available to talk to them?"

"I can arrange to be," Gould said.

Sarah took a slow swallow of tea to give herself time to weigh her thoughts. "Let me think it over," she said.

"Fair enough," Gould said with a wave of his hand. "Please let me get the check."

An actress must get her rest. It would never do to come on stage haggard with bags under her eyes, but that night was different. As Sarah walked back to her dorm room, she sensed that this was going to be an important night of her life, a time of potential change, like that fateful day at the Banyos three years earlier. In twenty-four hours, I may be a different person, she thought.

Back in her dorm room, Sarah stood before her mirror. Reflected behind her were all the books she had had to read to gain admission to Harvard Law. Who was the real Sarah?

She sat on her bed. It was an old struggle within her, the artistic and the practical. She had always chosen the latter. Now she could have both. She could take a year immersing herself in the arts while getting a prestigious degree. Then, a year later, she'd be safely enrolled in Harvard Law School. The best of both worlds.

That night, Sarah dreamed. She was in some kind of fantastic subway, riding high above a thrilling city. Her mother was with her, speaking some soft comforting words that she could not understand. Suddenly, the train stopped, and the doors opened onto a platform with a sign that said London, West End. Her mother pointed out the door, but there was a look of uncertainty in her eyes. Sarah turned to exit the car only to see a stern conductor in a black uniform blocking her way.

"You can't get out here," he said.

The doors closed, and the train moved on.

Melissa's questions pulled Sarah back to reality.

"Suretyships isn't really not so tough Melissa. I boiled the class down to 3 pages of notes. They got me an 'A', and you can have them."

"Thanks, Sarah, you're a true friend."

And so are you, Sarah thought. You just pulled me back.

Coincidences happen. On a fine day in mid-April, Sarah found two letters in her mailbox. That was all, no flyers, no junk mail, no magazines. One of the letters was from Goldsmith & Hammer, the other was from the Supreme Court of the United States.

The first thing Sarah did was to feel them. They were both thin, no more than one sheet in each. That was a bad sign from the Court, she thought.

She decided to open the letter from Goldsmith & Hammer first. Inside was a sheet of paper with the words "Appellate Division-First Department" in Gothic type: beneath it was the title General Sound v. Magnus. It was a very brief decision:

'The order of the trial court granting summary judgment pursuant to the terms of an unsigned contract is reversed and remanded.'

'The absence of a signature on the contract and the lack of any other proof in the record of the defendant's assent to the terms of the contract constitute questions of fact.'

We won, Sarah thought, unconsciously identifying with Goldsmith & Hammer for the first time.

What next caught Sarah's eye was a section of the decision entitled "Attorneys Present" that someone had marked in yellow hi-lighter. Under "Appellants" it read: "Harry Goldsmith, Esq. of Goldsmith & Hammer, with the assistance of Sarah L. Mendes, law student."

I've become immortal, Sarah thought. Whatever I do from this point on in my life, my name will be associated with a legal victory. Now, she opened the letter from Washington with confidence. She took it out and stared and stared....

"Sarah, Sarah." She suddenly realized Melissa was standing next to her, repeating her name. "Why do you have that funny look on your face?" But Sarah was speechless.

Then she held out the letter to Melissa. "I got

the clerkship with the Supreme Court."

"Sarah, you did it!" Melissa shouted.

The rest of Sarah's afternoon was predictable. There were joyful phone calls to family and friends, an absolute inability to concentrate on anything, and, by dinnertime, a realization for Sarah that she had several lucrative job offers that had to be diplomatically declined. She quickly drafted a form letter to send. However, when it came to Goldsmith & Hammer, she decided that a personal touch was in order.

When Sarah called the firm and asked to speak to Harry, she was put through immediately. "Hello, Sarah," Harry said. "What's cooking?"

She told him.

"That's wonderful," Harry said, and he sounded genuinely pleased. "Of course, you're going to accept. You'd be the biggest fool in the world if you didn't take it. Promise me you'll call the Court the moment you hang up and tell them you accept." Only then did it dawn on Sarah that she had forgotten to accept the clerkship. Sarah promised Harry she'd call the Court at once, and within two minutes, she did.

With that, Sarah's brief emotional roller coaster ride came to a halt, and she spent the evening as she usually did, in study.

The next day, Sarah found an overnight letter in her mailbox from Goldsmith & Hammer. It was from Harry.

"Dear Sarah, [it read]

Congratulations again on your achievement. In all honesty, I was fairly certain you were going to get it.

You are in for two of the most challenging years of your life. They will be years of hard work and tremendous professional growth. Your personal life may have to take a back seat, but you will have many years to catch up.

When you emerge from your legal cocoon in two years, you will see the world very differently than you do now, and that includes my firm. However, we are planning our own growth at the same time, so, perhaps, when you and I meet again, we will have metamorphosed into the kind of place where you would like to make a career.

Whatever you do Sarah, we wish you all the best.

Very truly yours,

Harry Goldsmith

P.S. If you ever find yourself in New York, stop by and we'll go to lunch."

Sarah held the letter from Harry in her left hand

and the letter from the Supreme Court in her right. She pretended to weigh them as if she were Justice herself with a scale in one hand and a blindfold across her eyes. To her, both letters seemed to hold the promise of a bright future. There was one other thing she knew. Harry Goldsmith had a lot of class.

CHAPTER VII

The next morning, Harry got to his office early and wrote to the Harvard Law School placement office, thanking them for the opportunity to interview their graduates and expressing the hope his firm could do so next year. He made no mention of either Max or Sarah.

As for Sarah, he really did not know what to think of her, except that he knew he had parted from her as a friend. Should their paths cross again, they would remain so. Then, Harry turned his attention back to running the firm.

Sarah still had four weeks of law school left, but, after getting the letter from the Supreme Court, she began to mellow, at least to the casual observer. She began to come to class in jeans, and she wore her hair long and loose. She could even be heard quietly singing snatches of old French songs as she raced from class to class. Three years of hard work and relentless pressure seemed to dissolve.

Of course, Sarah was still Sarah; she did not slacken her pace.

Jason even had his dream come true: Sarah went out with him for the evening, although to him it was a date while to Sarah it was time spent with a friend. They saw a Marx Brothers movie at a revival house. Then, they walked along the Esplanade by the Charles River. Finally, to his great joy, Jason got Sarah to join him at the Starbucks in Cambridge Square.

Jason brought two cups back to the table and offered Sarah a piping hot Earl Grey. "Life's doors should open very smoothly for you from now on, Sarah," he said. "After putting in your two years at the Court, you can write your ticket anywhere."

"You're in better shape than I am," Sarah replied. "How much are you getting again for starters, $135,000? I'll only be getting a fraction of that. My parents will have to help me out."

"But that's not charity," he said. "It's an investment in a sure thing."

"Thanks," Sarah replied.

Sarah never looked more desirable to Jason then at that moment. She was so close that night, and her eyes shone only for him, but Jason sadly knew that Sarah was at her ease only because she saw him as a friend and not a lover. He lifted his cup to his lips and sighed.

Jason had known Sarah for the three years of

law school, and now, as their lives were about to go off in different directions, he could not resist asking one question that had alternately intrigued and infuriated him for so long. "Tell me, Sarah," he asked, "why on earth do you work so hard?"

Sarah put down her Earl Grey. She sighed and looked off into space, and, for one moment, Jason thought he had stumped her. "It is a family tradition," she finally said.

Jason walked her back to her dormitory and they wished each other good night in the lobby. "Thanks, I had a great time," Sarah said. Then, she hugged him and kissed his cheek. For one moment, Jason felt her warm fullness pressed against him. And then, she turned and was gone.

He would replay that hug again and again in his mind for many days, each time more and more slowly until it seemed to go on without end. Then, it gradually faded away as the reality of life without Sarah became undeniable.

The last day of classes came and went, and Sarah headed off to her own private places for some uninterrupted study. During the five-day reading period before final exams, Sarah was only seen around the campus during her dawn runs.

Jason called her one night to ask if she had time to pay another visit to Starbucks. If she were too busy, he even offered to stop by with a few lattes.

"I can't do it, Jason," Sarah declined politely. "It'll break up my rhythm. Call me when exams are over. Until then, my motto is 'Absent thee from felicity awhile....' "

"You're irresistible when you quote Shakespeare," Jason commented.

"I played Ophelia in my senior year," she laughed. "I got great notices. Gotta' go now, bye," and then there was a dial tone.

Securities Regulation, International Conflict Resolution, Legal Ethics, Family Law: they were all that stood between Sarah and her graduation. Sarah knew that it was unlikely that she would fail any of them, but that was not the issue. She wanted to finish strong.

Only one thing disrupted her fierce concentration. One of the cases she had to read was the Tabat Arbitration case. That was a dispute between Egypt and Israel whether a few acres in the resort town of Eilat had to be returned to Egypt under the 1977 peace treaty. As she read the decision, her thoughts went back to her junior year in Israel.

⸺⸺⸺ ((◦)) ⸺⸺⸺

When Sarah went to Israel, she had not written to Victor in many months. She did not know where he was, nor did she think she wanted to know. But, one night, when Sarah was having dinner with a friend in a restaurant in Tel Aviv, she looked up and saw Victor sitting at a table across the room, talking to a young lady.

Sarah turned her eyes away from him for as long as she could. When she could no longer contain herself, she looked back, but Victor was gone. She never saw him again.

After dinner, Sarah walked with her friend along the Tel Aviv beach as the sun set into the Mediterranean. Then, they took a bus back to the university. High and fair, Jerusalem seemed to be a string of glowing jewels set against the starry night, suspended between heaven and earth. Sarah had been awed by the sight many times, but, that night, she sat in silence on the bus, not saying a word.

"Why are you so quiet?" her friend asked her.

"Oh, was I?" Sarah answered. "I guess the day just wore me out." That night Sarah took a long time to fall asleep; she kept thinking of the Banyos....

———◦《◎》◦———

Sarah snapped the book shut. Perhaps she didn't have to read the Tabat case to ace the final. She turned her attention to other books, other matters.

Reading week finally came to an end and examinations began. Sarah felt very little anxiety. Somehow, the Supreme Court's letter had put her at ease.

Jason tried to look up Sarah after exams were

over, but her phone went unanswered, and she was never in her dorm room. He finally called Melissa to ask where Sarah was.

"Oh, she's gone to Washington, Jason. She left right after finals were over. Sarah's gone apartment hunting. She'll be getting an orientation at the Supreme Court as well, but she'll be back in time for graduation."

"Thanks, I was just wondering," Jason said, fooling no one.

Sarah arrived at the Washington Hilton at noon. She opened the door to her suite, and then raced over to the tall, silver-haired woman who was waiting for her. "Hello, mama!" she exclaimed.

Over trout almondine in the hotel's bistro, Sarah and her mother discussed the future. "Your father and I are very proud of you, of course. He wanted to come himself, but he had a business meeting that simply couldn't wait."

"I understand, mama," Sarah replied.

"But your father has always invested in you and your brother Paul, and neither of you has ever disappointed him, and so...." Reaching into her pocketbook, her mother pulled out an envelope and handed it to Sarah. "This is your graduation gift. It's to help you buy your first apartment."

When Sarah saw the check, she was stunned. She simply couldn't speak.

Finally, Sarah spoke. "Mother, how can I possibly

take this?"

"A simple 'Thank you' will do, Sarah. After all, you and Paul are going to inherit everything eventually. You might as well have some of it now to help you get started."

As the two women left the hotel lobby to spend the rest of the day sight-seeing, they turned many heads. Both had eyes the color of the sea. One had raven black hair while the other's tresses were silver. But what impressed anyone who took more than a quick look at them was how at ease they were with each other. Besides being mother and daughter, Rachel and Sarah Mendes were the best of friends.

The following morning, briefcase in hand, Sarah walked slowly and proudly up the front steps of the Supreme Court, calculating her pace to arrive at exactly 9:00 A.M. When she got to the top, Sarah turned and looked back out over the gleaming city. Then, she turned and went inside.

Janet met her in the lobby. Now they shook hands like two proud equals. "Congratulations, Sarah," Janet said. "I thought you'd get it."

After a lot of preliminary paperwork, Janet escorted Sarah to Justice Bradford's office where they discussed upcoming cases. For an hour, Bradford spoke of cases involving vital affairs of state with the gentle manner of one of her professors explaining the law to new students.

And, when Justice Bradford offered Sarah a cup of tea, this time she accepted it.

It all seemed to Sarah like a walk on mountain tops with the rest of the world far below, but then, she was brought back to reality. The judge suddenly cocked his wrist and looked at his Rolex. "I'm afraid our time is up, Sarah. I've got to go now, but Janet will explain the rest of your duties to you. I'll see you in September."

After taking leave of Justice Bradford, Sarah was led by Janet to an empty office where she was invited to have a seat. The small size of the office was a disappointment to Sarah, but she made no comment. But Janet did. "You've already had a tour of the Court, Sarah, but there are a few realities of Court life that I would like to discuss with you."

"I would appreciate any advice you can give me," Sarah replied.

"Good," Janet said. "In the first place, this is going to be your office when you start. Don't you think it is a little small?"

"Well, a little," Sarah said politely.

"Well, it is small," Janet said in a sharp tone. "I felt the same way when I first had it assigned to me. Just remember that after you spend two years in it, you'll be able to command big offices anywhere for the rest of your career. That might make it easier to take."

Janet leaned back in her chair. "Now, here is my version of an orientation speech. It was given to me two years ago by my predecessor, and you'll probably be giving it two years from now to whomever takes your place. You must understand that Justice Bradford is a gentleman from the old school. There are some things that he thinks are too delicate to discuss so he leaves it to his senior clerk."

"First, the judge loves to talk about all the exciting cases we deal with here, but that's not what you'll start with. This Court is flooded with papers every day, and while every item is read by at least one judge, it is the clerks who read the documents first and synopsize them."

"I know," Sarah said.

"Good. You will be starting with submissions from people who may or may not be playing with a full deck. Here's an example." And she pulled out a thick document from a drawer and placed it on the desk. "This man lives in a town where the zoning board passed a law forbidding him from keeping goats. He claims this violates his constitutional rights although every court in his state has disagreed with him. Do you think this sounds stupid?"

Sarah saw a trap coming. "How can I know unless I analyze it?"

"That's the right answer," Janet said, and she tossed the brief to Sarah. "Why don't you write a three-page analysis of it, and I'll review it. No hurry. I'll be around until Labor Day." It did not sound like a suggestion.

"Okay," Sarah replied. She put the papers into her briefcase and snapped it shut. "What's next?"

"Just this," and here Janet took a deep breath.

"You'll never work harder than you will in your two years here. There really won't be much time to do anything else except work. You'll be pulling far more hours than you would on Wall Street or K Street."

"I know," Sarah said. "I accept that."

Janet looked sad for a moment, and, for the first time, Sarah took her full measure. Janet looked like a corn-fed blonde from the mid-west who had been hardened by a few years in the big city. Will that happen to me? Sarah wondered.

"Nevertheless, the judge feels that his staff should have personal lives. What I'm trying to say is that he expects hard work, but not martyrdom, and he will comment if you seem to be going to extremes. Do you think you can draw the line?"

It was obvious what Sarah was expected to say. "I think my record shows that I'm a hard worker, but I'm also a human being. I won't neglect that."

Janet stood up and offered Sarah her hand. "Well, I've said my piece, Sarah. Believe me, I wish you luck. Care to have lunch in the commissary? The food's great."

When it was all over, Sarah headed back to the Hilton in a cab when her cell phone rang. It was her mother. "Sarah, are you finished with the Court?"

"Yes mama, what's up?"

As always, Rachel Mendes spoke with a crisp, calm voice. "I'm with a realtor in Georgetown. I think I've found the perfect place for you, but you'll have to move quickly. It just came on the market this morning, and it won't be around for long."

Sarah gave her driver the address, and they sped off in a new direction.

Fifteen minutes later, Sarah found herself on a tree-lined street with brick-faced townhouses that recalled an era of butlers and horse drawn carriages. The neighborhood had the charm of the world as it was a hundred years ago, and Sarah fell in love with it at once. When she pulled up at the address, a pleasant, middle-aged man in a brown business suit opened her taxi's door and extended his hand.

"Ms. Mendes? I'm John Slater, I've been showing your mother properties all morning, and she insisted that you see this one immediately. She's waiting for you inside. I hope you like it."

Like it? She adored it. How could anyone resist a condo in an old-style town house with a den that boasted a fireplace and a large bay window? There were chandeliers in every room and a garden in the back.

"Mother, I really don't think I can accept this."

"And why not?" came the reply. "You've got the maturity to handle the place. If you don't like the idea of taking money from us, just remember that if you were going to work for a private firm you could pay for this yourself. Look upon our help as a subsidy for the low wages you'll be getting from the Supreme Court."

"Pardon me, Ms. Mendes," Slater interrupted. "Are you going to be working at the Supreme Court?"

When Sarah said yes, his eyebrows shot up. "Well," he said, "you certainly won't have any trouble getting approved by the board."

Mother and daughter had a busy day. They returned to the hotel, where Rachel Mendes took a nap while her daughter went to the health club for a sauna and a massage. That night they went to the theater.

Mother and daughter went to a performance of *Romeo and Juliet* in downtown Washington. Their taxi was caught in traffic, so they got to their seats just as the lights darkened. Then, the curtain rose, and the magic began. Sarah found herself whisked back to her college days when she had two paths in front of her--the law and the stage--and there was a painful choice to be made.

An actor in a Renaissance costume of gold and scarlet appeared from behind a curtain and spoke the opening lines, words Sarah knew by heart.

Two households both alike in dignity

(In fair Verona where we lay our scene) From ancient grudge to new mutiny

Where civil blood makes civil hands unclean.

From forth the fatal loins of these two foes

Two star-crossed lovers take their life....

Rachel saw that her daughter was already trans-fixed by the music of the words. Later, when Juliet mourned the banishment of Romeo, Rachel turned to see Sarah focused intently on the stage. Leaning forward, Rachel whispered in Sarah's ear. "Doesn't a part of you wish you were on the stage right now, saying those words?"

"I guess so, mother," Sarah answered softly. "I've made my choices, but part of me will always be there."

Rachel squeezed her daughter's hand. "Good," she said. "As long as part of you feels that way, you'll never go too far wrong."

Mother and daughter, they knew each other well.

After dropping off a deposit check with the real-tor the next morning, the two women parted company at the airport. Sarah kissed her mother at the gate to the New York shuttle. Then, Sarah headed off for the flight to Boston. It was now Thursday, and graduation was set for Sunday afternoon.

Once Sarah was back in Cambridge, she dropped her bag off at the dormitory, and then headed over to the Harvard law library with her trusty laptop to write up the 'goat memo' for Janet. This is the last time I'll ever use this library, Sarah thought. She felt sad. After a few hours of work, Sarah produced a snappy, three-page synopsis of the problem Janet had posed to her.

On Friday night, Sarah followed her custom

and went to services at the Hillel house. The rabbi wished everyone a good summer and bade farewell to those who would not be returning in the fall. There was joy and sadness in abundance amidst the tea and cake that followed the service. Sarah was so busy saying good-bye to everyone that she did not notice Jason standing in the corner with a sad look in his eye.

She gave a special hug to Melissa. "Thanks for all your help."

"It should be the other way around, Sarah. I'll probably drop off the Dean's List without your help."

"You'll do great," Sarah said. "And, whatever happens, let's stay in touch."

Sunday was the big day. Clad in a black cap and gown, Sarah was one of two hundred and seventy students who each walked across the platform set up in the Harvard yard to pick up his or her diploma. When the ceremony was over, there were hugs and photos with family and friends. Sarah's time at Harvard came to an end.

That night, Sarah moved back into her old room in her parent's apartment in Manhattan. This was temporary, of course. It was to be her base of operations for her next challenge: the bar exam. Then, it was on to the Supreme Court, and her future.

CHAPTER VIII

A few weeks after Sarah and Harry had parted on good terms, he closed the firm at twelve noon on Wednesday, July 3rd and wished everyone a long, happy holiday weekend. He stayed an hour later to do some paperwork. Then, Charlie drove him to his apartment to pick up Grace. Next, they headed out to East Hampton on the southern fork of eastern Long Island.

Twenty years ago, back when mere mortals could afford such things, Harry and Grace had bought a small cottage on a quiet street just a few minutes walk from the beach. As the years passed, they were offered many times the original purchase price. Some entrepreneurs had even offered them larger houses in nearby towns together along with a wad of cash to get them to part with their home. Harry and Grace always refused. This was their home, and they never wanted to leave it.

Harry and Grace headed out that weekend looking forward to four days of sailing, picnics and barbeques with friends and long walks under the stars at sunset.

But it didn't work out that way.

Three thousand miles to the west, things were going very badly for Goldsmith & Hammer. A Dutch company that manufactured submarines had signed a contract to build three diesel submarines for Taiwan. For political reasons, the deal was arranged through a California middleman, United Naval Engineering. Harry's firm brokered the deal. The California firm had to advance one hundred million dollars for the ships with an irrevocable letter of credit. The submarines eventually arrived in the port of Taipei in such a poor state of repair that the Taiwanese navy refused to accept delivery. United Naval was left on the hook for a great deal of money.

Lawsuits were being started all over the world when a lawyer in Harry's firm recalled a clause buried in hundreds of pages of contract language that required any disputes arising out of the deal to be resolved by the International Arbitration Association in California. For six weeks, Roy Cook, Brad McDonald and two associates stayed at the Mark Pierre in San Francisco in a suite filled with boxes of paper, arguing alongside lawyers from two other continents before a three-man arbitration panel.

In the last week in June, the panel ordered United Naval to post a bond of $25,000,000 as security pending a final decision. At a quarter to five on the eve of the Fourth of July, in the federal district court of San Francisco, Judge Looney (known to local lawyers as "The man who lives up to his name"), confirmed the order to post the bond and gave the opposing lawyers the immediate right to begin seizing the assets of Harry's clients if they didn't put up the money. The judge then wished everyone a pleasant holiday and walked off the bench.

Roy Cook was struck dumb, and if the court officers had not asked him to leave so they could lock up, he probably would have stood rooted to the spot for an hour. As it was, Roy found himself on the steps of the courthouse a few minutes past five California time, trying to reach Harry in New York by cell phone.

When Harry picked up the phone in his East Hampton foyer, the Rolex on his wrist said it was eight-fifteen. He and Grace were heading out for an evening stroll into town. As he spoke, she waited for him by the door.

"Hello, Roy," Harry said. "How are things in San Francisco?"

"The city is great, but there's real trouble," Roy replied, and he filled Harry in.

"My God," Harry said when Roy finished. "Didn't you ask the judge for a stay so you could post an appeal bond? That would cost us only two and one-half mil."

"Of course, I did, Harry. You know this judge's reputation. He just went wild."

Harry looked up at his wife and gestured her to come back inside. She breathed a sigh from long experience as she closed the door.

"Listen, Roy," Harry said, "we've got to go to the Court of Appeals to get them to stay Judge Looney's ruling until we can post an appeal bond."

"We can't prepare any papers out here," Roy said, exasperated. "We don't have the facilities."

"I know," Harry said. "I'll get a team together in the office tomorrow, and we'll get a set of motion papers together. We'll e-mail them to you at your hotel by seven o'clock Friday morning. You're admitted out there. You can sign the papers and walk them over to the Court of Appeals yourself." He looked at the captain's clock on the mantle over his fireplace. "It's twenty minutes to nine. Get some sleep and call me at the office tomorrow morning at five A.M. your time. Have a good night."

Grace walked up to Harry and put her hand on his shoulder. "Are you really going into the office on the Fourth of July?"

Harry took her hand in his and kissed it. "Yes I am. There's $25,000,000 at stake. But one way or another I'll be back for a late snack on Friday night, and I'll spend an extra day out here to make it up to you." He squeezed her hand. "Besides, I don't have to head back until tomorrow morning. We'll still have our walk tonight. Just let me make a few calls."

He chartered a helicopter from the local airport to fly him back to Manhattan at six the following morning. Next, he called up Helen and asked for a run-down of who was available to handle the emergency. He didn't like what he heard. Max was in town, but then, he never took time off. There weren't too many others besides him. His four best lawyers were sitting in a hotel room in San Francisco, unable to do much except answer questions by phone.

Most of his other lawyers had decided to head out of town for the holiday. One was getting married, and Harry was not about to disturb him. Finally, it seemed that only Jonathan Crane and Annette DeKoven would be available to help. Harry was worried; the two firms that were up against his had more than five hundred lawyers between them.

Then, a thought came to Harry. It delighted him. It was the kind of idea that Harry was famous for, an inspiration that would solve an immediate problem that everyone knew about as well as a problem in the future that only he could foresee. He called Manhattan information.

Sarah was locked in her room studying for the bar exam when her father picked up the telephone. As a man who was equally likely to be getting a telephone call in either English or French, he always answered the phone by saying "'Allo'." That way, he could switch into either language with ease. He knew who Harry Goldsmith was, and he knocked on Sarah's door to tell her that Harry Goldsmith was on the phone. Sarah took the call.

"Hello Harry," she said. "What can I do for you?"

"An interesting project has just come our way, and we've only got one day to solve it. Tell me, how is your studying for the bar exam coming along?"

Sarah let out a great sigh. "Harry, it feels like I never went to law school in the first place. I go to review classes five days a week, for six hours a day, in a room with a few hundred other people. Then, I spend the rest of my time studying."

"I'm sure you'll do wonderfully, Sarah," Harry said in his most reassuring manner. "Tell me, would you be interested in a day of hands-on legal experience at $250 an hour?" Harry explained the situation facing the firm. "I need every good legal mind I can lay my hands on in a hurry."

"I know the bar exam is in less than two weeks. Think of this as a chance to get some real experience. It might even be a stimulant to help you with the exam. It'll only be for one day."

Sarah thought quickly. She could think of many reasons for saying yes, and just as many for saying no. But she agreed to help for one reason, which she kept to herself. Her parents always had paid her expenses. Now, she had a chance to make some real money very quickly in a single day. "What time do you want me there, Harry?" she asked.

"A quarter to eight," he said, making no effort to disguise his pleasure. "I make it a rule never to dress down when going to the office, but that's just me. Feel free to come in casually. We'll bring in lunch and dinner from the best places in town."

After Harry hung up the phone, he reflected on all the long hours and missed holidays with his family that were part of the price he paid for building his practice. If I had just become a law professor as I had hoped to, I'd be leading a much quieter life now. Was it worth it, he wondered? Then, he took a long look at the foyer he was standing in, and he could see the Atlantic Ocean through the French doors that lead out to the patio. He thought of the two cars in his garage: a Cadillac for his wife and a Jaguar for himself. With a moment's sadness, Harry knew the answer to his own question.

After Sarah hung up the phone, she headed into the living room to speak to her parents. Sarah considered herself a grown woman, but while she was living in their home and taking their money, she felt an obligation to let them know what she was doing.

Her father didn't like what he heard. "Sarah, you have too much invested in the bar exam to interrupt your studies for a few dollars. If you need money, I'll be happy to give it to you." Sarah's father was much like Harry, except huskier and with slicked-back dark hair where Harry's was curly and white.

But what made people remember Maurice Mendes were his eyes. Pure brown verging on amber, they appeared to leap out with a vital energy that hardly seemed human.

Her mother did not look up from the book she was reading. "Let her do as she wishes, Maurice. You know she's going to pass the bar with flying colors.

Now might be a good chance for her to see what being a lawyer is really like." And that was that.

Sarah skipped her daily jog through Central Park the next morning. Instead, she headed to Harry's office on 42nd Street with a business suit in a backpack. She walked into Goldsmith & Hammer at seven-thirty. The place was deserted except for Harry. "Thank you for coming, Sarah."

"I'm not here officially yet, Harry," she replied. Can I use the shower and steam room before we get going?"

"Of course, Sarah," he said, and he was pleased at her request. It meant she was already starting to feel at ease in the office.

When she emerged from her morning ablutions, Sarah looked every inch the proper businesswoman. Then, she walked directly into the main conference room where Harry was waiting with his team. Harry sat at the head of the table with Max to his right and Jonathan and Annette to his left. Sarah could not help noticing that Harry seemed anxious for the first time since she met him while Max seemed to be perfectly at ease with himself.

"Good morning, Sarah," Harry said. "Let's get down to business." And he gestured her to a seat. Then he pushed a button on a speakerphone. "Roy, can you hear us?"

"Yes, I can."

"Would you please give us your version of what happened in court yesterday?" Harry asked. Calmer now, Roy took only a moment.

"Good," Harry said. "Now Max will discuss our proposed response."

Max put down his cup of coffee and began to speak. "The court has ordered us to put up $25,000,000. This is an injunction. According to. ...."

"Max," Harry said, "Perhaps you'd better explain what an injunction is." He shot a quick glance at Sarah, who had never practiced law before.

Max spoke with a hint of contempt, as if he were speaking to a group of idiots. "An injunction is when a court orders someone to do something, or, in some cases, not to do something. The classic example is a court ordering someone to take down a fence that was accidentally put up on someone else's property."

"Now, what can we do about this injunction, Max?" Harry spoke in a tone that revealed that his real calling was teaching.

Max suddenly seemed very pleased with himself. "We can get the Court of Appeals in San Francisco to reverse Judge Looney's injunction by showing the court that we are likely to win on the merits when the case is finally decided. We've got to review the entire case and prepare a detailed discussion of it for the Court of Appeals. There are a couple of thousand pages of testimony and exhibits to review, but with our computers we should be able to crank out some good papers in time to get them to the coast before the Court opens its doors on Friday."

"What will be our chief argument?" Jonathan asked.

"We're going to argue that United is only a middleman, and that the manufacturer of the subs is responsible for their screw-ups. There's no logical reason for us to have to post a bond because there's no way the arbitration panel could have possibly found against us unless they're on the take. Of course, we're going to have to go through several hundred inspection reports to document the defects in manufacture."

"I'm sorry, but I don't agree with your approach," Sarah said suddenly.

"I don't care what you agree with," Max snapped back at her. "You're just here to review documents."

But Harry had a different reaction. He put his hand on Max's arm to silence him and then looked at Sarah. "Your opinion is welcome, Sarah. What do you have to say?"

"Just this," she began. "First, all of you know a lot more about practicing law than I do, and normally I would just be quiet and take notes. But, as it happens, I do have experience in this one area of law."

Harry invited her to continue. Max shifted in his seat as if he were waiting for recess in kindergarten.

"I clerked for the Court of Appeals in Boston the summer after my first year. One of the things I did was to review motions in cases like this. This is not an injunction, it is a judgment, which is an order to pay money. According to the federal rules of procedure, you are automatically entitled to a ten day stay of execution of a money judgment to allow time to post a bond. And if you post a bond, your assets are safe. That judge was completely wrong. He had no right to refuse you a stay." Then she went silent and waited to see what affect her words would have.

Harry was quick on the uptake. "How long would it take to draft a motion your way, Sarah?"

"About an hour and a half," she replied. "Maybe less."

Now Max spoke up. "But if she's wrong, we'll have nothing in our hand come Monday, and our client's assets will be in danger."

Harry went silent, but everyone could see he was thinking. He held his gold fountain pen horizontal just a few inches above the table, as if it were the scale of justice. No one spoke until he finally said what was on his mind.

He looked at Sarah. "I think you're right, Sarah, but I can't risk everything on a single approach." He rose from his chair and leaned forward, resting his knuckles on the table. "This is what we'll do. We will argue for a bond as if Judge Looney's order were both an injunction and a judgment. We'll let the Court of Appeals decide what it is. Sarah will write the argument for the judgment portion, and Max will work on the other part."

Harry looked at the speakerphone. "You're pretty quiet, Roy," he said. "What do you think of all this?"

"It sounds good," Roy said. "But I've got to have the papers by the crack of dawn tomorrow."

"You'll get them, Roy," Harry said. Then, he looked around the table. "Okay, everyone," he said, slamming his open hand. "Get to work!"

Harry went to his office and closed the door, letting Max turn the conference room into a war zone. Boxes and boxes of papers suddenly appeared; yellow legal pads were rapidly filled up with notes as documents were painstakingly reviewed. Meanwhile, Sarah took her laptop and adjourned to the library. She took little more than an hour to put her words on paper. Her argument was so simple and direct there was no way it could be stretched out. Finished, papers in hand, she knocked on Harry's door with her work, and he invited her in.

Sarah was surprised by what she saw. Harry was seated at his desk, head in his hands and a small glass of brandy in front of him. There was only a little of the amber fluid left at the bottom. Sarah felt she was intruding. "Here is my part of the project," and she left it on his desk and turned to leave.

"One moment Sarah," Harry said apologetically. "I'm sorry you caught me this way. Max is more at home in tight situations like this than I am. He likes nothing better than a fight under the gun. I prefer a more leisurely pace to my litigation. Let me have a look at what you've written."

He picked up the papers and began to read. Within a few moments, the grim expression on his face became one of contentment. "Excellent job, Sarah. Now, let me pay you so you can enjoy the holiday and get back to your studies." He pulled out a ledger checkbook from his desk and started to write out a draft.

"Before you do that," Sarah asked, "do you need me to help out Max's team?"

Harry's pen stopped. "We could use all the help we can get," he replied. "But are you sure you want to take more time away from your studies?"

Sarah grinned. "I think you were right when you said this experience might stimulate me for the bar. I'm really enjoying myself, and I'd like to finish what I started."

Harry put the checkbook back. He didn't know whether he was nurturing a future star in the legal world or a monster. He adopted a neutral tone. "Sarah, as I said, we can certainly use your help. You're welcome to work here as long as you wish."

Sarah thanked him and headed off to join Max and the others. Once the door to his office was closed, Harry finished his drink in peace. In the conference room, Sarah found Max and his two associates nearly buried under endless piles of papers. Max was cursing the judge, the opposing lawyers, and life itself.

He threw papers around the table and barked out orders to Jonathan and Annette. Suddenly, Max looked up, and saw Sarah standing in the doorway. "What the hell do you want?" he demanded.

"I'm finished with my work. Harry said you might need some help."

"We're just fine here," Max half-snarled. "You can go home." Jonathan and Annette got pained looks on their faces when they heard these words.

But Sarah had a quick answer. "Okay, just thought I'd ask. I'll be in the library studying for the bar. Harry said I could use it." And she walked off.

Besides having an impressive number of books for a firm its size, the library at Goldsmith & Hammer was a cozy place. There were leather chairs, hand-finished wooden shelves for the books and even an unused fireplace. Sarah pulled out a textbook on property law, her weakest subject, and sat down to study.

However, Sarah was secretly waiting for something to happen, and, after about an hour, it did. Suddenly, she saw Max standing at the library door. There was a slew of papers in his hands, some type-written and others were yellow sheets with scrawled notes. When their eyes met, he walked over to her.

"Sarah," Max said, using her first name for once, "we're not going to make it if we don't get more help. Will you join us?"

Sarah thought of many things she could say to take revenge for the way Max had treated her, but Sarah was a lady. She snapped her book shut, stood up to face Max and politely asked how she could help.

For the first time, Sarah actually brought a smile

to Max's face. He held out the papers he had been carrying.

"Harry showed me what you wrote, and you know what you're doing. We need someone who can write well and write fast. We need you to turn this stuff into a sharp legal argument."

Sarah took the papers from him. "My pleasure," she said.

Max went back to the conference room while Sarah adjourned to a computer in an empty office. From that moment until late in the afternoon, Sarah was running back and forth from the library to look up points of law and to show Max each draft. He made changes in each revision. Sarah knew some were justified, but she thought other changes were just to keep her ego in check. However, it did not matter to her; she found it all exciting. She could feel the drive that had gotten her through Harvard Law burning inside her, and it was thrilling.

At five o'clock, Max finally announced that there would be no more changes to the motion papers. Now, they had to assemble several hundred pages of exhibits, scan the entire document and e-mail it to Roy on the West Coast. At eight o'clock, the assembly was completed; then, Harry, who had kept his distance from the fray, sat down and reviewed the final product. After nearly an hour, he looked up and said, "Good job," to everyone around him. Sarah felt like cheering.

Then, with the touch of a few keys, the document

went across country and was printed out at Roy's hotel in California.

Harry would not have been Harry if he didn't invite his gallant lawyers in for a drink at his private bar before sending everyone home in a limo. With his second brandy of the day in hand, Harry made a toast: "To honest hard work, may it always pay off."

Afterward, when everyone else had already gone home, Harry handed Sarah a check for $1,500 and a compliment to go with it. "You earned every penny today, Sarah. You have our thanks."

Sarah didn't bother to look at the check. She put it into a pocket and then shook Harry's hand. "I had a great time helping out," she said.

"Fine, Sarah. Now, go and ace the bar, or I'll feel guilty about taking you away from your studies."

She headed out to her waiting limo. Harry toasted his own cleverness with an extra thimbleful of brandy, and then had Charlie drive him to his apartment. He had spent fewer than a dozen nights away from Grace in their thirty-five years of marriage, but this was fated to be one of them. He had to be close to the office when the decision from the Ninth Circuit came down.

Sarah got home at a quarter to eleven, and she was not surprised to find both her parents watching television in the living room, awaiting her return. Her mother asked pleasantly how the day went while her father asked if it was worth the risk of failing the bar exam just to make some money.

"You don't understand, papa," Sarah explained. "For the first time I was really practicing law today, and I loved it. It was so exciting working with people on such a big project. Today was important to me because it showed me that I'm going to enjoy being a lawyer. And I promise you, I'm going to pass the bar with flying colors."

Before he could say another word, Sarah gave him a hug and kiss and then headed off to her room. Somewhat bewildered, Maurice Mendes looked at his wife. "Rachel, what do you think of all this?" he wondered.

"Let's just give her a small car after she passes the bar," Rachel said. "A big one might go to her head."

The mark of a good lawyer is the ability to turn from a project she has been engrossed in to a new one and never look back, and Sarah had that skill. After her morning jog across Central Park, Sarah spent the next day reviewing her notes on property law. By ten o'clock she had put Goldsmith & Hammer out of her mind, although she left their check on the corner of her desk so she could steal glances of guilty pleasure at it whenever she wanted to.

The afternoon was giving way to early evening when Sarah's father knocked at her door to ask if she wanted to go to Friday night services with him. Sarah was immediately agreeable, and she began to get ready. Her mother was going to stay home and prepare dinner.

Together, father and daughter walked to the Sephardic synagogue on 73rd Street. It was all marble with stone columns and stained-glass windows that reminded Sarah of Notre Dame in Paris.

Inside, the sanctuary's carpeting was thick and dark; soft light came from the gas candles mounted on chandeliers, and the seats of carved wood took up three sides while the marble ark filled the fourth wall. Sarah's father took his customary seat near the rabbi's lectern while Sarah adjourned to the women's balcony.

Then, the singing began. It was an open secret that the choir had a few paid singers from the City Opera Company on the Sabbath, so the voices were good. The hymns always touched Sarah. The melodies they sang had followed the congregation from Spain to Holland and then to America some three hundred years ago. "Rich and strange," that was the only way she could describe how they sounded to her.

At the conclusion of the service, Rabbi Harari shook the hands of the congregants as they left. When he met Sarah, he asked how her bar review was coming along.

"Pretty well," Sarah said, "we'll know in a few days."

"Sarah, you know that this congregation has had two Supreme Court justices over the years. I think you'll be the third."

Sarah smiled. "We'll see," she said. "Have a good

Shabbos."

Sarah gasped with surprise when her mother opened the door to the apartment. Sitting in the living room were Harry Goldsmith and Max Hammer. That was nothing. They were doing something she had never seen before. They were both smiling at the same time.

"What's going on?" she demanded.

"Easy, Sarah," Harry said, and he reached into his suit jacket and pulled out a folded sheet of paper. "Read this. It's a fax from the Ninth Circuit. We got it half an hour ago and got right over here."

She grabbed the paper and read it.

It read: "Pursuant to the Federal Rules of Civil Procedure 62(a) and Federal Rules of Appellate Procedure 8(a)(2) the judgment of the lower court is stayed for ten days to allow the respondent to post a bond. This matter is remanded to the lower court for the fixing of said bond."

"We won, Sarah," Harry said, "and it was with your arguments."

Max stood up and walked over to Sarah. "Ms. Mendes, you were right, and I was wrong. It's as simple as that." They shook hands.

"And saving a client twenty-five million dollars is nothing to sneeze at," Harry added. He pulled out an envelope and handed it to Sarah. "Here's a check for another $1,500 dollars. You've earned it."

Sarah didn't know what to say, but her father

did. "I don't pretend to know anything about law, but would you gentlemen care to join us for dinner?"

Max started to speak, but Harry got his words out first. "Thank you for your kind offer, but Harry and I have places to be. I'm sure we'll meet again on other happy occasions."

The two men got up and headed for the door, but just before he exited, Harry got another idea. He turned back to Sarah. "Tell me, Sarah, would you like to use our library to finish studying for the bar? I can give you your own office and complete use of our support staff."

Sarah didn't hesitate. "I'd like that very much. Thank you, Harry." They all parted in high spirits.

Once in the elevator, Max dropped his good behavior. "Okay, Harry," he demanded, "tell me why you're making such a fuss about this. So she hit it right. We already paid her for her time. Why the bonus?"

"Max, I'm surprised at you," Harry said in a happy voice. "Don't you realize that for every dollar I'm giving Sarah now, I'm investing in getting her back?"

"Just how can you be so certain she will be coming to us after the Supreme Court?"

"Where is your imagination?" Harry replied. "We just gave Sarah her first taste of legal combat, and she loved it. When she's done with the Supreme Court, she's going to want more of it and she'll make a beeline for the place that first got her excited about the law, and that's us. She'll come back to us the way salmon fight to get back to the stream where they were born."

The two men shared a laugh, and Max acknowledged to himself that Harry deserved to be the first-named partner in Goldsmith & Hammer.

Harry spent the rest of the weekend with his wife in the Hamptons, while Max spent a lot of time in the office.

The rest of the summer, or at least most of it, seemed to pass in a soft blur.

Sarah took Harry up on his offer. While she was finishing studying for the bar exam, Sarah became the uncrowned queen of Goldsmith & Hammer. Harry gave her an office next to his, and her desktop computer made studying a breeze. The perks didn't end there. Besides the membership in the firm's gym, there was a limo ride home every night, and, every day at noon, a partner or senior associate would stop in to ask how things were going. This was usually a prelude to a luncheon invitation. Harry, Brad and Roy all stopped in. Even Max, on his very best behavior, came by one day. He seemed relieved when Sarah begged off from lunch, but that was beside the point. Sarah knew she was being wooed.

The bar exam was no great hurdle. It was like acting, Sarah said to herself; if you've studied your lines, you have no anxiety. Forty-eight hours later, after it was over, a jet took off from JFK heading for Europe; Sarah was on it.

Belgium was wonderful; she became a French speaker again. Family and old friends filled her days, but a sadness slowly descended upon her. After so many years in America, Europe seemed so small. Knowing she could never bear to return, except for brief visits, Sarah cut short her stay and headed off to England.

London was as wonderful as ever, but somehow the city seemed to lack its old magic. She had been there on a high school summer abroad program, and the city had glowed with beautiful colors. Now, even the sight of Westminster Abbey, the Tower of London and Big Ben meant little. I want to be doing, Sarah thought, not sight-seeing. Within seventy-two hours of arriving in London, she was on a plane headed for Tel Aviv.

Israel stirred emotions in her that were very different than those she felt anywhere else. It was a scene of youthful hopes and visions and, while she always felt a wistful desire to go back there, every actual visit left her filled with the sadness of an unfulfilled dream.

Her brother Paul met her at Ben-Gurion airport and drove her to his apartment near the Hadassah Hospital in Jerusalem. They spent the afternoon catching up on each other's lives, and, that night, they had dinner with Liora, the lady in Paul's life. She was a Yemenite woman with dark eyes and black hair that hung in ringlets down to her shoulders. She's a knockout, Sarah thought to herself.

Sarah decided to spend the next day touring Jerusalem. The following day she flew down to Eilat, a resort and harbor town at the southern tip of the country. As she watched the Negev desert pass under her plane, Sarah wondered what would have happened if she and Victor had gone to Eilat instead of the Banyos? They might not have made love. She was old enough now to permit herself a wistful smile.

After two days of sun and snorkeling, it was time to head back to America. Sarah flew back to Jerusalem and met Paul at his apartment. As he drove her back to the airport, they exchanged thoughts.

"Do you think you'll be staying here, Paul?"

"I don't know. I'm enjoying my work at the hospital, but there's a big difference between being a tourist and staying here. It's the difference between romanticism and realism."

"But if you do stay on Paul, your children will speak Hebrew, mine will speak English and our family back in Europe will speak French. What will keep us all together?"

Paul paused for a moment before he answered. "Wherever we go, we'll work harder than anybody else. That's the Mendes family tradition."

Sarah agreed.

After passing through customs and security at the airport, Sarah sat alone in the departure lounge as she waited for her flight to be announced. With nothing to do, her mind wandered. Were her goals the right ones? What would be so wrong with staying, not going back to America, walking out into the cool dark night, throwing open her arms, and saying to the land "Embrace me."

But then, her flight was announced, and she reported to the gate.

CHAPTER IX

Sarah returned to New York on a Friday afternoon and announced to her parents that she was taking the first train to Washington on Sunday morning. She didn't want to wait any longer. Her parents knew their daughter by now. They questioned her no more.

At six o'clock Sunday morning, Sarah got into a taxi and headed for Pennsylvania Station. Within an hour, she was on a train heading toward Washington; it was filled with bleary-eyed tourists and a young woman with a Harvard law degree and all the world before her.

Sleeping cities whisked by her window: Newark, Philadelphia, Dover and Baltimore. Then, she arrived.

Union Station in Washington is a white marble cathedral of train travel, a monument to another age. It was always filled with light. But Sarah was not distracted by all its smart shops; she hailed a cab and headed for her new home. As always, Sarah was in a hurry.

The apartment in Georgetown delighted her. While Sarah was in Europe, her mother had supervised the decorating -- Rachel Mendes knew her daughter's tastes -- and, then, she had shipped down Sarah's books, clothes and computer. Nothing had been overlooked; even the refrigerator was fully stocked. On a table in her foyer was a brochure for the Jewish Community Center in DuPont Circle with a membership card clipped to it. Throughout her life, Sarah always felt the strong hand of her mother on her shoulder, never holding her back, but always guiding her and trying to smooth her path.

After she unpacked her bag, Sarah set off on a whirlwind tour of the city. The parks were scented with the sweet smell of the fertile earth. Her own Georgetown neighborhood was a world to explore; it was filled with cafes, boutiques and young people promenading hand in hand. In the heart of the city were government buildings, the Washington Monument, the Lincoln Memorial where she had paid her late-night visit months ago and the swirling sensations of a new world to conquer.

At the end of a long day, Sarah headed for the Jewish Community Center for a quick swim before getting a good night's sleep. Her mother's judgment was unwavering; it had a great pool.

For Sarah, 'a few laps' meant thirty. As she

toweled off at poolside, she suddenly heard a woman's voice behind her. "Hi, are you new?"

Sarah turned to face a woman a head shorter and a few years older than she was, with curly, brown hair. 'Perky' described her well. Sarah was always cautious. "Yes I am. Is it obvious?"

Her questioner laughed. "It's just that we have a pretty regular crowd here on Sunday nights. You stood out." She held out her hand. "I'm Ellen, Dr. Ellen Stein."

"Oh, my brother's doing a residency in cardiology. What's your specialty?"

"I'm a psychiatrist. I've got an office downtown, and I'm on staff at Georgetown Hospital. What brings you to Washington?"

Sarah felt on common ground. She introduced herself as a lawyer.

"What kind of law do you practice?"

Sarah hesitated. At Harvard, getting a stellar job was considered mundane. What would be a civilian's reaction to her job at the Supreme Court? It turned out to be laughter.

"It's tough over there. I treated a Supreme Court employee who almost quit because of the stress. Good luck."

Now it was Sarah's turn to chuckle. "Thanks. Everyone says I'll need it."

With a rapport established, the conversation continued in the sauna room.

"Tell me," Ellen asked, "will you be coming to any

of the social events here? They have a lot of them for young professionals."

Sarah wiped the sweat off her forehead. "I was planning on concentrating on my work at the Court for a while. By the way, how is the singles scene in D.C?"

"About the same as in every big city. First, you want to get established in your career, then you want to have some fun, but, finally, you want to settle down. I'm definitely at stage three, but Aaron, that's my fiancée, still acts like he's at step one." He's trying to make partner at one of the big law firms on K Street, so I don't get to see him as often as I'd like to."

"I understand perfectly," Sarah said.

The last rays of the sunset were in the sky as they left. Ellen hailed a taxi while Sarah walked off. They waved good-bye, and each said, "Nice meeting you."

So began Sarah's life in Washington.

The next day was overcast and a light rain fell, but to Sarah it only made the city seem even more romantic. On her dawn run, she imagined that the townhouses and apartments in the neighborhood were filled with fascinating people leading exciting lives. After changing from her running suit into her most severe business attire (Why not? she thought. It got me the job.), Sarah grabbed a taxi. Few things gave Sarah more pleasure than saying to the driver, "Supreme Court, please."

Half an hour later, Sarah sat in a conference room

with about thirty other people. The only person she knew there was Janet, who stood at the front of the room, clipboard in hand.

"Everyone help yourself to the buffet," she said. "Then please have a seat. We have some business to take care of. That's good. Now, we can get started."

Sarah slipped onto a bridge chair, a cup of tea in hand, a pen in the other hand with a yellow pad balanced on one knee.

Janet spoke with her usual crisp authority. "You have all had orientation. Since this is the first time you have all been assembled in one room, now's your chance to get to know one another. Will each of you stand up, say your name and law school, which justice you're clerking for and whether you're a first or second-year clerk."

There followed a litany of America's best law schools. Sarah counted three clerks from Yale, another Harvard graduate, two from Columbia and one from the University of Chicago. She knew she'd have to work harder than ever to shine. She never considered doing anything less.

When it was over, Sarah went to her new office and found a white cardboard box labeled 'Supreme Court' waiting on her desk. It was filled with neatly stacked legal briefs; on top was an envelope with her name on it. Inside was a note from Justice Bradford. "Dear Sarah, (it read) I enjoyed your 'goat memo.' I look forward to working with you over the next two years, John Bradford."

A yellow post-it note was attached to Bradford's note. "Here are twenty habeas corpus petitions. Have them reviewed by Friday. I'm out of here come Labor Day. Janet."

Sarah got to work.

One of the oldest features of common law was the writ of habeas corpus. In Latin, it literally meant, 'Produce the body.' If someone felt he was being held in custody illegally, he could appeal to a court for an order to set him free. The Supreme Court typically received thousands of petitions for habeas corpus each year. While some were the product of brilliant lawyers, many were handwritten by semi-literate men in prison. Sarah's pile of work had both. Each had to be reviewed and analyzed to lighten the burden of the overworked Justices of the Court. Sarah didn't mind the assignment. It was time to pay her dues.

Working alone in her office, Sarah became so involved in her work that she lost track of time. It was almost two-thirty when she looked up to see Janet in her doorway. "You don't have to prove you're an eager beaver, Sarah. I'm here to remind you that the cafeteria stops serving lunch in thirty minutes. Hurry up if you want to get something to eat."

After a day of excitement, comradery and hard work, Sarah was tired. When she finally called it a day, it was almost nine o'clock. Quietly leaving the building through the Maryland Avenue entrance, Sarah turned and looked back after a few paces.

There were still lights shining in many of the courthouse windows. Part of her wanted to go back inside; Sarah would be damned if she weren't the last clerk to leave each night, but a more realistic side of her nature said she had done enough for her first day.

There was still a bit of light in the late summer sky. Taxis cruised past her, but she decided to walk. She headed south down Constitution Avenue, past the Folger Shakespeare Library until she came to the great mall with the Capitol building standing in all its glory at the northern end. The towering alabaster dome was illuminated by floodlights. Sarah began to feel a sense of elation. She was where she always had wanted to be, at the center of all that was powerful and exciting. When she came to Washington for her interview at the Court, she would not venture out into the city at night, fearing that its excitement would seduce her. Now, Sarah decided that she wanted to be swept away in the moment. Believing herself alone, Sarah walked in triumph down the nearly deserted Mall.

Suddenly, a loud gruff voice barked, "Halt!" Out of the shadows stepped two Capitol Hill policemen. "Why are you her, Miss?"

Had she jeopardized her career in a foolish moment? Sarah quickly explained who she was and showed them her court I.D. "It was just such a wonderful day that my enthusiasm got the best of me."

The sterner of the two officers looked at her

identification and handed it back to her. "Please be enthusiastic somewhere else, ma'am. We have to keep this area secure."

Sarah thanked the officers and took a taxi back to her home. She used taxis frequently to get to her job for the next six months, but after she passed the bar exam her parents bought her a Honda Accord.

By the last week of December of her first year at the Court, Sarah had established a routine. Five days a week she would arrive at the Court at eight o'clock in the morning and leave around nine o'clock at night. She would show her face for a few hours on Saturday and put in time on her laptop at home on Sunday. Sarah had proven her worth at the Court, and now she was working on the kind of cases law students would read about one day. There was a rumor -- that Sarah helped start -- that Bradford would name her his chief clerk next year.

Her social circle was small, but that was by choice. The Court came first. For the time being, Sarah was satisfied with things the way they were.

By winter, Ellen and Sarah had become the best of friends, and their Sunday night swims in the JCC pool were a ritual. Being whom they were, Sarah and Ellen turned their swimming into a competition. On a cold night in December, Ellen, swimming like a fish, reached the far side of the pool first. She bobbed up and turned to Sarah, who came in a very close second.

Then the psychiatrist in Ellen made her ask a

question about a suspicion that Sarah had discussed with her before. "Why do you think that Bradford is trying to set you up?"

"I'm sure of it," Sarah replied. "He's been asking me questions about my personal life lately. It is always one question at a time, and he usually lets a week or two go by before he asks the next one. He is trying to be subtle. For example, last month he asked me if I had made any friends here in Washington. I hope you don't mind that I mentioned you."

"Of course not. But what will you do if he actually does play match-maker?"

Sarah hesitated. "I'm not really interested in a relationship right now. My work at the Court comes first. If he does set me up, I'll just go through the motions of a date." Then, she laughed. "Of course, if he's a terrific guy, then forget everything I just said."

"That's the right attitude, Sarah. As a shrink, I give you a clean bill of health. And are you still planning on coming here Friday night for the dinner? They say the speaker is supposed to be great, and Aaron promised he'd show up."

"It looks like I'll be free," Sarah said. Then, she nodded toward the other end of the pool, and they swam off.

Friday afternoon found Sarah holed up in a cubicle of the Supreme Court library researching to what extent a corporation enjoyed freedom of speech. Justice Bradford considered himself an authority on the subject, and Sarah wanted to be thorough. She was so absorbed in her work that she skipped lunch. It was only when the nine-to-five Court personnel began to leave that Sarah looked up and saw that it was getting dark. Well, do I go, or do I beg off? Sarah thought. She had built up such a strong rhythm to her work that she hesitated to call it an early day.

Suddenly, Justice Bradford appeared in the library. He walked over to Sarah and asked how her research was going.

"Fine," Sarah said. "I think we'll have some good ammunition for you at oral argument."

Then, Bradford said something to her he had never said before. "Sarah, you work so very hard. Why don't you go home at six today and be like the rest of the world for once?"

Sarah began to formulate a polite demurral. Then, she remembered Janet's warning about eager beavers. She quietly thanked the judge and went back to work. At five minutes to six, Sarah packed away her notepads and left a 'Do Not Re-shelve' sign on the books in her library cubical. With her winter coat buttoned up and her briefcase in hand, Sarah stopped by the judge's office to say good night as she always did.

"Good night, Sarah," said the judge without taking his eyes off a brief that he was reading. "There's no need to come in early tomorrow. I know how hard you work."

Thirty minutes later, Sarah was home. Typically,

when she got home on Friday nights, she would light her Sabbath candles, read or watch television, and then, fall asleep. She would be back at the Court the following morning. It was so rare that she came home with any energy that she wasn't sure what to do with it. The dinner at the J.C.C. started at eight o'clock. There was time to nap for half an hour, take a bath, fix her hair and dress up to the hilt. She decided to do it all, and then head over.

Sarah normally wore business clothing at the Court, and she would switch to light-hearted wear in her free time on weekends. In her closet were a few dresses meant for social life. She chose a black number.

Sarah arrived at the J.C.C. a few minutes before eight o'clock. The large red brick building was now mostly dark. However, the social hall on the first floor was lit up. She felt slightly intimidated in the foyer among the milling crowds of young singles that were there -- everyone looked like a professional -- and she hadn't been in a situation like this since the last Friday night service back at Harvard.

Upon entering the social hall, she heard Ellen's voice crying out "Sarah, Sarah." Grateful for the familiar, Sarah sat down next to her.

"Hello, Ellen. Aaron couldn't make it?"

Ellen's voice always seemed sad whenever she talked about her own love life.

"He had another big project, but he promised to get here for tea and cake. Anyway, I'm surprised to see you here at all. How'd you manage it?"

"Good behavior, I guess. Justice Bradford came up to me, and, out of nowhere, he told me to leave at a normal hour. He's never done that before. I am almost suspicious."

Then, a middle-aged man stood up at the front of the room and began to speak. He seemed to be the type who was professionally jolly. "Ladies and gentlemen, everyone, good Shabbos. I'm Ben Kahn, the director of social programs here. Would you all please find your assigned seats? Good. We have an excellent program tonight. Rabbi Silverman will start things off by making kiddush for us. Then, we're going to have a delicious Sabbath meal. After that, General Gad Na'or, from Israel, will discuss the current situation in the Middle East."

"A final thought. The idea of gatherings like this is to build a sense of community beyond our own little cliques. So, as soon as the rabbi finishes, why not go around your table and introduce yourselves?"

That set the agenda for the evening. After the rabbi said the blessings, the table was quiet, but Sarah, always the leader, spoke up. "I guess I'll go first," she said. "My name is Sarah Mendes. I just graduated from law school, and I'm clerking for a judge here in Washington." That was the abridged version of her life, the one designed not to intimidate people.

Ellen spoke next, and then the rest of the table took turns. Finally, a good-looking young man in his early thirties sitting opposite Sarah introduced himself.

"I'm Robert Weinberg, and I'm a securities partner at Schlesinger & Finch." Then he looked directly at Sarah. "Aren't you one of Justice Bradford's new law clerks?"

"Yes, I am," Sarah replied with surprise. "How did you know?"

"I read a write-up on the new batch of Supreme Court clerks a few months ago in *The Washington Lawyer*. Your name was unusual, and Harvard Law School stuck out."

"Thank you. But believe me, Harvard Law is no big deal."

"I agree with you there, but then I'm a Yale man so I may be biased." They both chuckled, and Sarah, deciding that this might be more than a passing encounter, checked him out. He was a tall, well dressed, dark-haired man, who wore a discreet gold watch that peaked out from under a shirtsleeve that bore a golden cufflink. But why did Yale ring a distant alarm bell?

Sarah wanted to keep up the conversation, so she said, "Schlesinger & Finch has quite a reputation."

"Ah, but the Supreme Court has a better one." His tone seemed to say, 'I am not intimidated.' Sarah liked that.

The more they talked the more the rest of the people at the table seemed to recede into the background. Sarah and Robert conversed about life in

Washington and how it left little time to do much of anything except work. Sarah explained that her chief recreations were workouts in the Supreme Court's gymnasium and a Sunday night swim at the J.C.C. Robert preferred a club near his office. His hobbies were his work and riding his bicycle on Sunday mornings. Would she ever care to join him? Perhaps, Sarah replied. Why don't you call the Court and ask for me sometimes?

Then, the speaker was introduced. The gray-haired general spoke about the political and military situation in the Middle East. Things were troubled, they always were in the Middle East, but there was reason to hope. Robert asked a few questions that showed he knew something about Israel from personal experience. Without saying a word, Sarah awarded him an additional ten points on an already impressive score.

After dessert, the rabbi said the concluding blessings and the dinner broke up.

Sarah and Robert left the building together, finding that they had a lot to talk about. It was a starry night, but they were more concerned with earthly matters, and the charming old neighborhood seemed to invite intimacies. After a few blocks, Sarah paused and said, "Well, here's my street." Then she offered her hand in a way that said: 'You will come no farther with me tonight.'

Robert shook her hand with enthusiasm. "Goodnight, it's been a pleasure, and I'll call you next week." He turned, but Sarah was not quite finished.

"By the way, what is your connection to Justice Bradford?"

She threw it out quickly, aiming to catch him off guard. But Robert did not lose his cool. Unfazed, he turned back to face Sarah. "How'd you know?"

"It struck me you both went to Yale," Sarah explained. "The judge has been acting peculiar lately, as if he were trying to set me up."

Robert had an easy answer. "My father and Bradford were classmates at Yale. I've known him since I was a kid. We've always kept in touch. A few weeks ago, he called me and asked if I was interested in meeting a nice Jewish girl who was a terrific lawyer and gorgeous to boot. Of course, I agreed. The catch was that he would only arrange the meeting. I had to get your number myself."

"And so you did," Sarah said with a grin. "Here, take down my home phone and my cell."

After he put the numbers in his phone, Sarah wished him good night. She turned and headed down her street. Robert watched her walk off, wondering if Sarah would take a backward glance at him. Halfway down the block, she did. They waved at each other. He headed off, wondering whether he would ever walk down that street with her to a warm place on such a cold romantic night as this one.

As for Sarah, she half-skipped down the rest of the block with a distinct lightness of step. She sensed it was going to be a beautiful spring that year.

Sarah typically was at her desk at the Court by 9:00 AM. on Saturdays. But, remembering the judge's stern warning, she came in at noon the next day. She finished her research around three and began to type up a memo for the judge. When Sarah finished the memo, she brought it into Justice Bradford's office to drop it off, only to see the judge leaning back in his chair, quietly reading a legal treatise.

"Oh, hello Sarah," Bradford said, and, true to his courtly manners, he stood up when she entered and motioned her to a seat. "I've finished my review of the Cheski case," Sarah said as she handed him her work. "I think the Court will want to reverse the Court of Appeals."

Bradford took the memo. "I thought the man was as guilty as hell from what I read in the newspapers, but, after I read your analysis, I'm sure I'll agree with you." He sat back in his chair, and put his feet up on the desk, something he only did on weekends, and prepared himself for a leisurely read. "Thank you, Sarah," he said politely. "Would you be so kind as to get me a cup of tea? Then, I think you can take the rest of the weekend off."

"Thank you, your Honor," she replied. She took no offense at getting him a cup of tea. The judge's manners were simply from another era.

Sarah had just reached the door when the judge stopped her with a question. "By the way, how did you enjoy your evening off?"

She paused and looked back over her shoulder.

"I had a very nice time."

"Good," the judge responded in an off-handed fashion. He returned to his reading. For the rest of Sarah's time at the Court, he never mentioned the subject again.

Sarah checked her office voice mail before she left for the day. There were several messages, including the one she anticipated. "Hello Sarah, this is Bob Weinberg. I enjoyed meeting you last night, and I was wondering if you might be free for brunch or dinner some time. I'm at my office now, but I always have my cell with me. The number is 917.555.6251. All the best."

Well, Sarah said to herself, I don't know where this is going, but I know it's on its way. She pulled out her cell phone....

CHAPTER X

Robert woke up in the middle of the night, and Sarah was not beside him. For a moment, he felt lost and confused. There was the darkness of the bedroom illuminated only by a streetlight that shone through the window and the warm indentation where she had slept next to him. He was alone. Where was Sarah?

Then, he slowly began to get his bearings. An illuminated clock radio on the night table said it was a quarter to four. It was a Sunday morning in March, little more than a year since he first met Sarah.

He reflected on his time with Sarah. There were the first tentative dates where they were simply getting to know one another. Occasionally, they would go bike riding on Sunday mornings, but with their schedules, a more typical meeting would be a late-night dinner in some out of the way cafe. His happiest memories were of Sarah gazing at him across the table.

Then, after they had drawn together, there was an evening where he escorted Sarah up to her door. She usually parted from him with a quick hug and kiss, but this time things were different. Sarah gave him an appraising look and said, "I guess it's time that I invited you inside." Hand in hand, they walked through her door and closed it against the night.

Now, with their intimacy so central to his life, he could not bear to be without her, even if they were only a few rooms apart. Wrapping himself in a blanket, Robert walked through the kitchen into the living room. No Sarah. But, as he stood there quietly, he heard the soft chatter of laptop keys coming from the study. Walking on tiptoe, he silently opened the door.

Wearing slippers, aviator glasses and a lace shawl (Where did she get that? he wondered.) Sarah sat in front of her computer, a cup of herbal tea in her favorite mug near her right hand. The room was dark except for the glow of the computer screen, which made Sarah look like a statue of bluish marble. He sighed; her loveliness never ceased to amaze him.

Sarah sensed he was in the room, but she kept on working. Robert walked up behind her and lightly ran his fingertips from the top of her shoulders down to her breasts. He cupped them and whispered into her ear. "Why couldn't you sleep?"

Sarah kissed his hands and put them back on her shoulders. "I'm sorry, Rob," she said. "I just thought of some sharper language I could put into this opinion, and I wanted to get it down before I forgot it."

He responded by wrapping his arms around her neck and kissing her. "Don't you think you work hard enough? You're just a ghostwriter. Even if you write a decision that gets printed in law books, you'll never get the credit for writing those words, the judge will."

"Oh, Rob," Sarah said, and she stood up and gave him a long, lingering kiss and an embrace with hands that had become wise and experienced since her younger days. "You know it's just the way I am. Besides, I'm Bradford's chief clerk now, and I've got additional responsibilities. I'll be back in the bedroom in just a few minutes. I'm almost done and after I e-mail this to the judge, I'll be free for the rest of the weekend."

He grabbed Sarah and pulled her closer. "Come back to bed," he asked. "You can finish in the morning." It was almost a plea.

Two parts of her nature began to fight with each other. "Oh, please Rob, just let me finish this. Then I'll be all yours."

"All right," he said with resignation. "Do you still want to go for a ride on Sunday?"

"Sure," Sarah said, but she really didn't. Rob lately wanted to drive through Alexandria, Virginia on Sundays to admire houses. She knew what he was leading up to, and it made her uneasy.

He kissed her again and headed back to the

bedroom. "Try not to be too long," he said. She returned to her work.

When she was alone again, Sarah thought back on all that Robert meant to her. It was great having him in her life, and there were times when Sarah almost convinced herself that this was the same as being in love, but she wasn't sure.

Sarah found herself, almost against her will, considering Robert from a purely practical point of view. He was a man who not only seemed to have everything in life but was prepared to lay it all at her feet. Utterly dedicated to Sarah, Robert gave her entry into the halls of power in Washington to satisfy her craving for success. Of course, Bradford had also opened professional doors for her, and Sarah had made her own connections with movers and shakers who could advance her career after the Court.

Sarah finished her revisions of the opinion, but then her fingers rested on the keys. Was she using Robert by being in his life when she was so uncertain about their future together? Sarah was so confused that she longed for some way to justify sleeping on the couch in the living room. Why was she over-analyzing a situation that made her so content just being what it was? Why was she trying to talk herself out of happiness? And how could Sarah even think clearly about her personal life when she was working eighty-hour weeks?

"You are a romantic and an idealist when it comes to love, Sarah," her mother had said, "and I don't think you will ever change."

Finally, after realizing there were not going to be any miraculous revelations at four o'clock in the morning, Sarah wrapped the shawl tightly around her shoulders and headed back to the bedroom.

It was late April, in her second year, on the Court and the time for Sarah to make decisions was fast approaching. Sarah had a dilemma that many people would envy: where do you go when you can write your own ticket anywhere? A senator wanted her for his chief of staff; she could go to some Ivy-League university to teach while writing books and making fat fees practicing law on the side. Of course, she could go to any law firm in the country. At the same time, Sarah needed a situation to give her some breathing room; the truth was she wanted to be alone for a while to sort things out in her personal life.

One day at the Court, while polishing up a draft on her computer, a thought occurred to her. She went to LEXIS/NEXIS, a powerful legal database that could search every reported court decision in the English-speaking world, in addition to hundreds of newspapers. She typed in the name of a certain New York law firm and was rewarded with a list of over 100 mentions. She printed it out and slipped it into her briefcase, resolving to study it in detail over the weekend.

Harry Goldsmith had never seen Sarah like this before. Usually, she was dressed at polar extremes whenever he saw her, either in severe business attire or in jeans and a sweatshirt. But, when Sarah swept into the King's Grille on East 50th Street, for their lunch date, she wore a light blue dress with a floral pattern. A handbag was cradled in her arm, and she carried no briefcase. Even though they were there to talk business, Harry felt flattered that she had made the trip from Washington when a phone call would have sufficed.

He rose to greet her. "Sarah, it's been so long."

"Hello, Harry," she said, shaking his hand. "You look more distinguished than ever."

What a polite way of saying that I have more gray hair, Harry thought. "And you look wonderful," he complimented in return. "Do sit down and make yourself comfortable."

"Thank you." Sarah admired the decor. "This is a lovely place. Do you come here often?"

"Frankly, no," Harry replied. "I save it for clients and special occasions. But, when a senior law clerk at the Supreme Court calls me and says that she would like to discuss coming to work for me, that calls for fireworks, or, at least, a special luncheon." He didn't mention that he had cleared his entire calendar for the afternoon just to see her. "But, you must be tired after coming up from D.C. today. Let's order and then talk."

Harry ordered a steak and a baked potato. Sarah asked for a salad.

"So, how would you describe your experience at

the Court, Sarah?"

"It was just what you predicted, Harry. It has been two of the most exciting years of my life. I've never worked harder, and I've never learned so much. Justice Bradford is an easygoing slave driver if that isn't an oxymoron. And the questions I've worked on and the people I've met . . . ."

"And yet you want to come and work for us after such vast worlds have been opened up to you ...." Harry gave her a quizzical look as if to say: 'prove to me you're not too good to be true.'

"Yes, I do, Harry, I've had offers from some of the bigger firms in D.C. and New York and even a few chances to teach, but I've decided that I want to get as much hands-on experience practicing law as I can over the next few years. And I know from first-hand experience your firm is the best place to do it. Besides, I already know Goldsmith & Hammer, and I feel comfortable there. Believe it or not, there have been times I've found myself missing Max."

Harry laughed. "I'll never tell. I promise." But then, he put a sad, serious look on his face, like that of a child who knew his parents could not afford to buy him a toy he saw in a store window. Harry took out a paper from his briefcase and handed it to her. "Sarah, this is what we offered you two years ago. There are only a few changes on it. I met with the partners before I came here, and everyone agreed we could only offer you $200,000 as a starting salary, plus an extra $10,000 as your hiring bonus, but that's all. We both know you can get a lot more elsewhere."

Sarah didn't bat an eye. She took the letter and put it on the table. "It's no problem for two reasons, Harry. First, I've gotten to know some people that I think will refer business to us. I'll gamble that I can be a rainmaker."

"And we would give you thirty percent of the net," Harry said. "What is the second reason?"

Sarah pulled out the computer printout and handed it to Harry. "I've kept tabs on Goldsmith & Hammer. Your firm is on the way up, and I'd like to be a part of it."

Now, Harry's face had the look of an attorney whose hard work at a trial had just resulted in a victory. "Well said, counselor. I think we can do business." Harry nodded to the maître d', and, by prior arrangement, two glasses of champagne swiftly appeared. Harry and Sarah each raised a glass and toasted one another. "To the law," they said.

After an hour of good food and even better conversation, Sarah walked out of the restaurant more than $200,000 richer. She could have done better elsewhere. But it was a lovely spring day in Manhattan, and Sarah walked up Park Avenue, content, nonetheless, with the prospects of her professional future.

Sarah spent that night in her parents' apartment before heading back to Washington the next morning. After her father had gone to sleep, she found herself sitting in pajamas on the living room couch, speaking with her mother.

"You've been with Robert for a long time, Sarah. How are you going to tell him you're planning on leaving Washington?"

Sarah was troubled. "I just don't know mother. I don't want to hurt him."

Rachel was direct. "You must tell him how you feel, Sarah."

"Mother, you know my friend Ellen, the psychiatrist? I called her a few hours ago, and we talked. She said the same thing you just did. She even offered me a free session to discuss it."

"Will you see her?" Rachel asked.

"I told her no," Sarah said. "What I have to do is clear."

Sarah wished her mother good night. The next morning, she caught the 6:00 A.M. train back to Washington.

When Sarah left Victor in Israel, she had excuses that placed her departure beyond her control. She could lay the blame on her parents. Now, her only reason that she could give for leaving Robert was to cite things within her power. She was choosing a job far away. How would she handle telling him?

As it turned out, it was easier than she thought. Telling Robert in a moment of intimacy, or over the phone, both seemed wrong. She had known him too long to use either situation to her advantage.

Instead, she chose a Sunday afternoon walk through her neighborhood.

Seated at a sidewalk cafe and sipping iced tea while eating a blueberry scone, Sarah waited for an appropriate opening. She did not have to wait long.

"Sarah," Robert began, "after lunch would you like to drive through Alexandria?"

"Maybe," Sarah said. "But, first, I've got to tell you something."

"Oh, what?" Robert now seemed concerned. He listened intently, suddenly alert to the slightest nuance.

"It's just that, well, Rob, I think I know why you always want to drive through Alexandria. You want to buy a home and settle down."

Robert paused for a moment, then he said, "I don't deny it. I kind of thought we were on the same page."

"But, we never discussed it openly. Probably, I should have been more forthright. It's just that so much has happened to me in the last two years, I need a little time to sort it all out."

"How much time?" Robert asked.

She couldn't read much emotion into his three words. "I just don't know," Sarah finally replied.

"Where will you be doing your 'sorting out?' Can we still see each other?"

She was silent a long time. Finally, Robert had to comment. "Sarah, it isn't like you to be at a loss for words."

"New York," Sarah blurted out. "An old employer of mine, Goldsmith & Hammer, made me an offer that included three years to a partnership."

Robert focused on her now. "That's a good deal in terms of the partnership, but with your c.v., you could write you ticket anywhere in Washington."

More silence, then Sarah spoke again. "It's not good-bye, Rob. It'll simply be a long-distance romance. We'll keep seeing each other."

At a loss for what to say next, Robert was saved by the arrival of their lunch. They ate it in relative silence. They didn't drive through Alexandria that day.

That night, Sarah phoned her mother.

"And how did Robert take the news, Sarah?"

"As well as could be expected, mother. He took the news I was thinking of going back to New York hard. I could tell, but he tried to hide it. He was quiet for a while. But we talked and finally we agreed to continue to see each other on weekends."

"What do you think will happen, Sarah?"

"I think it will simply fade away after a while. Bob wants to get married, and I just don't. Not now. He'll find whom he's looking for sooner than I will."

"I don't feel very good about myself right now," Sarah added.

"Sarah, listen to me," her mother said. "You are on a journey to love. Everyone is. Some people take longer to get where they're going than others, and some people tell themselves they've found their heart's desire when they really haven't because they are too weary, or too tired, to press on."

"And which am I?"

"Sarah, you'll find love, and when you do, it will be unmistakable and undeniable. Get some sleep now," her mother said. "You've got to be at your best if you want to finish up at the Court in a blaze of glory."

Sarah wanted to hug her mother. "Thanks, I feel better now."

And Sarah went off to sleep.

CHAPTER XI

Some weeks later, Justice Bradford threw a surprise party for Sarah and his other clerks who would not be returning to the Court in the fall. Sarah found herself missing them already. She packed up her furniture that summer, and then, headed back to New York. To Sarah's surprise, when she told Ellen she would be putting her apartment on the market, Ellen offered to lease it from her.

Finally, on her last day at the Court, Sarah went to see Justice Bradford privately.

"Your Honor, my two years on the Court have been the happiest I have ever spent."

She expected Bradford to be flattered, but he wasn't.

"Sarah," he said gravely, "I hope you have happier times that have nothing to do with the law. You see Sarah, I believe you are destined to return to this Court in some way, and I would like to think you would've had time for a life before you get back here. "

Sarah was touched, but now she weighed her words more carefully than ever.

"Thank you, Your Honor. I can't say I will be guided strictly by your words, but I will always remember them."

"Fair enough, Sarah Mendes." They shook hands.

Then, motioning with his arm as if he were throwing a football at Yale, Bradford joyfully cried, "Now, out into the real world with you!"

Within a few weeks, she started work at Goldsmith & Hammer as an associate extraordinaire. Harry proved as good as his word, and he guided Sarah every step of the way on the path to becoming a fine lawyer. When she showed a strong bent for securities litigation, Harry sent her to court to learn trial work from his best attorneys. Finally, the day came when Sarah was given her first high profile trial. It lasted a full month and concluded on a bright sunny day in October.

"Jury entering," called out the court officer. "Be upstanding in Court!" Everyone stood up. The twelve members of the jury slowly filed into the box, their faces severe and inscrutable. Most of them seemed to stare at Sarah's client, a Mr. Jackson Barnwell, who stood to her left at the defense table. He was a well-dressed, middle-aged businessman whom the government wanted to put away for a long, long time.

The judge looked as if he had stepped out of central casting. He was a distinguished looking older man with a full head of swept-back white hair. A stern look came naturally to his face. If I were directing a movie, Sarah said to herself, I'd cast him as a judge. When the last juror had taken his place, the judge said, "Be seated." Then, he picked up his gavel and continued to speak. "Before I ask the jury for the results of their deliberations, I caution all present that this is a court of law. If there are any emotional outbursts, the courtroom will be cleared, and I will immediately hold contempt hearings."

Sarah looked at her client out of the corner of her eye. At first blush, Barnwell was following her instructions. He looked toward the jury box without staring at anyone in particular. He had a confident smile on his face, and his hands were folded in front of him. Only Sarah was close enough to see that he was beginning to sweat.

"Members of the jury, have you reached a verdict?" asked the judge.

The foreman of the jury stood up, and said, "We have, your Honor." The foreman was clearly a man who took being a juror very seriously. He had come to court every day in a suit and tie and followed all the proceedings with rapt attention.

"The defendant will rise and face the jury."

Here it comes, thought Sarah, as she and her client stood at the table where they had sat every day for the last four weeks.

"How say you to the charge of wire fraud?"

"Not guilty, your Honor."

A murmur arose among the spectators. The judge rapped his gavel once, and the room was silent. "How say you to the charge of securities fraud?"

"Not guilty, your Honor."

Sarah saw that her client's face was turning red. She kicked him under the table and whispered, "Breathe!"

"How say you to the charge of racketeering in the first degree?"

Now, it was Sarah's turn to hold her breath. This was the one she was really worried about.

"Not guilty, your Honor."

It was over now. "Thank you, Sarah," whispered her client as he continued to stand at attention.

"The defendant may be seated," said the judge, betraying no emotion. He began to recite various formalities. He thanked the jury and dismissed them; he directed that the defendant's bail and passport be returned. Finally, the judge said the defendant was free to go. Then the judge rapped his gavel on his bench and said, "The business of this Court is concluded. Good day to all."

Once the judge left the bench, the courtroom exploded with activity. The prosecution team looked at each other dumbfounded. Sarah's client shook her hand. Friends and relatives of the defendant crowded around him, hugged him and patted him on the back.

Sarah walked over to the prosecutors' table and held out her hand to the lead attorney. He was a young man with a crew cut who had been as intense as a laser during the trial. Now he seemed dazed, almost like a new-born puppy. "Great job," she said.

Dumbfounded, he stared at her hand for a moment before he accepted it. "Not half as good as yours," he said ruefully. Then, he finally added the words: "Nice going, counselor."

When she walked back to her side of the courtroom, Barnwell held up a hand to silence his well-wishers. "How can you possibly shake their hands?" he asked Sarah.

"'In victory, magnanimity.' Churchill. Harry Goldsmith taught me that before I even started to work for him. Now let's get out of here!" She shoveled her papers into her briefcase and snapped it shut. If she had been alone, Sarah would've jumped into in the air and screamed "Yippee!" But she still had a job to do as a professional. She grabbed her client by the arm and headed out the courtroom door.

As she led her client through the hallway, Barnwell asked Sarah what the hurry was. "Charlie is waiting with the firm limo outside," she replied, "and besides, there are going to be reporters and TV people waiting for you. You don't want to say anything except 'No comment.' A lot of people want to sue you, and a foolish word could come back to haunt you. Now is not the time to stop and chat."

Sarah had predicted correctly. Walking down the steps of the federal courthouse, they faced a gauntlet of microphones and cameras. The questions flew thick and furious.

"How does it feel to be found innocent?"

"What worried you the most during the trial?"

"What are you going to do next?"

As they headed toward the sanctuary of the limo just a few feet away, Barnwell kept repeating "No comment." Sarah got in first, and Barnwell was halfway in when someone called out, "What do you think was most responsible for your acquittal?"

Barnwell paused, then turned toward the questioner and shouted out, "A hell of a damn fine attorney." Then, he got in and the car sped off.

"Thanks a lot for the compliment," Sarah said. "Can we drive you home?"

"Sure," he said. "I'm going to owe you people so much money that the cost of a limo ride won't make much of a difference."

"Mr. Barnwell's home on Park Avenue, Charlie," Sarah said.

As the limo headed north on the F.D.R. Drive, Barnwell began to act like a free man. He let out a deep breath and loosened his tie. "You did a brilliant job, Sarah. I still can't believe it's your first trial."

"It's the first big one that I've done alone. But believe me, they wouldn't have let me near the courthouse if they didn't think I was ready. Harry's strategy worked. People always side with David against Goliath and a single woman standing alone against a crowd."

"Well, I'm as grateful as hell, and I intend to throw a party and invite everybody in your firm who worked on the case. You can even bill me for the time you spend showing up."

"That would be nice," Sarah replied.

Her cell phone rang. Caller-ID let her answer, "Hello Harry, I was just going to call you. Did you hear what happened?"

"Hear it? It's all over the news channels. Great job! Where are you now?"

"Charlie and I are dropping Mr. Barnwell off at his home. Then I'm coming back to the office."

Barnwell tapped her on the shoulder and gestured for the phone. "Hello, Harry," he said. "Yes, she did a brilliant job. I think your whole firm is terrific, and you're going to get all my legal work from now on. Now, here's your shining star again...."

"Harry, what.. ."

"Sarah, right now you're flying so high your feet won't come back to earth for the rest of the day. And another thing, you haven't had a good night's sleep for a month. Take the afternoon off and come in tomorrow at ten sharp."

Sarah thought back to similar words Bradford had spoken to her. "Okay, Harry. See you tomorrow."

The limousine pulled up in front of a brick and stone apartment house with gargoyles on its corners and black iron grill works on its windows. The stately edifice seemed to shout, 'Old money lives here!' A uniformed doorman opened the car door. Barnwell shook Sarah's hand and thanked her again. Just as he exited the car, he turned back to her. "Are you sure you won't come up for a drink?"

"No, thank you. I'm tired, another time perhaps."

He shot her a friendly salute and headed inside. "Where to now, Ms. Mendes?" asked Charlie.

"Take me home," she said, "but would you mind driving me around for a while first?"

"Of course."

As Sarah sat back in her seat and collected her thoughts, Charlie gave her the Grand Tour of New York that Goldsmith & Hammer reserved for out-of-town guests. Sarah passed through the city like a Caesar in triumph. She drove past the United Nations, Grand Central Station and Yankee Stadium. Finally, Charlie headed back toward Sarah's apartment in the East 60's by passing through Central Park where the leaves were exploding in a riot of autumnal colors. This cheered Sarah, but she knew that, in just a few more weeks, the leaves and the grass would turn brown. But for now, the park was filled with green, red, yellow, and orange, and she savored it.

While in the limo, she made a few calls. Her mother warmly congratulated her. "Your father will be overjoyed. Can you come over for dinner Friday night so we can celebrate?"

"Of course, mama, I'll be there." She owed her

parents that and a lot more besides. But she thought she detected something in her mother's voice; perhaps Sarah only imagined her mother was saying 'Keep all this in perspective.'

Arriving at her apartment, Sarah threw her coat and briefcase on the sofa and made a beeline for her answering machine, which was blinking furiously. There were some heady surprises. Besides all the congratulations that she expected from friends, there were requests for interviews from the New York Law Journal and from the Sunday New York Times Magazine for an upcoming article about women in the law. She would accept them of course; Harry loved good publicity.

If you had just had your first big win in court, wouldn't you want the world to know? Sarah did. She sat down at her computer and sent off e-mails to all her lawyer friends who lived out of town: Melissa Klein, who was practicing law in Boston; Janet Meadows, who had gone back to the mid-West and was now the mother of two. Justice Bradford merited a handwritten note. Ellen in Washington also got an e-mail from Sarah announcing her victory. Even if Ellen weren't a lawyer, her husband Aaron could explain it to her.

After an early dinner, a bubble bath and her nightly cup of herbal tea, Sarah fell sound asleep.

At ten o'clock the following morning, Sarah stood next to Harry in the firm's library. More than thirty associates were gathered round. She stood almost a full head taller than Harry, but he riveted attention to himself by holding up his left hand to call for silence. In Harry's other hand was his customary brandy.

"Now, that you've all had some refreshments, I just have a few words to say. We're all very proud of Sarah's first big trial, but I'd like everyone to remember several things. She may have come here from the Supreme Court, but Sarah worked her way up to the right to try cases just like anyone else, and the same path to the top is open to every attorney here. We do not hire second-rate people at this firm. Every lawyer we hire has the same opportunities for professional growth that Sarah has had, and I'd like nothing better than to make every man and woman in this room a partner. Now, I'm turning the floor over to Sarah ...."

Sarah knew what she had to say. "I'm very proud to be working here, and not only am I grateful for all the people who have been my teachers, but I am also grateful for the comradery and team spirit we have here. I couldn't have won this trial without the help of a lot of people back in the office, and I look forward to teaching younger associates as both a duty and a privilege."

Everyone applauded.

After twenty minutes, Harry looked at his watch and said that it was time to get back to work. "Oh yes," he added in a casual matter, "would Max, Brad and Roy stay behind? You too, Sarah." Without explicitly announcing it, Harry had just called a partner's meeting.

The small group left the library and adjourned to their usual conference room adjacent to Harry's office. Harry sat at the head of the table. Sarah sat at his left, taking notes. Max was at his right, waiting impatiently for the meeting to be over so he could get back to work.

They disposed of several mundane matters quickly. Then, Harry said, "You all know my flair for the dramatic." He reached inside his suit jacket and pulled out a folded sheet of paper. "The Second Circuit just decided the Metcalf appeal this morning. I got this off their web site just before the party. I'll read it to you, but I'll tell you up front that we lost." Everyone was silent as Harry opened the paper.

Metcalf was one of the biggest cases Goldsmith & Hammer had ever handled. The firm represented the plaintiffs in a huge securities fraud. It took two and a half years to bring the case to trial; thousands of pages of documents had to be reviewed and dozens of witnesses were examined under oath. Goldsmith & Hammer had to shell out hundreds of thousands of dollars in pre-trial expenses against a third of any recovery. Many of the partners didn't want to take the case, but Harry persuaded them. "We've got to take this case to grow as a firm," he had explained, and they believed him.

Even more controversial than taking the Metcalf case was Harry's decision to assign it both to Sarah and Max. Neither was thrilled at the prospect of working with the other, but Harry had absolute discretion in such matters. As it turned out, except for an occasional flare-up, the arrangement worked, but Max and Sarah never dropped their guard. They were like two wolves locked up in a small cage.

Metcalf was tried in the U.S. District courthouse at 500 Pearl Street in lower Manhattan. The trial got good media coverage but, somehow, although Max was the lead attorney, Sarah was the one who was most often photographed and interviewed. Max wasn't pleased.

After deliberating for one day, the jury came back with a verdict that stunned everyone: only $2,000,000 in actual damages, but, $80,000,000 in punitive damages - meant to punish the defendant for near-criminal conduct.

But then, the judge did something that made the front page of the *New York Times*. He explained that the Supreme Court had ruled in <u>Connor v. Sierra-Monarch Insurance</u> that punitive damages could not exceed ten times actual damages. He then cut the jury award by $60,000,000.

Goldsmith & Hammer immediately filed an appeal with the Second Circuit Court of Appeals. Sarah had written the brief while Max had done the actual argument before the higher court. They had been waiting two months for a decision.

"This is the key passage of the decision," Harry said, as he began to read: "'Despite the well-reasoned arguments of plaintiff-appellant's counsel the rule in <u>Connor v. Sierra-Monarch Insurance</u> is controlling. Any change in the rule must come from the Supreme Court.'"

Harry threw the decision on the table. "Where does this leave us?"

Brad McDonald tried to be hopeful. "I've crunched some numbers. If the judge's decision stands, we get a third of $22,000,000. Not bad."

"But what were our expenses?" Harry asked.

"Our out-of-pocket expenses, mostly attorneys' time, came to just under a million."

"Figure five point eight mil, Harry," Max calculated. "We lose half to taxes, but we still don't do too badly."

Harry lifted his chin, took a deep breath and tapped his pen on the table. "I'm not interested in 'not doing too badly' I'm afraid. I want our third of that $60,000,000. Let's go back to the decision. Sarah, you know more about federal practice than any of us. Why did the Second Circuit write their decision this way?"

Sarah answered Harry. "I think the court was saying they agreed with us, but, they couldn't fly in the face of what the Supreme Court decided. I think they were hinting that we should take a chance and go for 'cert.'" Sarah used lawyer's slang for certiorari, asking the Supreme Court to hear an appeal from a lower court.

"What are our chances on appeal?"

"The Supreme Court gets several hundred petitions a year to reconsider Connor. It always rejects them."

"Ah, but how many of those petitions do you suppose are written by a former Supreme Court clerk?"

Sarah saw what was coming and decided to face it. "Probably very few. I'll do it, Harry."

"Excellent, Sarah." Harry faced forward. "That concludes our business. He started to get up from his chair but then sat down again. "Almost forgot. We need to hire a new round of attorneys for document review in the TGV case. Whose turn is it to do the interviews?"

With a sour look on her face, Sarah held up her hand. "It seems to be my lucky day," she remarked.

"Thank you for speaking up, Sarah. Helen will set up the interviews, and she has the resumes. Okay folks, we're done."

Temporary lawyers: Sarah hated to deal with them because they made her feel so sad. Most of them were young lawyers looking for their first break, but what really hurt were the older lawyers who'd been let go from firms where they'd worked for years and now had no idea what to do. Still, big cases like TGV, a huge bankruptcy case, needed thousands of documents reviewed by lawyers, and the money was green. Goldsmith & Hammer needed a lot of temporary lawyers quickly, and, as the newest partner, Sarah had the job of interviewing them. Two days later, she was doing just that.

Her sixth interview was with a young law school graduate nervously looking for his first paying job as a lawyer; he was still waiting to find out if he passed the bar exam. His briefcase is probably empty, Sarah thought. He is probably carrying it around for show. Dashing someone's hopes was something Sarah hated to do, but she felt it was best that temporary help come in with no illusions.

She lowered his resume and peered at him over the rim of her glasses. "You understand, of course, that this job is temporary. When it's over, it's over. You will not be considered for a permanent position here."

"I understand," the young man said with a calmness that seemed forced.

But Sarah had not completely turned into Max. The influence of Harry and her own humanity made her add a hint of kindness. "Of course," she added, "if you do your work well, you can count on a good recommendation from us, and that will help you get a real job. Anyway, you're hired. Can you start tomorrow?"

"Yes, I can," he said, and the joy in his voice was unmistakable. "And thank you very much."

After he left her office, Sarah took a few moments to get a cup of herbal tea in the lounge. She had never had to struggle like most people, but she always cared about others' feelings. Anyway, she drank up, and then, went back to the interviews.

Sitting back at her desk, Sarah buzzed Helen and told her to send in the next applicant. (She had to fight back the urge to use Max's favorite term, "warm body.") "All right," Helen replied. "By the way, his name is Allen Wasserman. Do you have his resume?"

Sarah shuffled a few papers around before she plucked it out of the pile. "Got it," she said triumphantly. "Send him in."

Skimming over the resume, Sarah did not like what she saw. This guy has been out of law school about as long as I have, she thought, and he's had a lot of jobs. Unstable, she said to herself. She expected the interview to be short.

True to form, Sarah kept her eyes riveted to the resume until she heard Helen come in, followed by a second set of footsteps. She glanced up with an insouciant air at the tall, dark-haired, handsome man in his early thirties and said, "Hello, I'm Sarah Mendes. Please have a seat."

"My name is Allan Wasserman," he said.

Sarah began to speak, but there was something about this man that gave her pause. He did not have the look of a typical litigator, constantly ready for the kill, nor did he have the slightly sad, slightly pathetic look most of the applicants did. There was a sensitivity in his face, a kindness in his eyes that she only saw in a Justice Bradford or Harry Goldsmith in their unguarded moments.

Sarah rallied her professionalism and prepared a salvo of questions designed to cull the weak from the herd. At the same time, without thinking, she straightened out her skirt. "I see you've had three jobs in five years. One of your jobs was with Culpepper, Smeaton & Denham. You started with them. They're not such a bad firm. What happened?"

He was quiet for a moment before answering. "Culpepper simply didn't work out. I'm still looking for the right position. As they say, 'All the world's a stage, and in his time a man plays many parts.'"

Sarah put the resume on her lap. "I don't get much Shakespeare in this office, but, any way, you left out something. This is the way it goes:

'All the world's a stage,

And all the men and women merely players:

They have their entrances and their exits,

And one man in his time plays many

parts. His acts being seven...'

"I played Rosalind in *As You Like* It in my sophomore year. Tell me, don't you feel a little odd quoting Shakespeare when you're looking for a job?"

He paused again, then quietly said, "The words are so wonderful that it's hard to forget them, and it's hard to keep something beautiful out of your mind."

"Do you have a favorite poem?"

There was a sad look in his eyes. Finally, he said, "'Absent thee from felicity awhile.' I think that's the most beautiful line of poetry I know."

To her surprise, Sarah found herself wanting to keep the conversation going. "Let me give you some advice. It's wonderful to love the arts, but only a few lucky people get to live in that world. Most of us wind up doing more mundane things, like law. Too much poetry can make people think you're not taking life seriously."

She scolded herself. Sarah, what are you saying? Why are you getting personal with a temp?

She scrambled to get the interview back on track. She straightened her glasses, cleared her throat, and tried to affect the manner of a stern teacher. "This job involves reviewing documents and preparing one or two sentence synopses of each. Do you think you would enjoy doing that?"

"I can't say that I would enjoy a steady diet of it, but, I could do it and do it well."

"What would you rather be doing with your life?" Sarah couldn't believe she asked that question, but it flowed from her as easily as water in a stream.

"Is that relevant?" he asked.

"No, it isn't," she replied. "But I've already decided to hire you. I was just curious. You're not the run-of-the-mill temp attorney; that's pretty obvious."

"Well," he said, "I guess I'd like to be living in that

world you were talking about."

"Just a moment," Sarah said, and she sat back in her chair, trying to make sense of the resume, the man and the way she was acting. She looked at his educational background on the bottom of his resume and sat bolt upright. "You were at the University of Chicago undergrad and for law school?" Sarah nearly shouted. This man had spent more time in the heights of academia than she had.

"That's right," Allen answered quietly.

"Are you from Chicago?"

"Yes," he said quietly. "My father's a lawyer out there."

"You know we'll do a background check."

"I know. Go ahead," he replied calmly.

"Well, can you tell me why you were magna in college, but, you didn't get honors in law school?"

Silence.

She felt sympathy for him and lightened her tone. "Well?"

"It's nothing I like to talk about, but...I took a master's in English while I was going for my law degree, and I think it slowed me up."

She dropped his resume on her desk. "Excuse me for asking, but what the hell are you doing looking for a temporary job reviewing documents?"

Before he could answer, her phone rang; it was Helen. "Is everything all right in there?" she asked. "You're taking a lot of time, and you've got more people to see."

"I'll be done in a few more minutes," Sarah promised, hanging up the phone brusquely.

She ended the interview by standing up. "I know document review can be tedious, but you might want to remember something Oscar Wilde said: 'We are all of us lying in the gutter, but some of us are looking up at the stars.'" Then, Sarah did something she never did with any applicant; she shook his hand. "Be here tomorrow morning at nine o'clock sharp, and we'll get you started."

His effusive thanks told Sarah how much he wanted a job. But as he turned to go, a question jumped out of her mouth before she realized it. "By the way, we are trying to fill openings for associates. Would you like to be considered?"

He whipped around and faced her. "Yes, I would," he replied with a look of surprise.

"I'll submit your resume," she said. "See you in the morning." After he headed down the corridor, Sarah felt a desire to go to the doorway and watch him walk away. She managed to resist it. If Helen hadn't buzzed her again to ask if she were ready to see the next applicant, Sarah might have remained lost in thought indefinitely, trying to figure out what the hell had just happened.

CHAPTER XII

The following morning, Sarah found herself facing five newly hired temp attorneys. Allen was one of them. Sarah tried so hard to avoid looking at him that her neck began to feel stiff. Still, she couldn't help shooting glances in his direction.

I am mean, Sarah said to herself, lying, and she spoke to the gathering as if they were a bunch of unruly children and she, their keeper.

"This case involves the TGV corporation; it's an international conglomerate based in France. I'm sure you've all heard of it. The case involves a possible accounting fraud mixed up with a massive bankruptcy. Your job is to read each page of the records assigned to you and dictate a two or three sentence summary of it. You are not expected to give an in-depth legal or forensic accounting analysis, just to prepare a quick synopsis so more experienced eyes can save time later."

Oh, dear God, he caught me looking at him! She jerked her gaze away from Allen, only to feel her eyes slowly drawn back to him.

"Of course, if you come across something interesting, put a yellow stickie on it. If you come across something really interesting call me in my office, and I'll come down."

Oh, he caught me again!

"Your hours are from 9 to 6 with an hour for lunch. You're welcome to put in as much overtime as you wish, but please don't push yourself beyond your limits just to earn a few more dollars. You won't be helping yourself or your client. Any questions?"

She looked around the room. There were no hands. "Okay," Sarah said. "Let's go down to the twelfth floor, and I'll get you started."

Sarah looked Allen right in the eye as if to say she was not intimidated by him. But, when she did, she found herself wondering what he thought of her, whether he liked her. The work area on the twelfth floor did not have private offices with red leather chairs. It was a large open space with white-washed walls, long tables and metal folding chairs. The room was filled with boxes of documents. Forcing herself to concentrate on the work at hand, she set the temps to work with as much emotional detachment as she could muster. But, as Sarah walked out, she stopped at the doorway. She called out over her shoulder, "Mr. Wasserman, I'd like a word with you."

Somewhat anxious, Allen came over to her.

"Nothing to worry about," she said, making sure they were out of earshot of the others. "I just wanted to tell you I'm not going to submit your resume until next week. I think you should put in a little time here first."

"Thank you very much," Allen said quietly, and then, he headed back to his work. As he walked off, Sarah felt joyful that she had pleased him.

But the following week, Harry Goldsmith was not a happy camper. "Is this a joke?" he fumed, slapping the resume on his desk. For one of the few times in their years together, Harry was angry with her.

"I would not have hired him when I was starting out. I don't care if he is University of Chicago. He doesn't have a stable work history. Sarah, when we hired you, it was the start of a new era for this firm. Now, we get resumes from top schools all the time. Why on earth should I even think of hiring this man?"

"Call it a woman's intuition, Harry."

Harry's answer was not soothing. "Sarah, this is the first time you've ever explained yourself by saying you're a woman."

"Perhaps, it's overdue. Anyway, I'm a partner, and I'm asking you to consider this man."

Harry was silent for a long moment before he spoke. "All right, Sarah," he muttered, "I'll interview him, but only because you're entitled to ask a favor. I want to see this man's work product before I meet him."

Sarah was overjoyed. "Thank you, Harry. You

won't regret this. I promise."

He looked her right in the eye. "Sarah, I'm starting to regret it already, but I've just given you my word."

She walked out of Harry's office, leaving him to wonder what was making his best lawyer lose her better judgment.

Sarah then took an elevator down to the twelfth floor where the temps were sitting hunch-backed examining reams of documents. They were slowly sifting through them and dictating summaries. It's a modern-day Roman galley, Sarah thought. She pitied anyone who had to work in such a place, especially Allen.

She felt it would give the wrong kind of impression if she walked directly to Allen, so Sarah first went to every other attorney and mechanically asked how each one was doing. When that was over, Sarah felt a kind of relief because she could now turn all her attention to Allen. But she forced herself to put on one of her sternest expressions.

"How's it coming?" she asked, pretending she really didn't care.

Allen looked up at her. "Well enough," he said. "You were right. It is pretty boring, but I think I'm making headway."

Keep looking at me. I like it when you look at me.

"I'd like to see some of your finished work if you don't mind."

He was concerned. "Is there a problem?"

She spoke softly, not wanting the other attorneys to overhear. "No, they want to see some of your work product upstairs before they interview you. Oh, and have you got a regular writing sample?"

Allen could not believe his good fortune. "I see, well, here are a few pages. And I'll have a writing sample for you tomorrow."

"Thanks," Sarah said.

Can't you think of something to say that will give me a reason to stay here and talk to you awhile? But he didn't. She turned away and headed back to the fifteenth floor, back to the world of the partners.

One afternoon, Sarah was walking briskly down the main corridor at Goldman & Hammer while proof-reading a contract. Her peripheral vision detected Max heading her way. She attached little importance to his approach. As he passed, she breathed out a faint "Hi" and kept walking.

Max lacked many social graces, but he had impeccable timing. He waited until he was almost out of earshot before he said, "Heard you got a boyfriend down in document review."

Shocked, Sarah whipped around quickly, only to see Max turn the far corner. But what horrified her was that, although she was poised to fire off a blistering retort, she couldn't think of one. Max had spoken the truth, and Sarah had no idea what to do. She just kept walking.

Later that same day, Sarah was so busy at her

desk, it took her a moment to realize someone was standing in her doorway. It was Harry. In his hands were Allen's writing samples; on his face was an expression that she could not interpret. She had no idea what he was going to say.

"I've read his writing samples, Sarah, and, he does have a way with words. But I still have my doubts." Harry put the pages down on her desk and sat down in one of her chairs.

Sarah gave a soft, almost inaudible reply. "Sometimes a person's worth doesn't show up on a piece of paper. I just have a feeling that he would be a good attorney with a decent firm. Besides, now you've seen that he can write."

Harry began to regain his normal composure; he really found it hard to remain angry with Sarah for long. "It sounds to me like you're pleading woman's intuition again, Sarah. That isn't like you at all."

"I just have a feeling about him," she said.

I think I know what that feeling is, Harry said to himself. But there were many considerations. Sarah had never asked for any special favors in all her time at Goldsmith & Hammer except the chance to work hard. She had brought in business to the firm and now, especially with her last trial, she had put the firm on the map. If he didn't grant her a wish like this once in a blue moon, she might start looking for another firm that would.

"All right, Sarah," Harry said at last. "It seems to me that we took a chance on you, and I'll consider taking one on this fellow. I want to re-read his writing samples. Then, I'll talk to him. If he's as good as you say, I'll see what I can do."

"Thanks, Harry," Sarah said.

"Now, you'll pardon me, Sarah. I still have some work to finish up." Harry took his leave.

Sarah had gotten the opportunities she wanted from Harry: to bring Allen up to the fifteenth floor where the real lawyers worked, and to be closer to him. Sarah asked herself why she wanted this so badly, but there was not time to ponder the question. There was a lot to do before going home.

However, Sarah discovered she didn't want to read the document summaries coming up from the twelfth floor. She wanted some reason, any reason, to go down there and strike up a conversation with Allen.

Get a grip on yourself. Are you in love with a stranger with a lousy resume, who happens to know a little Shakespeare?

Sarah was surprised to realize that she was not answering her own question with a resounding 'No!' Alarmed, she rallied herself and began to pore over the documents. Soon Sarah was probing deeply into the world of TGV, and, when she concentrated with that fervor, nothing could distract her.

Nine o'clock came, and Sarah got up to leave. She put on her coat but did not take her briefcase. Why should I? she thought. When I get home, I'm just going to make some herbal tea and get into bed, and I'll be back here tomorrow at 7:00 A.M. I won't have five minutes free all night.

At 5:45 the next morning, Sarah emerged from her apartment building wearing a running suit with a backpack. The streets were nearly empty, and there was only the barest hint in the sky that the sun would be rising later. Sarah loved this time of day. Jogging briskly, she headed to the Central Park entrance at 69th Street and Fifth Avenue. Racing through the Sheep Meadow, Sarah was in a full sweat by the time she reached Columbus Circle. Then, she jumped into a taxi and headed downtown.

After a quick shower, Sarah stepped out into the office in her typically severe business suit. (Sarah kept a fresh one in her office.) She sat down at her desk and ordered breakfast delivered from her favorite cafe. Then she got to work.

It was sometime after lunch when Sarah realized that someone was in her office with her. She glanced up and again saw Harry standing in the doorway, writing samples in one hand. "What's the matter, Sarah?" he asked. "You've got a funny look on your face."

"I guess that's because I can't read your expression," she said. "You seem to be happy and serious at the same time."

"It's probably because I'm so puzzled," Harry explained sitting down. He threw the papers in front of Sarah. "I've re-read his papers, and yes, Allen writes well, but if he's so good at it, then I have to wonder why he hasn't been able to latch onto a steady job until now. I worry that he has another side that's going to come out after we hire him."

"Will you give him a chance?" she asked and instantly regretted it.

"Frankly, Sarah, I'd rather not, but, I owe you too much not to extend you this consideration. Have him in my office at four o'clock tomorrow and I'll interview him."

"Thank you very much, Harry."

He gave her the sternest look in his repertoire. "I'm only agreeing to meet with the man. No promises after that. Meanwhile, when do you expect the cert petition in Metcalf to be ready?"

"In about two weeks."

"And when will we be able to report to the client on TGV?"

"We'll have a preliminary report in about ten days."

"Fine," Harry said as he stood up. "I don't have to tell you that the future of this firm depends on doing both jobs fast and right." Then, he turned and walked out of the room without saying another word.

After a moment of pleasure at getting her way with Harry, Sarah began to consider the practical consequences of what she was doing. She was laying years of hard work on the line to get a job interview for a stranger.

Still, she wanted to tell Allen quickly. Once on

the twelfth floor, Sarah walked over to each temp, making small talk and complimenting them on their work. Upon reaching Allen, she assumed her most serious mien. "May I see you outside?" she asked. Her tone suggested Allen had done something very wrong.

She walked out, and Allen quietly followed her. The other temps looked up briefly from their labors and wondered if he was in some kind of trouble, but there was too much work to spend time wondering. It was not their problem. The temps returned to their documents.

Once out in the hall with Allen, Sarah felt a kind of secret pleasure. She was alone with him. But she had to act as if this were simply business.

"Harry Goldsmith has read your writing samples, and he's agreed to interview you. He'll see you in his office at four tomorrow. Be ready. I'll come and get you fifteen minutes before."

He smiled but seemed puzzled. "Thank you very much. May I ask you a question?"

"Shoot."

"I'm very grateful for all your help, I just don't understand...."

"Why I'm doing this?"

He nodded.

"I think I see talent in you, and that's always welcome." Sarah wasn't sure that this was the truth, but it would do until she figured herself out. "Dress for an interview, and please don't mention this to your co-workers. Well, I've got to go now."

"Thanks again."

Sarah turned and headed for the elevators, wishing she could find some reason to stay there and talk with him, on and on. Suddenly, she paused and looked over her shoulder; Allen was standing there, still looking at her.

"One more thing," she said. "Don't quote poetry." Then she turned away.

"I won't," he called after her.

But he made no promise not to think about poetry. As he headed back to his documents, he thought of some lines he read years before:

"And ne'er did Grecian chisel trace,

A nymph or naiad or a grace,

Of finer form or lovelier face"

The next day, Sarah appeared on the twelfth floor as scheduled. She didn't enter the room where the temps worked; she just stood in the doorway. "Mr. Wasserman," she called out in the most disinterested tone she could muster. "Would you please come with me?" Then she turned and walked away.

Sarah was such a good actress that Allen was mildly alarmed that something had gone wrong, and that she had come to toll his death-knell at Goldsmith & Hammer. He put down his papers and walked after her.

In the elevator, she gave him a few tips. "Harry

is very tough, or, at least, he knows how to come across that way. Meet him eye-to-eye, keep your answers short, and when he asks you why you've had so many jobs, tell him what you told me. But don't quote poetry."

Save it for me, she thought.

Sarah felt that she wanted to straighten his tie, but her facade never cracked. Once on the fifteenth floor, they went straight to Harry's office. He was standing by the globe when they came in. Sarah recognized this as Harry's body language for saying 'I'm in charge here.' He turned to face them and gestured toward his desk. "Have a seat," he said, spoken like a doctor greeting a patient he couldn't stand.

Then Sarah did something that horrified Harry. It was a small thing, but it spoke volumes. Sarah adjusted the visitor's chair in front of Harry's desk and then motioned for Allen to sit in it. What the hell...? Harry thought. He walked over to his desk and sat down; then, Sarah moved over a chair and sat down next to Allen.

Harry stared at Sarah for a moment before he spoke. "Sarah, may I see you outside?" His voice was the calm before the storm.

Outside in the hall, out of earshot, Harry stopped being polite. "Sarah," he said in almost a hiss, "you're not his mother, and this isn't an interview to get into a good kindergarten. If he can't handle himself alone in a job interview, then I don't even want to talk to him."

"He can handle himself, Harry," she protested. "I just thought...." But he cut her off.

"Sarah, I really don't want to know what you think about this man. Frankly, your attraction to him is upsetting me, but I gave you my word. Go to your office, and I'll call you when the interview is over."

Sarah had never seen Harry like this before; he was angry--at her. Was she actually putting her career at risk for someone she hardly knew? Quietly she said, "Okay Harry," and walked off.

Sarah went back to her office and proceeded to get absolutely nothing accomplished. She tried going through the document summaries, but her heart wasn't in it. She put the papers down, turned on the radio and tried to lose herself in soft music. It was with great effort that she didn't reach for the phone to ask Helen if the interview was over. She knew it was just a case of nerves. Harry would let her know what he thought the moment the interview was over. Harry could be as blunt as Max when he wanted to be.

At times, when Sarah let her mind wander, her thoughts drifted off to her romantic past. But now, these thoughts gave her no comfort. She was with Allen, alone in that room with Harry. She wondered how it would be to work with Allen every day. How horrible it would be if Harry banished him back to the twelfth floor or even cast him out the door.

The phone rang several times before she snapped out of her reverie. Helen was on the line.

The interview was over, and Harry wanted to see her. No hint as to what happened.

When Sarah walked into Harry's office, Allen was nowhere to be seen. Bad sign. Harry greeted Sarah at the door with a handshake and smile and motioned her over, not to his desk, but rather to the couch by the globe. He's softening me up for bad news, she thought.

But she was in for a surprise. "I've spoken to the fellow, Sarah. I can see why you want to give him a break. He's got brains, and he speaks and writes well."

What's he leading up to?

"He evens knows his Shakespeare...."

Oh, no, I warned him!

"On the other hand, he has a spotty work history, and I'm frankly not sure he's cut out to do litigation. I just don't know if he has the guts...."

"What is your decision, Harry?"

"Oh, he's hired, of course. For your sake I'm willing to give him the benefit of the doubt. Right now, he's needed to review documents, but, in about two weeks, the backlog should die down, and we can bring him up to the fifteenth floor."

Sarah glowed. "Thank you so much, Harry, I'll start planning his first few assignments."

Harry spoke harsh realities with soft speech. "Sarah, I'm not at all sure that he's going to work for you when that the time comes."

A note of fear sounded. "What do you mean?"

"What I mean Sarah is that he'll go where the need is greatest. It may be you; it may not be. But I must tell you that because you want him aboard so badly, I'd rather see him prove himself with other partners first."

"But Harry...."

Harry responded with the words he only used on rare occasions: "Sarah, my name is on the door."

She knew the matter was closed. Standing to take her leave, she put her best face on things. "Thank you, Harry," she said quietly. "You won't be sorry."

"Time will tell, Sarah. Time will tell. Meanwhile, get your preliminary report ready for TGV. The strategy meeting is coming up fast."

A few moments later, Sarah was back once again on the twelfth floor. By now, Sarah suspected the temps knew there was a special bond between Allen and her, so she resolved to show no more interest in him, at least not in public. She walked into the room where the temps labored and passed among them, speaking to each one briefly. When Sarah got to Allen, she did the same. But as she left, she told him to stop by her office when he was finished for the day.

Back in her office, she found herself concentrating on TGV for the first time in days. She knew it was because Allen would be coming to see her, and they would be alone together.

When things were all settled, she could tackle

the cert petition.

Except for a ten-minute break around six for a cup of tea (the regular kind, she felt the need for a little caffeine), Sarah kept busy at her desk, working. The sun set, and associates passed by her office on the way home, but she didn't notice. A bomb going off would not have made her flinch, but a knock on her door did. It was Allen.

"Oh, come in please," she said. "Have a seat."

He did; he honestly didn't know what was going to happen next.

"I have some good news for you," she said casually. "You did such a good job at your interview with Mr. Goldsmith that he has decided to give you a try-out as a regular associate."

"Thank you very much," he said.

I like making you happy, she thought.

"You're welcome," she said, but I have to tell you that this comes with a few catches. You probably won't be working with me at first. You'll go where you're needed most."

"Whom will I be working for?"

A horror flashed before her. What if Harry assigned him to work with Max? Max, who could smell weakness the way a shark can detect a drop of blood in seawater and act accordingly? "I don't know," she replied. That depends on the needs of the firm in two weeks. You'll be temping until then."

Then, a better thought came to mind. "Why don't we have a cup of coffee somewhere, and I'll fill you in on the various partners. It's better to talk about this sort of thing outside the office. I can wrap up the stuff on my desk in five minutes."

"It sounds good to me," Allen said.

"Wait for me in the lobby downstairs."

Sarah knew where to go to be seen and talked about the next day. She also knew quiet little bistros where no one would ever recognize her. A few blocks away from the office was a late-night pizza shop with a red brick interior and a latticed bay window fronting the street. On the walls were photos of old New York. As they sat down, Sarah looked at a picture of a store on the lower East Side, a century ago, with a Yiddish sign. That isn't how my family came to New York.

They both ordered deep-dish pizza. Then, the conversation began in earnest. There wasn't much to say about most of the partners at Goldsmith & Hammer; they were decent, hard-working family men. And, of course, there was Max. Tall, broad-shouldered, big-bellied Max, who seemed to make a joke out of every expectation of polite behavior; Max, who had no fear of the wrath of judges; Max, who devoured young associates like Moloch. Even after two years of clerking on the Supreme Court, Sarah had found the four months she spent working for Max very hard to take. Now, she and Max were partners working together on the biggest case of their careers, and they still acted as if the other might bite without warning.

But Sarah did not discuss this side of Max. Instead, just like Harry did at Harvard, she talked about Max's clownish antics. Sarah repeated all the old stories and added a few of the newer ones: Max falling asleep at a securities arbitration and defending himself by saying the proceedings bored him stiff; how Max upstaged her at a press conference, and how she retaliated by walking off, leaving him alone to answer questions for half an hour.

Then, Allen asked the same question she had asked five years ago: "How does anyone stand him?"

Sarah found herself giving the same answer that had been given to her: "Oh, he's just a joke, and everyone knows it. Just show Max you're not afraid of him, and he'll leave you alone."

"Tell me, if you do wind up working for Max for a bit, do you think you'll have any trouble?" She tried to make her question sound as casual as possible.

"I think so," Allen replied.

"Any way I can help?"

"You've got to understand," he said. "I'm just very uneasy about all this. Since I left Culpepper, I've worked mostly for ambulance chasers. Goldsmith & Hammer is the road back."

Sarah decided to change the subject. "What do you do to relax?" Sarah asked.

"Mostly I've been looking for work. It's rough out there. What about you?"

"Oh, a movie here and there. I can't remember

the last time I read a book for pleasure. But I like to get together with friends, and I work out a lot."

They ate largely in silence, and, when they finished, Sarah asked, "What were your interests before you started law school?"

"Reading," he said. "'My library was dukedom enough for me.'"

"Prospero, *The Tempest*," she said with a chuckle.

"Don't tell me you played Miranda."

"No, I did do *The Tempest* during my freshman year at Brandeis, but I played Caliban."

"You played a monster?" he laughed. "I don't believe it."

Sarah told him a secret. "I asked to play the role. Even if it meant grease paint and a fright wig on my head. I thought it had the best speech in the play."

Allen began to recite: "Be not afeard, for I think the island is filled with noises, sounds and sweet airs that give delight and hurt not...."

"That's the one," Sarah said.

"I beg your pardon," said a waiter in a white apron covered with tomato stains. "We'll be closing in a few minutes."

Sarah looked at her watch. It was 9:30 P.M. "We've got to be going." She pulled out her cell phone and hit speed dial. "Hello, this is Sarah Mendes of Goldsmith & Hammer. I need a limo." She gave them the address. "They'll be here in five minutes."

"Well, thanks for the company and the great advice," Allen said. I'll see you tomorrow." Then, he headed out into the night.

The two weeks passed slowly for Sarah. She didn't dare go out with Allen again while he was still doing the document review. She couldn't risk it. Sarah still went down every day to the temps, but she tried to treat Allen as indifferently as she could. That was a mistake. Sarah worried that Allen wouldn't understand why she was acting this way and that he would resent it. Sarah kept asking herself how she could have let this situation happen, but she found no answer.

Finally, when the two weeks were almost over Sarah had a paralegal bring Allen to her office. He arrived with a worried countenance.

"Would you close the door?" Sarah said.

"Is anything wrong?" Allen asked.

"No, there isn't," she hastened to reassure him. "I was just concerned that you might have misinterpreted the way I've been acting toward you lately. My interest in you is professional; I think you've got talent that this firm can use. Frankly, I didn't want anyone to get the wrong idea, so I've tried to be, well, more even-handed with all the temps and not show any favoritism."

"I see. I thought it was something like that. Thank you for telling me."

"You're welcome."

Suddenly, unspoken words passed through Sarah's head. I wonder what he's thinking about me? Unsettled, she cut the conversation short.

Allen headed out, but then, he paused at the door. "My hour is almost up when I to most sulfurous and tormenting fumes must once again render myself."

Sarah peered at him over the rims of her aviator glasses. "Watch the poetry," she said with mock sternness. It was now a private joke between them, and, after he left, another phrase from *Hamlet* suddenly popped into her head. She thought about Allen's eyes and said to herself: "He bent their light upon me."

On Friday afternoons, at four, the partners held their regular weekly meeting to discuss where each department was going and what needs might crop up in the near future. They met in the small conference room that connected to Harry's office by French doors. The room was furnished with a long mahogany desk and hand-carved wooden chairs with black leather cushions. To Sarah, it was the 'power room.'

After snacking from a cart Helen had wheeled in, they took their seats. Harry sat at the head of the table. Max sat at his right. Sarah was to Harry's left with a cup of her herbal tea at hand.

Harry called the meeting to order by lightly rapping his coffee cup with a spoon. "Let's go everybody. All right, let's look over the past week. Max, lead off."

Max leaned forward. "Well, we're up on our

usual business, but the Nasle case has thrown my department for a loop. It's going to take a few weeks before we're up and running on it. The trouble is, we may not have that much time. Judge Malone, down in federal court, wants a conference in ten days, and he sanctions people who are un-prepared. I don't think he'll buy the explanation that we're new attorneys on the case."

Harry touched his fingertips together. "Are you saying that you might need more help?"

"It's not a question of 'might'. I didn't have a chance to tell you this because it happened only a half-hour ago, but Jonathan Crane has given no-tice. He's out of here in two weeks."

"I see," Harry said. His face became its most se-rious, and he shot a quick glance at Sarah. Then, he looked away. "We'll discuss staffing after we do the calendar. Brad, how is your department?"

Sarah listened with growing anxiety as the other partners discussed their needs. By the time she spoke, it was clear that Max really was short-handed and that everyone else was taken care of. Sarah had to confess that her litigation group was running well.

Then, Harry turned to Max. "You've obviously got a real problem coming up, Max. We've got a new associate starting Monday. His name is Allen Wasserman, and he is going to work for you. Helen will give you his resume and his writing sample."

"Thanks Harry."

Sarah saw Max look at her with triumphant glee. For the first time in many years, Sarah felt that events around her were slipping out of control. And she felt something else: fear.

CHAPTER XIII

After the meeting, Sarah approached Harry in his office as he was getting ready to go home. "Harry, I've got to talk to you about assigning the new associate to Max. I just don't think it's a good idea."

Harry didn't want to have this conversation, and he let it show. "Why not, Sarah?"

"I just think that Max won't get along with him."

Harry snapped his briefcase shut and looked directly at her. "Sarah, he's staying with Max for three reasons. First, right now Max needs help more than anyone else in the firm. Second, every new associate spends some time working for Max, and everyone survives the experience. You did. Third, I've never questioned your maturity or professional judgment until this new fellow came along, and I don't like having doubts about people I work with. So drop it! He's working for Max."

Harry picked up his briefcase, flung his coat over his shoulder and headed for the door. He didn't say another word. Sarah stood alone in Harry's office for a moment, then she shut off the light and left.

Sarah went to her office and sat down in her chair, wondering what to do. Suddenly, there was a knock at the door, and one of her associates, Masaka Mifune, popped her head in to wish Sarah good night. Sarah was about to ask with a slight barb why she was leaving early when she glanced at her clock: it was almost seven. She had been staring off into space for nearly an hour. She mumbled best wishes for the weekend, and Masaka left. A few moments later, Sarah left too. Friday night in New York began.

Sarah's personal time was spent much the way she worked, never coming to a rest until she was stopped by the sheer exhaustion of being fully alive.

Friday nights were a sharp break from the rhythm of Goldsmith & Hammer. In the warmer months, she would walk out of the office at six (working a half day, she called it), and head up Fifth Avenue, savoring the warm air as she merged with the vast crowds of people, so many excited to be even a small part of the thrilling city, filled with wonders.

Winter was a time for bundling up and going with friends to some warm intimate place. Her memories of winter were full of happy smiles and glasses of wine, toasts in front of roaring fires and dreams of a future that seemed as broad as the sea.

But, no matter what the season, early every

Saturday morning, Sarah would do her morning run around the Central Park reservoir. If it rained, she would swim laps in the pool on the roof of her building. Then, she would dress to the nines and head across Central Park to her family's synagogue, always arriving for the last 20 minutes of the service. Then, there would be the congregational Kiddush — the blessing over the wine accompanied by tea and cake -- and the comfort of family and old friends.

After saying hello and exchanging the latest news from home -- and somehow the West Side of Central Park would always be her home, even though she technically declared her independence when she moved out -- Sarah would head to the office for a few hours. Sarah did not resent putting in a few hours on the weekend. Everyone did except Harry. It let her plan her work for the upcoming week without distraction.

Near to Sarah's heart were the two associates she supervised. Like herself, Natalie Joann was Belgian. She had an L.L.M. from Columbia and wanted to spend a few years working in New York before heading back home. Masaka Mifune originally came from Japan to study filmmaking at NYU. But, somehow, she found her way into its law school. Masaka explained there were so many movies about lawyers that it was hard to believe there was any other profession in America. Sarah always looked forward to the slower pace of the weekend.

Sunday was regimented casual pleasure. Sarah

would occasionally spend time at the office, but not often. But she would be busy: shopping with her mother; skiing with her friends in winter; sailing with them in summer or doing one of a hundred other things. She was never alone except by choice.

It was only on Sunday night at nine o'clock that Sarah would make her inevitable cup of herbal tea and step into a warm bubble bath with Mozart wafting in from the living room. Sunday night was the time of the week Sarah reserved for her deepest thoughts and sweetest dreams, surveying her world as if she stood on a mountain top.

But, when Harry dropped the bombshell that Allen was going to be working for Max, Sarah's carefully orchestrated routine went out of the window. Quickly wishing Masaka goodnight, she grabbed her coat and headed out. If Sarah didn't hurry, she would be late for *Carmen* at the City Opera.

Skipping dinner, Sarah met her friends at the fountain at Lincoln Center and sat through the music as if it were a dull duty she had to get through. She spent the rest of the night sleeping fitfully, wondering what she should do, to whom she could turn.

It was Saturday morning, the Sabbath, and although it was winter outside, the voices of the choir of the Sephardic synagogue filled the sanctuary with warmth. Sitting high in the women's balcony, the tall, stately, gray-haired woman thought how sad and melancholy the music was, and, yet it always ended on a high, hopeful note. She was transported so far into the realm of the timeless that she didn't notice anyone approaching her.

But then Sarah walked up behind her and whispered in her ear. "Good Shabbos, mama."

"Good Shabbos, Sarah," Rachel Mendes replied. She looked at her watch and asked with surprise why Sarah was a full hour early.

"Mama, I need to talk to you and papa."

Rachel touched Sarah on the shoulder to reassure her. "We'll go into the chapel after services and ask for a little privacy. I'm sure there won't be a problem."

At the appointed time, Sarah and her parents headed down the carpeted stairs into the small sanctuary, a room decorated in colonial style with furnishings dating back to when the congregation met in a rented house near Wall Street during the American Revolution. Sarah's mother sat down in a leather chair, crossed her legs, and folded her hands in her lap. Her father Maurice sat near her on an upholstered bench.

"Now then, Sarah," he said, "tell us what is troubling you."

"It's hard to explain." But then Sarah proceeded to do so. She laid out what was happening in her head and her heart as if she were arguing before a court. Sarah explained how she met Allen and how he had quickly become part of her world. Now, it seemed he had become her life. Without realizing it, Sarah wrapped up her exposition by placing her hands on a wooden railing and leaned forward as if her parents were indeed a jury. She was a wonderful trial lawyer.

"What does it all mean?" Sarah asked quietly when her tale had finished.

Nothing was said for what seemed like an eternity. But then her mother stood up, walked over to Sarah, and gently kissed her on the cheek. "It means you're in love, Sarah, and we're so happy for you."

"How is that possible?" she cried. "I've never had a shortage of men who wanted to go out with me."

"Tell me," her mother gently chided. "Have you given them any thought since Allen came into your life except perhaps how to get rid of them?"

"No, I haven't," Sarah admitted.

"See what I mean?" her mother asked. "Now we're not printing up wedding invitations just yet, because you've still got a way to go. But you are on the path." Rachel Mendes radiated happiness as she hugged her daughter. But, one party to the conversation had yet to be heard from. Maurice sat still. He seemed to be both lost in thought and deep in concentration. Finally, when Rachel asked him directly how he felt, he replied, almost reluctantly, "He sounds like un âme perdu."

Sarah was shocked. Her father had returned to his native language to call Allen a lost soul.

Rachel came to the rescue. "Maurice, you've got to at least meet him before forming an opinion like that."

"Perhaps, you're right." He stood up and put his arm around Rachel while he kissed Sarah. "Let us see where this goes. We'll put off meeting him for now. We love you Sarah, and we trust you. Enjoy this time of your life."

They rejoined the congregation for wine and cake in the social hall, and then they went separate ways. Sarah headed off to her office while her parents walked home, hand in hand.

When Sarah was far away, Rachel asked her husband this question. "Maurice, what are you really thinking? I don't believe what you said back there, and I'm sure Sarah doesn't either."

He took a deep breath and then spoke slowly and deliberately. "If I told her what I really felt, she wouldn't listen to me. The truth is I don't see how this can end well."

Rachel said nothing. She held her husband's hand that much tighter, and they headed home.

An hour later, Sarah was back in her office, preparing to wage war. She sat at a circular table in a small conference room; sitting around her were Natalie, Masaka, a paralegal, and a part-time law student from Fordham. Sarah had a big securities trial coming up in two weeks and still much needed to be done. There was also the cert petition in

Metcalf that had to go out soon, so Sarah had no choice but to delegate tasks. Memoranda of law had to be written, subpoenas prepared, and exhibits assembled. Sarah politely queried her subordinates about their various assignments, patiently listened to what they had to say and then gave instructions in a warm, kind voice, but there was no doubt who was in charge.

Everyone ran in and out of the conference room except for Sarah, who sat as still as a queen on a throne. Finally, about five p.m., Sarah saw that things were falling into place, so she headed off to the commissary for a snack.

The quickest way was through the library. On a late Saturday afternoon in early February, there was only one person who could be reliably expected to be there -- "Moses." His nickname was easy to explain. Moses was the law-giver of the Bible.

C. Elliot Drucker was the "law man" of Goldsmith & Hammer, a man so enamored of the law he would come into the office on his own time just to read the latest cases. Aviation law, oil and gas law, landlord-tenant regulations, it made no difference to him. He loved them all.

Moses looked up when he heard her footsteps. "Oh, hello, Sarah."

"Hello, Elliot," she replied. No one called him Moses to his face.

"Have you seen the latest maritime regulations? Fascinating."

Sarah confessed she hadn't, but she promised to look at them when she had the chance.

Then, she heard a kind of stumbling sound from the back of the room. On a corner of a table near rows of bookshelves was a stack of legal texts that was definitely bigger than a molehill. Suddenly, out from between the shelves came a strange figure. The bottom half was a pair of legs struggling under a heavy load; the top half was two armfuls of law books, high enough to cover the face of the person struggling with them.

"Let me help you with those," Sarah said.

Grabbing some books from the top, she saw who it was. "Allen, what are you doing here? I thought you'd be enjoying your last few days of freedom before you started."

"I thought I'd be doing that too," Allen said. "But, then, Mr. Hammer called me last night around midnight and told me he needed a memo of law on his desk first thing Monday morning."

"I see," Sarah said, wondering what was going on. "Why are you using all these books? Why not use computers? You'll save hours."

"I wanted to," Allen said. "But I wasn't due to get a computer password until Monday morning, and Mr. Hammer said he wasn't allowed to let me use his."

There's no such rule, Sarah thought. She decided she'd investigate that later. "Did he say you couldn't ask for help?"

"No, he didn't say that."

Good, Sarah thought. She called out to Moses. "Elliot, can I see you for a moment?"

Holding his book open so he could keep reading law, Moses smiled pleasantly as he walked over. "Can I help you with something?"

"Yes, you can," Sarah said. She introduced the two men. "Elliot, Allen has to write a memo of law over the weekend. It's a rush. I don't want you to help him write it, but please help him with the research. You can use the computers, of course."

"Gladly," Moses said. Anything involving law made him happy.

Sarah left the two men, but, exiting the library, she shot a quick glance back. Allen and Moses were huddled over the stack of books, but Allen was looking at Sarah. When their eyes met, they both looked away, and Sarah hurried off.

In the commissary, Sarah helped herself to a banana, a quarter of a bagel with cream cheese, and, of course, a cup of herbal tea. Heading back to the war room, she took the long way, skirting the library completely. She avoided it for the rest of the weekend.

Sarah was not very good at being nonchalant. It was against her nature, but when Monday morning came around, she gave it her best shot. When she got to work that morning, she casually asked the receptionist if Max had arrived yet. The answer surprised her. "He's not due in today. He's in Houston."

Sarah was startled. "Was this an emergency?"

"No. He knew about this last week."

Sarah decided to go about her business and wait for developments. She didn't have to wait very long. Before ten o'clock, Allen knocked at her door, holding a memo of law.

"I've got a problem. Here's the memo of law Mr. Hammer wanted. But now, I find that he's in Texas, and I don't know when he's coming back. I don't know what to do with this memo, and I don't have any other assignments to keep me busy."

Sarah's reply was carefully measured. She could not afford to get involved. "Give a copy of the memo to Max's secretary and explain to her what you said to me. Max is supposed to call in every few hours, and if he wants the memo, she can fax it to him."

Allen thanked her and turned away, but then, she said words she would later regret. "As long as you're here, let me review your memo." He handed it to her.

"What's the case about?" she asked.

"It involves a wrongful death action, a nineteen-year old drove into the back of a parked truck and died. We're arguing that when you hit a parked vehicle you are presumed to be at fault."

"Sit down, and I'll review it," Sarah said. Her eye scanned the memo. It was good writing she said to herself; in fact, it was too good. One particular passage alarmed her. "Tell me why you wrote this," she asked, and she read aloud the closing paragraph:

The plaintiff concludes his arguments with an open appeal for sympathy, suggesting that procedural and substantive rules be relaxed because this case involves the death of a nineteen-year-old boy. However, this writer has known the death of a loved one as has everyone who has ever lived or will live. Yet, our legal system is based on law, not on emotional arguments. Were it otherwise, our judicial system and indeed our way of life would be very different.

"Is there something wrong with it?" Allen asked. His voice showed his concern.

"Here's the problem," Sarah said. "This is good writing. I'd give you an 'A' if this were a class in composition. But Mr. Hammer has a particular taste in legal writing. He's very blunt, and he might not find this to his liking."

Allen's face fell, but Sarah tried to be upbeat. She hit a few buttons on her computer, and the printer behind her desk started to spew out paper. "As long as Max isn't looking for the memo right now, why don't you re-do it in his style?"

"Thank you," he said, and he took the memo and headed out.

Sarah put the matter out of her head for the rest of the day. Goldsmith & Hammer was bidding for business from an insurance company that wrote errors and omissions insurance for directors of large companies, and she was entrusted with writing a proposal letter. Then, Sarah had to start preparing her witnesses for her coming trial, but, at three-thirty, she looked up and saw Allen standing in the doorway.

"I re-wrote the draft," he said. "Thanks for your help."

She held out her hand for the draft and motioned him to sit down. It was a better draft, at least, the kind that Max would enjoy, but it gave Sarah no pleasure to read it. That same passage now read:

The plaintiff has obviously never attended law school, or, if he did, he paid little attention to such basic rules as that courts decide cases by law, not on sob stories. The plaintiff was nineteen years old when he died. Sad, but it would be even sadder if courts threw out the law whenever someone came to court with a bleeding-heart saga. Defendant did not cause the accident, the plaintiff's negligence did, and the case should be dismissed.

"He'll love it," Sarah said. But she looked at his expression. "You're not happy?"

"To be honest, I don't like the personal attacks."

"It's all a game," Sarah said. "You'll get used to it." Yet, she had the feeling that she had broken something. She could not tell whether it was something in Allen or herself.

The day came to an end, and Tuesday arrived. Sarah was so busy with cases that she gave little thought to Max. She even gave Allen short shrift, but then, her phone rang. It was Harry.

"Sarah," he said, "please come to my office."

"What's up, Harry?"

"Just come," he said. Harry was seldom so brusque.

Helen was holding the door to Harry's office open for her. Looking ahead, she saw Harry sitting behind his desk and Max sitting in one of the two chairs in front of it.

Sitting down in the empty chair, Sarah asked what was up. Harry held up two documents, one in each hand. "Do you recognize these memos, Sarah?"

"I do," she said. 'Those are two drafts of memos Allen was doing for Max."

"Can you explain why one is so different from another?"

"Editing."

Now Max weighted in. "That's not the point. One is written like someone fresh out of law school. One is written like a guy who's been in the trenches for a couple of years. I got the first version from a friend of mine in the word processing department. The second was what that new guy gave me this morning. I'd like to know what's going on here."

Sarah turned to Max. "I'm just curious. Did you think of asking Allen?"

Max was not in a mood to be put on the

defensive. "No, I preferred to go to the source, and this has your fingerprints all over it."

Sarah raised her voice. "I resent that. You were out of the office, and I was simply offering him a style guide. As a matter of fact, it was the same format you gave me when I worked for you."

"That doesn't give you the right to interfere with the way that I bring along one of my associates."

Sarah looked right at Harry. "Am I forbidden to speak to him?"

Harry stared right back. "Sarah, this is not the Montagues and the Capulets. You're a mature adult, at least you've come across as one for years, I just want you to act like one." Then, he shifted his gaze. "By the way Max, that goes for you too." Silence. Finally, Harry spoke. "I'm sure we all have better things do."

Suddenly, Sarah and Max both started to shout at each other, each determined to have the exquisite last word.

Starting to get up, Max couldn't resist taking a parting shot. "Just leave him alone."

Sarah had no more self-control than Max. "You leave him alone."

Harry slammed his fist on his desk. "Shut up both of you. I'm looking at two highly compensated partners, in this firm, who are acting like children. Sarah, I have to ask you not to interfere with Max's relationship with his associates. And Max, just cool it! Helping someone revise a memo is not the end of the world."

Everyone sat there fuming. Finally, Harry spoke. "Look, we've worked together for years. Just go back to work, please." Without a further word to each other, Max and Sarah walked out of the office.

"Only spare his life ...."

Max was the antithesis of a religious man, but there was one Biblical passage he knew well. God tells Satan of the great piety of Job, and Satan replies that it is an easy thing to love God when all is going well. Put Job to the test, Satan suggests, and he will break. God replies that Job is in Satan's hand to do with as he pleases, the only restriction being "Only spare his life."

Harry did not think he was doing anything unusual when he assigned Allen to work exclusively for Max while telling Sarah not to interfere. But, to Max, the words of Job rang in his ears: "Only spare his life ...."

Once the meeting with Harry and Sarah was over, Max promptly went to Allen's office. He entered without knocking. "You can go home now," he said. "But, I want you in my office at 7:30 tomorrow morning. Sharp. I've got a big project for you."

"I'll be there," Allen said.

"And another thing," Max added with a triumphant grin. "If Ms. Mendes ever speaks to you about anything related to your work, I want to know about it promptly. You are my associate." He paused. "You got a problem with that?"

Allen answered as matter-of-factly as he could. "No, I don't."

"Good!" Max turned and walked off in triumph. It was only after Max got up and closed the door that Allen felt the full impact of Max's words. He was being ordered to stay away from Sarah. Perhaps it would be better to do document review at another firm than to treated like this, Allen thought. But then, he wondered what Sarah would think. He resolved to fight it out.

Max had put Allen on notice that, starting the following morning. he intended to make his life hell. But Max had given him no assignments for the rest of the day so, in theory, he could go home and get some rest. But somehow Allen had to speak to Sarah. It was just past 6:00 p.m. Allen knew that Max typically left the office around 6:30 p.m., and Sarah left an hour later. He stayed in his office until a quarter to seven and then walked past Max's office. The door was closed. Max was gone. Further down the corridor, Allen could see that Sarah's door was open.

He paused by her door. Sarah looked up. "Yes, Allen?"

"Oh, I was heading to the library, and I wondered if you had any books you wanted to return."

"No, thank you, "she said. "But I might have to head down there in a few minutes."

Allen sat down at a table in the back of the library. As he expected, Sarah walked into the room a few seconds later, holding a yellow legal pad and a pen. She got a book off a shelf, sat down and started to read. Then, she got up and walked past Allen as she headed deep into the bookshelves. After a discrete pause, he followed. Shielded by the books, they spoke.

"It seems I'm forbidden to speak to you," Allen said.

"That's not exactly what Harry said, Allen," Sarah replied, attempting to draw a lawyer's fine distinction. "He said I can't interfere with your working relationship with Max."

"That's the same thing," Allen said. "To Max, law is co-extensive with life."

"Listen to me," she said. "We can still meet at the pizza place after work, and I'm going to help you anyway I can. I still think you're a fine lawyer."

Allen felt something that he could not define, so he said simply, "Thank you."

Sarah found herself looking into Allen's eyes. "Just remember he's a big bag of wind from the night division of the Bronx Law Institute and you're University of Chicago." They devised a series of signals by which they could communicate with each other.

Allen stole out from between the bookshelves; Sarah followed a few moments later.

At 7:30 the next morning, Allen walked into Max Hammer's office. Max had a cigar in his mouth, and there was a gray haze above his head. In front of him was a thick stack of papers in a manila envelope. "Don't sit down," Max said.

Max gathered up the papers into a folder and slipped a single rubber band, under heavy tension, around the mess. He casually tossed it in Allen's direction, and he instinctively caught it.

"Let me tell you about the case," Max said with a grin. "Man runs a restaurant, on 51st Street, called 'La Boheme.' It features a great salad bar, and he makes his own dressing. They're famous dressings. They get written up in the *New Yorker* all the time. He's thinking of bottling them.

"Anyway, he employs the same chef and salad man for years. Treats them like his kids. Then, one day, no warning, they quit and open their own place three blocks away, and they advertise salads in the tradition of 'La Boheme.'"

Max pounded his fist on the desk. "What our client wants is to shut them down, or at least keep them from using his salad dressings. Your job is to prepare an Order to Show Cause for an injunction, and it's got to be ready by five o'clock when the client comes in."

Max leaned back in his chair, took his cigar out of his mouth, and folded his arms behind his head. "Think you can handle it?"

"No problem," Allen replied.

Allen took the stack of materials to his office and set to work. This was a fairly routine problem in trade secret law. Fortunately, Goldsmith & Hammer was heavily computerized. Every memo of law done in the last ten years was thoroughly indexed and available with the touch of a few buttons. He was pressing those buttons when a box popped up on screen: "You have a new e-mail." It was from Max. "By the way (it read), don't use the memo of law in the computer about trade secrets. I know it, and I don't like it. Do something original."

Suddenly, ten minutes work became a day's project. Allen groaned, but then, his cell phone rang. It was Sarah. "What did he give you?" she asked.

After Allen explained his assignment, Sarah thought for a moment. Then she said, "I've got the perfect format for you. It's my personal work product, and it's not on the office network. All you need to do is update the cases I cite with some newer ones. I know you; you're a whiz at research. You can have the whole thing wrapped up by lunch."

Allen wanted to sing her praises, but the wiser part of him calmly thanked her and asked if she'd be free for lunch. She was, at a discrete restaurant no one at the firm patronized.

It was a small vegetarian place on Seventh Avenue, wedged in between an adult bookstore and a shop specializing in tourist trinkets and cheap electronics. Sitting way in the back, believing themselves unseen, they relaxed.

"Did you bring your work product?" Sarah asked.

"Yes, but I feel guilty about this."

"Don't," Sarah replied. "You've got the right stuff.

But you don't know how to fight dirty the way Max does. I do. Let me do a quick edit."

She pulled out a pen and began to mark up the pages, but it was hard for them to keep their minds on the project. After a brief spell of editing, Sarah put down her pen to order food. Somehow, she forgot all about the manuscript till they were done eating. Their conversation was too delightful. Then, Sarah looked at the time, was horrified, and hailed a taxi.

Sarah finished the edits before they reached Goldsmith & Hammer. She put the papers into Allen's hand as they bolted from the cab and headed inside. "Good luck," she said kindly.

CHAPTER XIV

The following morning, Sarah found herself summoned bright and early into Harry's office. What she saw there alarmed her. Harry was at his desk, not at the couch where he normally held his relaxed meetings. In one of the two chairs fronting his desk sat Max, who had a broad, insufferable grin.

"Sit down, Sarah," said Harry. His face had never been more stern. When she had taken her seat, Harry handed her some stapled papers that had been lying on his desk. To her horror, she saw it was the memo she had helped Allen with yesterday. Her handwritten corrections were all over it.

"Where, where did you get this?" Sarah demanded.

"Your boyfriend forgot to shred it," Max said in a taunting manner. "He should've been more careful. Why anyone could come along and find it in a wastebasket."

Sarah turned to face Max. "Haven't you got anything better to do than to check out garbage cans, Max?" It took little imagination to see she wanted to add the words 'You bastard!'

"Now, now," Max continued in his most condescending manner. I'm simply trying to bring along an associate, and you keep interfering."

Sarah was furious. "You're not 'bringing him along' as you put it. You're piling on pressure to break him."

"Shut up both of you," Harry shouted, and he slammed his fist on his desk. "You're acting like babies." Harry rarely shouted. Max and Sarah stopped their battle and faced forward, like little children fearing discipline in kindergarten.

"Allen can stay in the firm. But Sarah I want your word that you won't help him." Sarah froze, a defiant look on her face. In response, Harry adopted a fatherly tone. "Sarah, your word please."

Finally, she said, "You have it."

"Good," Harry said. "You must also promise not to see Allen or talk to him during business hours. It goes without saying you are expected to observe the firm's sexual harassment policy."

"Unfair," Sarah cried. Max could not suppress a chuckle. Sarah turned on him, and now, she forgot that she was a lady. "Bastard!"

Now it was Harry's turn to be furious as Max broke out in gales of silent laughter that shook his big belly. "Sarah, I've known you seven years, and this is the first time I've heard you curse. Enough. This isn't worth it. I'm giving Allen his walking papers."

Now, laughing out loud, his face red, Max stammered out, "No, don't send him away. This stuff is better than *Romeo and Juliet*." His convulsions of laughter lasted nearly a minute before he regained control of himself. Given his bulk, his laughter drew more attention than the fine beads of sweat on his face.

Sarah left Harry's office a badly chastened woman. The only concession she had wrung from the whole business was permission to meet with Allen for a few minutes to explain the situation. Surprisingly, Allen took it calmly when she did.

"But, we can still see each other," Sarah concluded. "Even if I can't help you with your specific tasks, I can give you general advice."

"Sarah, I can't keep seeing you like this."

Sarah's face fell. "Why not?"

Allen, who had been sitting at his desk, now stood up and faced her. "Sarah, you've taken me out twice to welcome me to the firm and three times to 'mentor' me. These have all been dates. Dates. Dates. Dates. But you refuse to call them that. I don't know why, but I don't want to see you anymore under false pretenses. I want to date you."

And then, Allen put his arms around Sarah and kissed her. The partner in Sarah raised her hands to push him away, the woman moved her hands across his back to tighten the embrace. The woman won.

When it was over, Sarah said, "You're right. They've all been dates, and I want to date you now."

Allen spoke. "I love opera. Do you?"

Sarah said. "'Love it. Mozart is my favorite."

Allen grinned. "Great. Wednesday night ... City Opera ... *Don Giovanni* ... eight o'clock. Meet me at the fountain."

"I will, Allen," Sarah replied. "Now, we both know I have to go, and we can never talk again on premises."

As she left, Sarah added, "Max was right about one thing. This is just like *Romeo and Juliet*."

"But we'll have a happy ending," Allen said.

Wednesday night was cold, but somehow the chill air made the city lights shine more brightly. There was not a cloud in the night sky. It was ten minutes to eight, and the last of the latecomers were racing into the opera house while Sarah stood by the fountain in the plaza, waiting for Allen.

She looked at her watch again. "Damn," she said to herself. "We'll miss the first act." Sarah thought about calling Allen's cell phone but decided it would make her look too anxious.

Suddenly, a taxi jerked to a halt on Broadway, and Allen jumped out. He ran up to Sarah, making apologies. "There were so many last-minute details to straighten out," he said. "Max gave me hell for leaving early."

"It's okay," she said. "You're here, I'm here, let's go inside." The house lights were going down as they got to their seats. Then, the orchestra began to tune up. But then, the conductor rapped his baton for attention. All was silent as he raised his arms.

He held them over his head for a few seconds, then brought them down as the orchestra played two powerful notes of music. Allen put his arm around Sarah's shoulders and whispered, "It's begun." Then, he went silent, and they surrendered to the music.

When the lights came on at intermission, Allen turned to Sarah. He was going to comment on the opera, but then, he realized that this was his first look at Sarah without her coat on that evening. "You look great," he said.

She did. Her dark hair fell gracefully to her shoulders, and she wore a black evening dress. "You didn't go to work like that," he finally said.

"No," she replied. "I've got a pretty big closet in my office. Shall we get some wine?"

"Maybe at the second intermission," Allen said. "Right now, I've got other plans. Come with me."

"Okay, I love a mystery," Sarah said as she followed him. They walked through the red-carpeted lobby that was filled with elegantly dressed men and women. Finally, they reached an elevator.

"Can you tell me where we're going?" Sarah

asked.

"You'll see," was the reply.

They got out on the fourth tier, and Allen led her to a stairwell. They walked one flight up, but there was no fifth tier in the opera house. Instead, they came to a sign forbidding them to go further, warning them that the roof lay ahead.

"Why did you bring me here, as if I couldn't guess?" she asked.

Allen kissed her passionately.

Up in the stairway, the house lights never blinked to signal the end of intermission, and the warning buzzer never sounded, so Allen and Sarah never got back to their seats in time for the second act. They didn't care; they bought wine at the concession stand and watched the opera on the monitor.

"You know," Allen said at one point "*Don Giovanni* is like *Hamlet*. It has everything: comedy, romance, tragedy and the supernatural. If *Hamlet* is the best play, *Don Giovanni* is the best opera."

"Why did you become a lawyer?" Sarah asked him.

The question caught him off guard. "I can't go into that," he said.

That led to a long silence. Finally, the opera ended, and the audience rose to its feet in thunderous applause. Amid the crowd leaving the theater, Allen gave Sarah a good-night kiss and announced it was time for him to head back to Brooklyn.

Don't go back to Brooklyn, Sarah wanted to say.

It's such a long trip, and the night is so cold. I've got a couch in my living room -- but she said no such thing. Instead, she reached into her purse and pulled out her cell phone and a voucher.

"Let's go home in style," she said. I'll have our night car service pick us up and drop us off."

"Don't you have to bill it to a client?" he asked.

Sarah shrugged. "Who cares? I'm allowed an occasional sin," she said. "After all, I'm a partner." That was that.

The limousine came quickly enough, and ten minutes later, they were heading across Central Park. Allen was singing and humming snatches of Mozart while Sarah leaned against him. They felt at peace with each other.

When they arrived at Sarah's home in the East 60's, she gave Allen still another kiss and then headed inside. After a short elevator ride, she found herself looking in the mirror. Her face was flushed, and she had a smile that could not be erased. It was then Sarah realized she was in love.

The following day, Sarah was at her desk, still preparing for that big trial. She suddenly realized that now she saw her fellow attorneys in a different light. They were no longer her comrades in arms, they were her potential betrayers. Sarah even began to wonder if she could trust Masaka and Natalie, and she decided that she could not.

Sarah waited anxiously for the call or e-mail that would summon her to Harry's office for her night at the opera, but it never came. Finally, by day's end, she realized she was safe.

Allen and Sarah's next date was *Tosca*, the following Monday night. That seemed an eternity away for Sarah. Where was the woman who had sworn off men in exchange for three years of success at Harvard? She was nowhere to be seen. The days passed in slow agony. Even when she would bump into Allen in the hallway, there was no relief. She had to studiously ignore him.

During the days of waiting, Sarah turned to harder workouts than ever at the gym, along with steam baths and massages.

On Saturday morning, she again pulled her mother out of services and told her what was going on.

Her mother only smiled when Sarah finished. "Now you are on the path, Sarah. Enjoy your romance."

Monday night finally came, and again, Allen made it only at the last minute, jumping out of a taxi and into her arms in a single step.

"What happened this time?"

He was out of breath. "Max ...at 7:30 ... I had my coat on when he ordered me to do a quick memo. He wants it on his desk tomorrow morning when he comes in."

"Allen," she said. "You should have called me and canceled. I would have understood."

"You're too important," he said. "C'mon, let's

go hear the opera. I'll run back to the office and finish it. It'll only take about an hour."

When the intermission came, Sarah and Allen did not head for the stairs. Instead, they each settled for wine. "Allen, I've been thinking. Don't exhaust yourself for my sake. Skip the rest of the opera. Go back to the office and do the memo."

"No, Sarah. I want to be with you, and this is my only chance." Sarah hesitated before she spoke again, but not for very long. "How about this: After the opera, you can do the memo, then you can spend the night at my place. Don't get the wrong idea. I've got a big couch in my living room."

"'Love you, Sarah. I'll do it. And by the way, I've copied one of your ideas. Now, I always keep a change of clothes at work."

The opera soared, and at its conclusion, Allen and Sarah were on their feet applauding. "Bravo," Sarah shouted. "Bravo."

Suddenly, amid the cheering crowd, Allen held her gently and gave her a kiss. After Sarah composed herself, she wanted to know why he needed to kiss her right then and there.

"It's just the excitement of the moment. A lot of the people who applaud just do it out of habit. You love the opera. When I saw that, I just couldn't resist you."

She whispered in his ear. "Let's find a stairwell. Even for five minutes."

He arrived at her door at one-thirty that

morning. Sarah greeted him at the door in a full-length blue bathrobe. She led him to her couch, which was fitted out with bedding. On a nearby table was a steaming cup of herbal tea atop a coaster.

A scene is being set here, Allen thought. Relying on instinct, he began to gently put his arms around her, but Sarah slipped out of them. "Allen," she said. "You must know I have feelings for you, but I'm still sorting them out. Besides, it's almost two o'clock in the morning on a school night, and we both need our rest."

"I understand, Sarah," Allen said. He kissed her on the forehead and adjourned, alone, to the sofa bed.

The next morning, Sarah woke up Allen with a hearty shake of his shoulders.

"Can I make you breakfast?" she offered.

"No, Sarah," Allen replied. "You're too kind. I'll grab something near the office, and I can shave and shower at my health club." After a quick kiss, he put on his clothes in the bathroom and headed out the door.

Sarah stood facing the door for nearly a minute after he left. She was trying to remember something *from Romeo and Juliet* -- Juliet's words of agony at parting from Romeo -- but they would not come back to her.

Well, there was nothing to do but get dressed and head to the office herself. Once Sarah got there, she yielded to the dark angels of her nature and checked on Max's whereabouts. Sure enough, Max was in court and wouldn't even be in the office until noon. So much for needing that memo the first thing in the morning.

Sarah was slowly becoming more and more conscious of the two sides of Allen. Passionate at the opera and when she was in his arms, but seemingly so misplaced in the world of the law. It was something that she sensed she would have to face, some day. Right now, she was simply too happy to worry about it.

In an unguarded moment, the two of them spoke at work when they happened to meet in the library. They spoke in the back of the library, behind a shelf of books that were never used.

"*Fidelio* is playing at the Met on Thursday night. I can get tickets, Sarah. But I've got a question. Why does it always have to be the opera?"

The answer was immediate. "Because I love it," Sarah said. "I always have. To me, theater is the most wonderful thing in life, and opera is the most sublime form of theater."

"Good enough for me," Allen replied. "We'll do it."

A hard rain fell that Thursday night. Sarah had to wait inside the lobby. Eight o'clock came and there was no sign of Allen. At five minutes past, she got a text message from Allen saying he was trapped in the office, but he thought he could make the second act. Nevertheless, Sarah decided to miss the start of the opera and wait for him by the entrance under the mezzanine balcony. By nine o'clock he had still not arrived. Finally, at 9:30, Allen showed up soaking wet. Even ten steps away, she could see he looked haggard.

"My God, Allen, what happened?"

"Max again," he replied calmly. "Now, he's got a computer in his home, and he wants my work product e-mailed to him when it's done. No more having it on his desk the next day."

Sarah was angry. "No one else at Goldsmith & Hammer works the hours that you do. Enough is enough. I'm complaining to Harry."

"Please don't. I can handle this."

"Allen, at least, come back home with me tonight. Don't go back to Brooklyn." He nodded agreement.

They enjoyed what little was left of the opera. After it was over, Sarah summoned a limo, and they were at her apartment before 11:30 p.m. It was still raining when they got out of the car. Then, Allen suddenly turned her around to face him. "What's more romantic than kissing in the rain?" he asked. She answered, but not with words.

When they finally arrived at her apartment, there was a pot of hot coffee -- Allen preferred it -- an extra bathrobe and a hot shower. Sarah took his wet clothes and hung them up to dry.

Allen felt he belonged there.

Under the stream of hot steamy water, Allen's

concerns seemed to fade away. He was only conscious of his body. Then, for long moments, of nothing at all. Suddenly, he heard Sarah's voice calling his name from the other side of the shower curtain. Sticking his head out, he saw Sarah standing in front of him, wearing a short, terry cloth robe.

"Allen," she whispered softly. "Aren't you going to invite a lady in out of the cold?"

"Where are my manners?" he asked, spreading wide the curtain.

The long night passed, but, afterwards, they could not sleep for a long time. They lay next to each other, holding hands and talking nonsense they would never remember. Then, Allen turned to Sarah and said, "I love you."

Sarah rolled over to face him and said the only thing she could think of. "And I love you."

Then, Allen suddenly asked, "Sarah, can I tell you something?"

"Sure."

"It's about my family," Allen sat up. "Did I ever tell you that my father was once the acting Attorney General of Illinois?

"No, you didn't Allen. All you've ever told me was that you're from Chicago, and that there were a couple of lawyers in your family."

"I'm afraid I didn't do them justice, Sarah. My grandfather was the founding partner of

Wasserman, Smith & Knight. They're now the second largest law firm in Chicago, two hundred lawyers in the Sears Tower. And I've got an uncle who
is a federal judge."

Sarah was wide-awake now. She switched on
the lamp by the bed. "Why are you telling me this
now?"

"I guess intimacy leads to telling secrets," Allen
said.

"How many of them love poetry the way you
do?"

"No one really. I guess I'm the black sheep of
the family."

"Not to me," Sarah said. "Never." Then, she
kissed him.

Sarah's alarm clock sounded promptly at 5:30
a.m. She leaned over Allen and shut it off. "Go back
to sleep," she said with a quick kiss. "I'll fix you a
breakfast you'll never forget."

Then, she hopped out of bed, grabbed a blanket and wrapped it around herself as if it were a
toga. As she headed off to the kitchen, she heard
Allen say, "I love you."

She turned around and put her closed fists on
her waist, looking like a cross between an Amazon
general and a Roman matron. "I know," she said.
"And that's why we've got to keep this quiet, or
we're both in trouble. Deep trouble. We're outlaws
at the firm now." Then, brushing the hair out of her

eyes, she turned and headed off into domesticity.

Breakfast for Sarah was usually yogurt and a bowl of cereal with skim milk, but now she had given herself a challenge. Every pot and pan as well as her trusty microwave was called in to service as she made a morning meal for the ages: omelets, pancakes, waffles and oatmeal for substance; tea, coffee, juice and bottled water for beverages.

Fifteen minutes later, Allen appeared in the breakfast alcove. He seemed only half awake, as if, deep down, he was still asleep. With a muttered, "Thank you, it looks great!" he began to eat. After he had some food inside him, he seemed more himself. He grinned and offered a mischievous proposition, "How about we both call in sick and spend the day together?"

"Can't do it," Sarah replied. "Too much talk in the office as is. Harry and Max would ask questions."

"Are you that afraid of them?"

"No, I'm cautious."

That was a lie. Sarah knew she was strong enough at the firm to survive one scandal, but she didn't think Allen was.

But Sarah now had a question; it came from the practical side of her nature. "Allen, why did you go into the law?"

He turned away. "I can't answer that."

Sarah laughed, but only a little. "Allen, we've just been as intimate as two people can be, and I can't know why you entered your profession?"

"I just can't talk about it now," he said quietly. Sarah saw there would be no more questions for now.

She got up from the table, put her arms around him and kissed him. "I love you," she said. "It will all work out." Then, she changed the subject. "Would you like to come back here tomorrow night?"

"Well, after work, I could run to my apartment and pack a few things, and, then race back here. I could make it by a quarter to nine or so."

"Do it," she said. "I'll have dinner waiting." And then, they kissed again.

Thirty minutes later, a cab stopped in traffic three blocks from Goldsmith & Hammer. Sarah jumped out while Allen continued onward. A very pleasant double life had begun.

Sarah was content to let Allen keep his secrets. Their lives quickly assumed a kind of rhythm: lovers by night, lawyers by day. As attorneys, they pretended to be indifferent to each other's existence; as lovers, they laughed over the situation.

But Allen's behavior, at the firm, changed in a way that alerted the sensitive antennae of Max that something was afoot. Somehow, Allen had become cheerful and contented and seemingly immune to whatever Max could throw at him.

One day, Allen was walking past Max's office. He was almost out of earshot and getting ready to turn the corner when Max's voice, in a tone equally friendly and sarcastic, called out, "O, Allen!"

That stopped him. He turned around and, in a moment, he was standing in front of Max. Max had picked up one of Allen's briefs and was studying it carefully. Allen stood still for a few unpleasant minutes. Finally, Max slapped the pages on his desk and looked up.

"They're good," he said dryly. "They're excellent. What I want to know is why. Has Ms. Mendes been ...?"

Allen cut him off. "No, it's all my work. Now, if you don't mind …." But Max did.

He got up and blocked Allen's path to the door. "But I do mind. You're different somehow. You're happier, and I want to know why."

Allen simply shrugged. "I guess your influence is rubbing off." Silence. "May I get back to work?"

Max shrugged back in turn. "You can go."

Max didn't like what he was seeing. He was used to wielding life-and-death power over his underlings, and he resolved to do something about the situation. He checked his Rolodex and called up someone who owed him a favor.

One day, Sarah came back from court in a foul mood. A rare thing had happened: she lost. Law is an adversarial profession, as she always said to her associates. That means someone is going to win, and someone is going to lose. But now, she added to herself, "Why did it have to be me?"

She was already writing out the appeal in her

head when she walked in the door of Goldsmith & Hammer. Sarah didn't get far before Helen intercepted her and told her that Harry wanted to see her immediately.

As soon as Sarah set foot in Harry's office, she began to make excuses for herself. "It was those crazy rulings the judge made, Harry. We'll win on appeal...."

But Harry brushed it aside. "That's not what we're going to talk about Sarah," he said. "Sit down."

Something in Harry's manner told Sarah she had to be all business. She sat down in her most lady-like fashion. "Yes, Harry?" she asked calmly.

"Sarah, how long have you and Allen been living together?"

Sarah wasn't a trial lawyer for nothing. "Old trick, Harry," she shot back. "Asking a question that assumes a fact not yet proven."

But Harry had tried a few cases too. "And it's just as old a trick to answer a sensitive question with an accusation, hoping to confuse the questioner."

"Are you accusing me?"

Harry paused, then he continued with a shade more gently "Sarah, Allen resigned this morning."

"What!"

"Yes, Sarah. He sacrificed himself to protect you." Then Harry opened his desk and pulled out a DVD. "You see this? An investigator has been following Allen for several weeks. Allen walks in your front door every night, and you leave together in the morning."

"I can't believe you're capable of this, Harry," Sarah shot back. "Who did it?"

Harry seemed sad. "Believe me, Sarah, this wasn't my idea. I was just as shocked as you are when I was shown the disk. But now, we all have to suffer the consequences. Allen admitted your relationship and resigned to protect your career here."

Sarah was furious. "This is Max's doing, isn't it? I'll bet he paid for the investigator out of his own pocket."

Leaning back in his chair, Harry drew a deep breath as he looked off into a corner. He said nothing.

Sarah rose from her chair, but Harry made a gesture for her to remain seated. "Max isn't here Sarah. I know you. I sent him away because we all wanted to avoid a confrontation. Here, take the disk. It did what Max wanted. It got Allen out of the firm. But you're still working here, and you've got to act like a lawyer and a partner."

Sarah flushed. She took a few deep breaths and regained her temper sufficiently to stammer, "I'm taking the rest of the day off."

Harry looked down at his desk. "I can't blame you, Sarah."

Then, Sarah left his office and the building.

She was walking out onto Fifth Avenue when she realized that she had no idea where Allen was.

When he answered a call to the apartment, she breathed a sigh of relief. "Allen, are you all right?" she asked.

His voice was calm. "Yes, I am Sarah. I'm all right. I was expecting your call."

"Listen," she said quickly. "I'm taking the rest of the day off. If you haven't had lunch yet, I'll pick up some steak sandwiches. This will all work out, darling."

"Thank you, Sarah. Steak sandwiches sound fine. I'll be home when you get here."

Walking in her front door thirty minutes later, she saw Allen sitting in the reclining chair, smoking a cigar. There was a fine, gray haze about his head.

"Have you taken up cigars, Allen?"

"Relax Sarah," he said gently. "I only smoke on special occasions. Losing a job is one of them. As I was leaving the office, I passed by Max's office. He wasn't there, but there was an open humidor filled with Cubans. I don't know where he gets them. I just took one."

Sarah sensed it was her turn to be mild, so she only gave him a gentle scolding. "Well, whatever you're trying to prove, you have. Please put it out. I don't like the fumes."

They ate in silence. Then, Allen asked a question. "May I tell you why I became a lawyer?"

Sarah put down her sandwich. "Why tell me now?"

"Like they say, 'The essence of legal ethics is full

disclosure to your client.'"

Her first thought was to cross her arms. She did not know why. But Sarah knew enough about body language to sense Allen would view it as a wall she had suddenly erected. To counter the impulse, she spread her open hands on the table and spoke in a warm comforting tone.

"Whatever you say, I'm still going to love you."

Allen took a deep breath. "I wasn't exactly honest with you when I first told you about my family." He took another deep breath and continued.

"Sarah, the name Wasserman doesn't mean much in legal circles in New York, but, it has a very different impact in Chicago. My grandfather was the first member of our family to go to college. He went to the University of Illinois and to law school at the University of Chicago on scholarship. He was brilliant."

"So are you," Sarah said quietly.

"Not like him. Nobody was like him. My dad and my uncle both went to U of C undergraduate and for law school. But they didn't need scholarships. By then, my grandfather had founded Wasserman, Smith and Knight. I told you how big they are."

Sarah cocked her head. "If this is too painful, you don't have to tell me."

"No, I want to tell you. As I told you that wonderful night, my father is a partner in the firm now, and my uncle is a federal judge. Dad was once the interim Attorney General of Illinois, and he teaches criminal procedure at U of C. My earliest memory is U of C Law pennants on my bedroom walls."

Words poured out. "For my bar mitzvah, I was given a bound copy of Cardozo's *The Nature of the Judicial Process*, and, from my junior year in high school on, I worked summers at the family firm. I even had my own office there until I moved to New York."

"How did that happen?"

Allen contorted his face, as if he couldn't decide whether to speak or be silent. "I felt trapped. It was my last year in law school. Everything was set for me to start at old Wasserman, Smith & Knight in the fall. My family was going to set me up in an apartment and give me a car as a graduation present. But then, suddenly, a friend of mine told me about a New York recruiter on campus for Culpepper, Denham & Smeaton, who still wanted to see people. I went to see him, and, suddenly, I had a job offer in Manhattan that paid more than my dad's firm, and it had a bigger name too. How do you say no?"

"It sounds like you can't. I couldn't have if I were you. But what happened at Culpepper?"

Allen shook his head. "I can't really say what went wrong at Culpeper because I don't know what I was working on."

"What do you mean?"

"Culpepper is a mega-firm," Allen answered. "They can put fifty lawyers on a case. I was hired at $140,000 a year, to start, given a lovely office, and they assigned me to write memo of law after memo of law on one aspect of one big case."

Sarah was naturally curious. "What was the case about?"

"I don't know," Allen replied. "I asked my supervisor to explain the case to me, but he always said he was too busy. Then, one day there was a crisis in the case. They put me in charge of preparing a big order to show cause in the Second Circuit. Money was no object. They assigned two lawyers to work under me and as many paralegals as we needed. We worked on sheer adrenaline for three days ...."

"What happened?" Sarah asked.

The sad tone in Allen's voice mocked his words. "We won, Sarah. We won. And I was a hero."

"Allen, I think you should calm down."

"The following week, I was called into a meeting with the clients, and my boss said to them, 'Look, we've stalled paying the money we owe them for five years. Thanks to the hard work of young Mr. Wasserman here, we can stall for at least three more. By then, they'll be ready to settle for pennies on the dollar.'"

Allen laughed. "So that's what I was doing for all that money, stalling. I needed something to believe in, so I left."

Then, Allen asked Sarah a question. "What do you believe in as a lawyer?"

Sarah remembered how surprised Bradford was

when she gave him an honest answer to a similar question. The judge had taken it in his stride, but she didn't think Allen could, at least not now.

Sarah did not answer his question; she couldn't.

"Allen," she asked. "Why did you put up with such misery working for Max?"

He quietly said, "I guess I did it for you."

"What will you do now, Allen? Where will you go?"

"I'll look for another law firm," he said. "There are thousands in New York."

"Do you have to be a lawyer?" Sarah asked. "It makes you so unhappy. There are so many other things you can do."

"My fate is sealed," Allen said. "That was decided long ago. For me, my law degree is a Mark of Cain." He thought for a moment before he spoke again. "Sarah, I think I'd better move out, at least, until I get settled again somewhere else. I may not be too pleasant to be around until I find another job."

"No," she said. "Don't go. Stay."

"Sarah, we're not in the same league. I'm nothing without a job."

"Oh, no, no." She was determined. "You're so wrong. Stay here with me."

"What are you saying, Sarah?"

"Allen, I want to marry you."

"But what will your family say? What will Harry say? Can you imagine the jokes Max will make?"

"I don't give a damn what anyone else thinks. I'm over twenty-one."

She kissed him.

"Then neither do I," Allen said. "Listen, I've got some cash in the bank. Before I become poor again, I want to buy you the biggest diamond ring I can."

Throwing caution to the wind, they headed out arm-in-arm.

Maurice and Rachel Mendes got the word of their daughter's engagement later that night. They were both happy for Sarah, but Maurice's feelings were tempered with doubt. Taking the phone from his wife's hand, Maurice wished Sarah and Allen well and then invited them over to the apartment for lunch that Sunday. The time had come to meet Allen.

"Yes, papa," Sarah said. "We'll be there."

Hanging up the phone, Maurice told his wife that he wanted a fully catered lunch with hired help to serve it. "Spare no expense," he said.

"Why are you being so formal?" Rachel asked.

"I want to take his measure," was the reply.

But Sarah knew her father. She turned to Allen and told him the news and what was in store for them. "But don't worry," she assured him. "Papa is easier than Harry, and darling, there is no Max in sight."

If only she could believe that.

Before the big day arrived, Sarah made sure

that Allen was ready. Fortunately, Allen had studied French in school. Sarah reviewed with Allen a few phrases of greeting in the language to put her parents at ease when they all met. Meanwhile, Sarah wondered what her parents would think of Allen. Sunday was a beautiful spring day in New York City. Sarah and Allen took a taxi over to her parent's home. Riding up to the Mendes' apartment on Central Park West, Sarah turned to Allen, and she gave him a kiss. "Don't be nervous," she said. "I'm with you."

Rachel Mendes opened the door. "Sarah," she said with a smile. "And you, of course, must be Allen."

Before they could cross the threshold, Maurice came to the door and shook Allen's hand. "Maurice Mendes. Do come in. It's a pleasure to finally meet you." The men were a study in contrasts. Allen was tall and slender. Maurice was not as tall, but he was strongly built and husky; he looked like he could walk through a brick wall.

Now, Sarah was glad that she told Allen they must dress formally. Her mother wore a burgundy dress with a discreet diamond pin, and she had obviously had her hair done. Maurice wore a dark, three-piece suit. Peeking out from under his right cuff was his gold Rolex, which he only wore on special occasions. The battle lines were already drawn.

Now, Allen offered his few words in French, and both Maurice and Rachel were pleased. Then, he and Sarah walked in.

At Maurice's invitation, the men took off their jackets, and they all sat down in the living room where the maid took orders for drinks. Rachel asked for wine, Maurice asked for cognac while Sarah took bottled water and Allen, ginger ale.

A fine meal followed, accompanied by well-wishes, anecdotes and light banter. There was happy talk against the background of a meal most people would eat only for Thanksgiving dinner.

But then came a moment Sarah dreaded and had hoped would never arrive. Maurice stood up, looked at Allen, and said, "Sarah tells me you have a Masters' degree in English from the University of Chicago. You got it while taking your law degree. I am impressed. Would you like to see my library?"

Allen stood up, and Sarah did too, but her father gently chided, "Sarah, this is for the men." Sarah sat down, concerned. The library was where her father went when he wanted to think through a business deal or to have important, private conversations. Maurice took a cup of coffee, and then, lead Allen into the library and shut the door.

"Do sit down," Maurice said. He gestured Allen toward a couch.

After Allen took his seat, he glanced around him and was impressed by what he saw. The library was three walls of books with a broad window overlooking Central Park. The polished desk with its swivel chair and the brown leather couch had obviously been placed there by a professional decorator. Even the plastic frame of the computer screen matched the warm earth tones of the room.

Maurice did not sit on the couch or on any of the chairs; instead, he put his coffee down on the desk and sat next to it. This gave him a height advantage over Allen, and both men knew it.

If he's trying to impress me, Allen thought, he has succeeded.

Then it began.

Maurice sipped some coffee first. "You know," he said, "my daughter is very deeply in love with you. She has had other men in her life, but none like you."

Allen was silent for a moment. Then, he quietly said, "I am honored by her love. I try to be worthy of it every day."

Maurice spoke. "That brings up something I wanted to talk to you about. You and Sarah are alike in some ways, but different in others. You are both brilliant. That is obvious. You are both lawyers, and you both have strong feelings for the finer things in life. Books, music, theater and the like."

"How are we different?" Allen asked.

Maurice swallowed more coffee, almost draining the cup. He took a deep breath before he spoke, and Allen sensed what was coming. "After you both finished law school, your lives went in different directions it seems. Sarah went to the Supreme Court, and now, she's a partner in a growing firm.

But, it seems your career has not prospered, and . . . ."

"Yes, Mr. Mendes?" Allen suddenly became more formal.

"Call me Maurice, please. My wife and I would, at least, like to see you steadily employed before any marriage. I hope you understand our concerns."

A very long silence, then, Allen said, "I've discussed this with Sarah. We want to marry now."

"But how do you really feel about this, Allen? Would it make you uncomfortable to enter into a marriage like this?"

Trapped. If he said he would be comfortable, it would mean he was at peace with living off his wife even temporarily. If Allen said the opposite, he was denying himself marriage to the woman he loved. He had to make a choice. He did.

"I'm a lawyer, and I can always make money, even if it's day work," Allen said. "I love Sarah, and I want to marry her. And I've told her I'd be happy to sign a pre-nup leaving me nothing if we were to divorce."

Maurice looked honestly sympathetic, and he shifted to a chair directly oppose Allen. "You have a sense of honor, and I admire that. I did not know about the pre-nup offer."

Maurice continued to speak. "I'm not asking you to break up with Sarah. I only ask that you postpone marriage until you are settled in a career. Do you think I'm being unreasonable?"

Allen started to answer the question, but he was silenced by a knock at the door. It was Sarah. "Is everything all right in here? You've had plenty of time to show off your books."

Maurice smiled and slapped his knee. "You're right. How can you come into a library and not talk about books? We'll be out in a few moments, Sarah."

After Sarah closed the door, Maurice said to Allen, "Well, what do you think of my collection? I'd be curious to hear your impressions."

Allen stood up and moved around the room slowly, peering quizzically at each volume. With permission, he took certain volumes off the shelves and examined them. He is not stalling for time, Maurice thought, he is honestly curious. At last, Allen finished circumnavigating the room, and, instead of sitting, he stood and faced Maurice.

"Well, what do you think?" Maurice asked.

"Excellent," was Allen's reply. "You have a genuine love of French love poetry, and you admire the plays of Molière. You also love English poetry, even if you haven't had enough time to read as much of it as you would like."

"Why do you say that?"

Allen had a ready answer. "Your books show that you know a great deal about literature, but many of the spines haven't been broken. You buy them in hopes of reading them. On the other hand . . . ." Here, Allen reached for a tattered copy of the

Tax Code and held it out to Maurice. "This alone tells me you are a shrewd businessman."

Maurice had brought Allen into the library to probe his weaknesses, but now, Allen had turned the situation around and shown his strengths. Worse, Maurice sensed he could no longer question and pressure Allen as before. Realizing the game was lost for now, Maurice remarked, "And, you are a very observant young man."

The talk turned to theater and books.

Half an hour after they had entered the library, Maurice and Allen emerged. Allen is smiling, Sarah thought. Good.

Sarah and Allen left shortly after the library episode amid a final round of well-wishes.

During the day, the Mendes apartment had a sweeping view of the greenery of Central Park with Fifth Avenue off in the distance. At night, Fifth Avenue was ablaze with light while the Park was dark except for scattered pole lamps. Maurice and Rachel sat quietly by the window in their night clothes, waiting for sleep to come. Maurice didn't mention Allen until night fell. Then he spoke.

"Rachel, what do you think of Allen?"

Rachel put down the magazine she was reading. "What do I think? I think he's a fine young man who hasn't found himself yet. Sarah can help him do that. Besides," and here she touched her husband's hand, "they happen to love each other."

Maurice spoke slowly. "I agree that he is a decent human being, but he will never be a successful lawyer. I've spent my life dealing with top lawyers, and he just isn't one of them. The Bible forbids a man to place two different types of animals under the same yoke. The stronger will eventually break the weaker one's neck."

Rachel leaned over and kissed him. "Sarah and Allen are not animals; they are two young people who love each other. Let's go to sleep."

CHAPTER XV

From the journal of Harry Goldsmith ...

Why am I putting pen to paper to record the story of how Sarah got married? God knows, I do a lot of writing, but it is all for business. I started keeping a diary when I was twelve and gave it up in a week. Still, something is making me write it down. Perhaps, it was all so beautiful I just want to hang on to it a bit longer.

It was a morning in late March. The unpleasantness about Allen seemed to have been forgotten, and the office was running smoothly. He was never mentioned, and Sarah seemed to be all business as usual. But then, on that morning, I found the envelope on my chair. It bore just one word 'Harry.' It was in Sarah's handwriting.

Inside was one of the most beautiful wedding invitations I had ever seen. In gold leaf on parchment, it read, "Rachel and Maurice Mendes request the honor of your presence ...." Before I read any further, I dropped ahead to the date. June 15th. Perfect.

It was only then that it hit me whom she was going to marry -- Allen Wasserman. I couldn't believe it. How could Sarah marry such a loser? A man who had no business practicing law. But I found it impossible to generate real anger.

I set off for Sarah's office, invitation in hand, to offer my congratulations. Her door was closed, which was not her style. I knocked and entered at her invitation. I found her seated at her desk. She looked up at me with the most radiant smile I had ever seen on her, but she still spoke cautiously.

"Now you know," she said.

"Yes, now I do," I replied.

At that exact moment, I realized the dizzying complexity of my relationship with Sarah. I had discovered Sarah's talents at Harvard and given her the excitement of legal combat. I lured her back from Washington to Manhattan, and I gave her a short, quick path to legal stardom.

I knew what she wanted from me -- absolution. "You have my blessing, Sarah," I said.

"Thanks, Harry," she replied, and then I left.

Max provided the comic relief as usual. Later that day, he burst into my office and threw his invitation down on my desk in front of me. "Can you believe the gall of that woman?" he demanded.

"What is the problem?" I replied calmly, "I got

one too."

"That's different," Max said. "You're her friend."

I leaned back in my chair and spread my arms in a show of sympathy. "Maybe it's meant as a peace offering. Most people want to be at peace with the world when they get married."

For one moment, I actually thought Max was going to explode. "She's not getting away with it," he finally yelled. "I'll be at that wedding just to spite her. I'll bring my computer and sit there doing work." With that, he turned and stomped off, like a dinosaur heading into extinction.

Two weeks later, when the initial euphoria over Sarah's wedding had died down, I got a fax I'd been expecting for months. It was from the Supreme Court. Metcalf. They were going to hear the case. I had to tell everyone, starting with Sarah, whose legal wizardry had pulled it off.

Her door was closed when I got there -- not her usual practice, but hardly unconventional. I knocked once and said, "It's Harry," and Sarah said to come in.

I opened the door and stood there stunned. Sarah's office was filled with people; it was standing room only. Everyone was milling about except Sarah. She stood in the center of her office wearing a white wedding gown but no head covering. A woman stood in front of her holding up several veils as if waiting for Sarah to decide which one to wear. A tailor was measuring and pinning the gown. Another man held open an album filled with pictures of floral arrangements, and her office was filled with recorded music.

"What's going on here?" I demanded.

A young man walked up to me and produced a business card. "Hello," he said. "You must be Mr. Goldsmith. Ms. Mendes has said so much about you."

I looked at the card:

"All In One Wedding Planners" [it read]

"We Bring the Work of Wedding to You."

Thanking him, I handed back his card. Then, I asked Sarah to step outside. We must have been quite a sight. Sarah dressed in white standing next me.

"Sarah, couldn't you take one day off to make your wedding preparations? Was this really necessary?"

"I'm sorry," Sarah said, and she was truly apologetic. "It's just my style."

Now, I felt I had to say I was sorry.

"I guess you're right, Sarah," I said. "I cannot criticize you for being the woman I hired. Just try to enjoy getting married. That way you'll only have to do it once."

"Thanks, Harry!" She put a hand on my shoulder, and then, for the first and only time, she gave me a kiss, a little peck on the cheek.

It was time to retreat. A senior partner cannot show weakness. I handed her the fax which I had nearly forgotten. "By the way, congratulations. The Supreme Court will hear Metcalf. Just take care of it."

Then, I went back to my office, leaving Sarah staring at the fax. But, once behind my desk, I felt a strange emptiness that took me some time to understand. Finally, light dawned. When Sarah started at the firm, she had a raw hunger for the law, and her loyalty to the law and to me were un-questioned. Now, she was getting married, which meant that, while she would still work here, her heart would be elsewhere. It took a bit of brandy to deal with that sadness.

On Sarah's wedding day, Max was true to his word. Grace and I had been to several weddings at the Sephardic synagogue over the years, but never one as opulent as this. Flowers and white lin-ens were everywhere. The buffet was magnificent. And, of course, Max tried to spoil it.

In a crowd of tuxedos and evening gowns, Max wore a checkered sport jacket and red tie. True to his word, he had his laptop with him. Pushing his way through the guests, he loaded up a plate with food, got something with alcohol at the bar, and then, sat down at a table and got to work. At first, everyone was having such a good time talking about the bride and groom and speculating about their future that they ignored him. But gradually, the re-ality of Max noisily typing away imposed itself, and people began to stare at him and whisper.

Finally, I had to do something. I found the rabbi -- a dignified gentleman -- hurriedly introduced myself and explained the situation. Then, together, we approached Max.

"Hello, I'm Rabbi Harari. Mr. Goldsmith here tells me you're Mr. Hammer, one of Sarah's co-workers."

"Yeah, that's right," Max said, still typing.

The rabbi cleared his throat, "Mr. Hammer, if your work is so important, you can use my office."

"That's okay, I'm happy here," Max said contentedly.

Now, the rabbi's voice turned as cold as ice. "But, you're making everyone around you very unhappy. Put your computer away or leave the building, and please don't drink anymore. You strike me as a man who can't hold his liquor."

Max was the most irreverent man I'd ever met. Nothing was sacred to Max, but somehow the rabbi's words got through, and he shut his laptop. I expected him to grin broadly, delighted he had irritated everyone, but, instead, he looked like a schoolboy ordered to eat spinach. (And Max bills $450 an hour, I thought.)

"Thank you," the rabbi said with a slight bow. "Now, let's all go into the sanctuary. It's time for the ceremony."

As we took our seats, a strange, beautiful music filled the air. There was no doubt in my mind it was Russian, only a Slavic composer could so clearly evoke in me a clear, starry night sky above a landscape of snowy hills and virgin forests. And then, a new theme burst in suggesting to me horse drawn sleighs racing through the wilderness to some romantic destination.

The music distracted me from my surroundings. We were in the small synagogue, one adapted from the first chapel the congregation built in colonial times. The walls were white, the pews were carved wood and running up the center aisle was a burgundy carpet. At one end, a chuppah -- a wedding canopy -- had been erected and decorated with flowers. The rabbi stood under it with the cantor by his side. I hurriedly took my seat. At my left was my wife, Grace, of forty years; at my right was Max, my partner of thirty-seven years.

Then, I noticed he had somehow walked in with a glass filled with some amber fluid. I took it out of his hand.

"I need it," Max said. "I refuse to sit through this sober."

"Shut up," I whispered. "You'll get it back when they're married. Then, it can be a toast."

The music suddenly ceased, replaced by a violin and a xylophone heralding the coming of the bride and groom.

Allen came in first, flanked by his mother and father. He had a more confident look than I had ever seen on his face during his time at Goldsmith & Hammer. For the first time I realized, or, perhaps allowed myself to realize, that he was a handsome man. He was more than six feet tall with thick black hair and well-chiseled regular features.

Barely a moment later, all eyes turned to Sarah as she entered the room. She was ineffably beautiful. Her fair skin and black hair were accented exquisitely by her veil. In her hands was a bouquet of red roses. But the thing I will remember most was the look on her face; it was the visage of a woman who had been seeking something and had now found it. She seemed so happy that I felt the same way.

Once the ceremony was over, there was dining and dancing for hours. Then, Sarah and Allen left to cheers and well wishes. They went by the firm limo to a secret location for their wedding night. I gave them Charlie as a wedding gift and ordered him never to tell me where they went. (By the way, Sarah told me after she came back from her honeymoon that they had gone to the Waldorf.)

I caught glimpses of Sarah's parents several times during the wedding. Her mother seemed to rejoice. Her father seemed morose and solemn.

Just after the happy couple left to begin married life together, I spotted Maurice standing forlornly at the bar, still looking unhappy. He had an empty glass in his hand. I got two snifters of brandy and offered him one.

"Thank you," he said. "I prefer cognac, but I try to be flexible." He took a sip. "Excellent."

"Tell me," I asked him, "how does it feel to have a married daughter?"

"Fine," Maurice said. "It's the son-in-law . . . ." He didn't finish the sentence, just his snifter.

"I agree with you completely," I replied. Then, I rapped the bar with my knuckles. "A brandy and a cognac, please."

That night, as Grace and I shared our evening tea before going to bed, I thought of Max in his apartment, huddled over his computer. Suddenly, I shuddered thinking of being alone.

Whatever need compelled me to write this narrative has now been sated. I close knowing a chapter in all our lives concluded today and that tomorrow a new one will open. I will write no more.

There were more memories of Sarah's wedding day. In between dances, Sarah saw a man in a dark gray suit slip into the ballroom and stand discreetly by the door. Sarah felt that she knew him from somewhere, but what alarmed her was her knowledge of body language from her years in Washington. He's packing a gun, she thought. Before she could say a word to anyone, things fell into place. She recognized him as a federal agent assigned to the Supreme Court, and that gave her a fraction of a second to prepare for the next person who walked through the door, Justice Bradford.

The lawyers in the wedding party recognized him first; then, Bradford's height and natural grace drew the attention of the rest of the guests. Sarah turned to Allen, but, before she could speak, he anticipated her. "It's okay, Sarah. I won't be jealous."

Sarah glided across the room to greet Bradford, who clasped her hand and kissed it. "All the very best on this wonderful day, Sarah."

"Your Honor, if we had known you were coming ...."

"I didn't know I'd be free until yesterday," he said. "Besides, this is your day, not mine. Ah, but the music is playing, and I happen to know this number. May I have this dance?"

Bradford proved to be as commanding a presence as a dancer as he was in a black robe. At the end of the music, Bradford asked to be introduced to her new husband. When Allen saw Bradford approaching, he stood bolt upright and extended his hand. "Many congratulations," Bradford said. "You're getting a very wonderful woman."

"And a very fine lawyer," Allen said.

"Ah, yes, that too," Bradford said. Then, he looked at his watch. "Sarah, in thirty minutes, some bar association is determined to give me an award of some kind. I'd like to meet your parents, and the people you wound up working for."

Sarah made the introductions, and, in the process, Sarah saw a look on Max's face that suggested for the first time there were some people that impressed even him. Then, with a final wave of his hand, Bradford was gone.

"He's your world," Allen said.

"It's only our world that matters now," Sarah replied.

Then they left for their wedding night.

For their honeymoon, Sarah and Allen wanted to go to a warm climate where there was nothing to do but be together. But Sarah had so much work waiting back at the office that she wanted to be away no more than a week.

Sarah's mother and a travel agent took care of finding such a place. They found Zueno, a small island about thirty miles off the southern coast of Puerto Rico. One could only get there by ferry or seaplane. There were two beaches on the island, a big one and a small one and a single hotel. Zueno also boasted a tiny, sleepy fishing village and a remnant of a rain forest that had once covered the island. It sounded perfect.

At seven-thirty on their first morning as husband and wife, Charlie picked up Sarah and Allen at the hotel and drove them to LaGuardia airport. Hours of flying awaited them, but love made the time pass quickly. After changing planes in Miami, they arrived at San Juan airport at 6:00 p.m.

It had been a cool rainy morning when they left New York, and they had dressed for it. When they exited the plane in San Juan, they were met with a blast of heat and close humidity that made them take off their coats. Waiting for them was a man in a white shirt, peaked cap and tie holding a sign that read "MENDES/WASSERMAN."

With only a few words, the man loaded their bags into a waiting black taxi, and then they drove off to the southern port of Ponce. Shadows were already forming when they left San Juan, but Allen and Sarah held hands and paid scant attention to the landscape outside the window.

At the Ponce harbor, the car pulled up to a sign saying, "Water Taxi." A heavy-set, swarthy man whose very presence seemed to say 'sea-captain' greeted them.

"*Buenos tardes*," the man said. "I am Eduardo. The last ferry left more than an hour ago. My son and I are taking you to Zueno tonight."

Ten minutes later, their luggage loaded, the boat set out for the island. The captain escorted them to two swivel chairs on the open stern. They were designed for sportsmen seeking big game fish, but they were set close enough to each other for hands to touch. That was what mattered.

The sun was setting when the boat set off. Allen and Sarah sat in awe as Ponce's lights receded into the distance, and gentle night descended on the sea. Sometimes, the boat would bounce on the water, and the spray on their faces would make them laugh.

The captain came on deck and set a large cooler down at their feet. "Everything inside is from New York. It was sent on ahead." Then, he walked away.

Opening the Styrofoam box, Allen and Sarah found the makings of an informal dinner. There were a dozen bagels, peanut butter and jelly, Nova Scotia salmon and a bottle of champagne. There was also an envelope wrapped in plastic. Inside was a card that read, "With our love, Mom and Dad."

"Well, I'd say you are part of the family now," Sarah said.

Night had unequivocally fallen when Eduardo rang a bell and then came onto the stern. "The lights of Zueno are just ahead of us," he said. "Would you care to see them?"

"Oh yes!"

Zueno, at night was not like the New York sky-line; that was for certain. It was a small dark is-land with only a few lights clustered in the center. "Those lights are the hotel," Eduardo said. "The rest is the beach. The village is on the other side of the island."

As they drew near, details became clearer. The beach ran nearly the length of the north shore of the island. The hotel itself looked like a Victorian summer house. Two stories tall, it had a huge porch with a hammock and swings.

Near the front of the hotel was a wooden dock that stretched out some thirty feet into the ocean. "The dock for the ferry is by the village," Eduardo explained. "This is just for the hotel." When they were just a few hundred yards away, the captain sounded his horn, and a man bounded out the front door, picked up a coil of rope and headed for the end of the dock.

"That's Ib," the captain said.

"What kind of a name is Ib?" Sarah asked.

"Oh, he'll tell you," Eduardo said. His expression suggested they had an experience in store.

Indeed, they did. Ib met them at the boat with a hearty greeting. A man of medium height, the sun had dyed his skin deep brown and bleached his hair dirty blonde. Somehow, Ib carried all their bags by himself and showed them to their room while telling them the story of his life.

Ib was a Dane. After finishing college in Denmark, he had set off to see the world and wound up on Zueno, where he decided to stay for a while to earn some money. He took odd jobs in the village, working as a fisherman and as a jack-of-all-trades at the hotel. He fell in love with the hotel owner's daughter ....

But, enough of that. Ib was surprised that they didn't want any food, so he showed them to their room. Sarah had only two questions: would it be okay if she took a morning run on the beach, and was there a place where she could get on the internet?

Ib said morning runs on the beach were no problem. As to the internet, there was a jack near the fireplace in the lobby. Perfect.

Allen overheard all this. "Sarah," he said. "You promised."

"Just to let mom know I'm okay," she replied with a guilty look on her face.

Sarah and Allen were dead tired, but, after they unpacked, they took a walk on the beach and finished off their champagne. That got them ready for a sound sleep in a place that felt like it was on the far edge of the world.

"On a night like this, all the world seems peaceful and good," Sarah said.

"But we both know it isn't," Allen replied.

That was the last time they mentioned the outside world for a week.

The following morning, Sarah came down from their room in a running suit and sneakers. A towel was wrapped around her neck, and she carried a laptop.

She got online at the jack, near the fireplace, and checked her messages from the firm. A few problems had developed in her absence, but nothing she couldn't handle long distance. She sent off replies, and she then slid her computer under a couch.

Running on the beach just after dawn was utterly unlike running in New York. The air was warm, the breeze was steady, and there wasn't a soul to be seen. As she ran, she passed seashells, mermaid's purses, crabs, and sea birds. The sky was violet, not yet blue. She ran and ran, back and forth, gradually forgetting about life in New York until the only reality was the beach and the sea.

When she returned to her starting place, she kicked off her sneakers, pulled off her socks and headed into the water. The Caribbean was smooth, dark blue without waves. With powerful strokes, she headed out into the bay and then dove under. Beneath the surface were small, brightly colored fish, but, without a mask, she could only stay under a few moments. Then, she came up and floated on her back.

It was the night of her triumph as Ophelia, Hilton Gould was in the audience, and so were her mother and father. Afterward, at the reception, Sarah introduced them and explained Gould's offer.

But, when Hilton Gould spoke to Sarah's parents, her father did not agree. He answered Gould in a calm, proud voice.

"Mr. Gould, you have honored my wife and me by the praise you have heaped on our daughter. However, I cannot agree to your proposal, and, if Sarah accepts it, I'm afraid she will be on her own."

Sarah looked directly at her mother, who remained calm and silent while her husband continued to speak.

"Let me tell you something about our family. We lost everything in the war. Only my father survived, and he rebuilt the family. I was born in the ashes. I helped him rebuild the family diamond business. I had little time for school. I had to work, but my father always told me about the value of books. I vowed my children would have the best in life, starting with the best of educations. I can't let Sarah give up Harvard Law for the stage, even for only one year. One year leads to another. My wife and I give generously to the arts, and, if Sarah wants to continue that tradition when she is established in her profession, she is welcome to."

In response, Sarah's mother continued her silence.

Sarah sighed as a dreamer and obeyed as a daughter.

Sarah felt as if she were being consumed by her memories, but then she realized she was still floating in the sea. She tasted saltwater on her lips. Once she awakened from her revery, she knew she had to get back to Allen. With a few strokes, she righted herself, and, in minutes, she was back on shore and heading into the hotel. She had a new husband who was entitled to her attention. There was no need to tell him every secret. Not yet; maybe, not ever.

After a breakfast that consisted mostly of bread and fish, Ib herded them into a jeep and gave them a manic tour of the island. Sarah felt resentment at first; she just wanted to be alone with Allen. He felt the same. But Ib was like a force of nature. He loved his island and wanted to show it off to every visitor.

The fishing village wasn't sleepy; it was nearly comatose, with only one small general store that doubled as a post office. There were no paved roads, only dirt paths with tire ruts. The rain forest somehow managed to be both small and endless. But a great surprise came when Ib suddenly stopped the jeep in what seemed to be the middle of the forest.

"What's here?" Allen asked.

"Just listen," Ib replied in a whisper.

Then, through the trees, they heard the sea. Ib motioned them to follow him. A few feet off the road, they came to a wire fence with a padlocked gate that Ib opened with a key. Just beyond it was a low bluff overlooking the broad Caribbean.

"How beautiful," Sarah said. Allen agreed.

"But, what do you think of the beach?" Ib asked.

Sarah looked down and lost her breath. It was the most pristine beach she had ever seen, so pure, so white.

Ib finished her thought. "This is the honeymoon beach," he said. "It's yours."

Now, they understood why Ib insisted they pack swim gear and a picnic lunch. He gave them a walkie-talkie in case they wanted to come back before sunset; otherwise, he would fetch them then.

No laptops. No wireless internet. No cell phones. Except for the walkie-talkie, they were out of touch with the world. They swam, the sun warmed them, they danced, they loved, and occasionally, they would speak of future hopes beneath a blue sky that seemed eternal.

But, on the afternoon of the last full day there, reality did intrude. Lying on the beach, Sarah turned to Allen and asked him what he was going to do once they were back in New York.

He kept looking up at the sky. "I'll get another job as a lawyer, Sarah. Until then, I'll find day jobs. I'll keep earning money, Sarah."

This is wrong, Sarah felt. Terribly wrong for him. Instead, she said, "I love you," and let the matter rest.

CHAPTER XVI

Months passed . . . .

Goldsmith & Hammer had only a small real estate practice. But this deal was going to put them in the big leagues in one stroke. One of their corporate clients, a holding company based in Montreal, was exchanging property in London and Canada in return for a New York office building and a lot of cash. The laws of three countries were involved, as well as national and local tax codes.

The real estate department under Brad Cook had labored for weeks on the deal, checking every detail. Each morning, Harry would review their work at his desk. Finally, the day came when all the parties descended on New York to sign the contracts. The large conference room on the fifteenth floor was a beehive of activity. Brad Cook moved from one group of lawyers and accountants to another while Harry sat quietly at a large table with his back to the windows overlooking Fifth Avenue. Sarah sat next to him, quietly taking notes on a yellow pad.

Max was pointedly not invited to be part of this deal. There was already enough tension in the air. Once, at the signing of a major contract, Max broke up a log jam in the negotiations by jumping up, slamming a door to get everyone's attention, and then, screaming, "All right, everyone trying to make this deal work stand on this side of the room. Everyone trying to fuck it up, line up against the wall." Somehow, that deal survived, but Harry was taking no more chances.

The key players were waiting quietly in nearby hotel rooms, expensive ones, for phone calls telling them to come over and sign the papers. Harry was about to make those calls when a last-minute hitch developed. A team of Quebec lawyers suddenly decided they wanted a key term changed to require all disputes be resolved in Canadian courts. This threw everything into chaos, and, for a few minutes, it looked as if the deal would fall apart. But then, Harry and Sarah entered the fray. Harry stepped in and calmed things down while Sarah used her French to keep the Canadians from walking out.

The tide slowly turned, and the deal was almost completely wrapped up when Sarah's cell phone rang. She looked at the number, and then, quietly said, "Excusez-moi pour cinq minutes." She said "wait" into the phone, and then, left the conference room.

Down the hall near the library, Sarah felt it was safe to speak. "Hello Allen, what is it?"

"I just got a court appearance for tomorrow. It pays $175."

"Allen, that's wonderful," she said.

The line was quiet for a moment. "No, it isn't. You're just being kind. You can earn that in fifteen minutes. I just had to let you know I was doing something."

"Allen, we've been through this before. I love you. The fact that I may make more money than you does not bother me, and it shouldn't bother you. You'll find your niche. The important thing is that we love each other."

"All right," he said in a voice that could not disguise sadness.

"I'm running late tonight, but I can't wait to see you. Bye. 'Love you.'" Sarah hung up the phone and turned around to find Harry standing right behind her, his face a portrait of barely contained rage.

"How long have you been standing there?" she asked.

Harry answered in a voice that seemed too controlled to be natural. "Long enough, or perhaps, I should say too long. Let's get back to the conference room. You and I have to have a talk, but first we've got to close this deal."

And, after a few more hours of haggling, the deal

was closed. The executives came over from their hotels for the signing, Harry led everyone over to a freshly stocked buffet table, and the long day came to a peaceful conclusion with Goldsmith & Hammer nearly a million dollars richer.

Sarah headed for the door, hoping Harry had forgotten what happened earlier. No such luck. Harry cleared his throat and asked her to stay for a few moments. After the last person had left, he motioned her to a chair.

Harry stood across the table from Sarah, knuckles resting on the glass surface. "Sarah," he said in an even voice, "you walked out in the middle of a major deal when it was about to collapse."

She was silent.

He pointed at her, something he had never done before. "Don't we have a policy for this?" he demanded. "Your family calls the switchboard, and a note will be discretely handed to you."

Harry then sat down and rubbed his face with his hands. Finally, he spoke, his voice gentler. "Sarah, no one involved in this deal has slept for more than two hours at a stretch for the past week. I don't want to speak when I'm so weary, but I must tell you that since Allen came into your life, you're off your game. You're not the woman who made partner in three years."

"My billable hours are virtually unchanged," she replied.

"True, but the old Sarah would never have let

anything keep a big deal from closing." Then, Harry abruptly stopped his reprimand. He saw that he was upsetting Sarah, and that even if she were off her game, Sarah was still the star of the firm. She was the one who was regularly written up in the *New York Law Journal* and interviewed by the Lawyer's TV Network. She could walk out the door and have a dozen offers by noon. Harry changed his approach.

He took his glasses off and twirled them in one hand. "Sarah, I want you to take a week away from the office. It won't count toward your vacation time. Go off somewhere with Allen and think about what you want from life. What would really make you happy. Find some place with no e-mails and no cell phones, if such places still exist. Sometimes, the hardest thing a man and woman can do is just sit and talk. Do that, and then come back and we'll discuss what you've decided."

Sarah knew he was making a peace offering, and she took it. "Thanks Harry," she said. "We'll do it."

"Let's go home," Harry said. "Charlie can drop you off." Wordlessly, they gathered their papers up and put them in their briefcases, put their coats over their shoulders and headed out the door. With Harry only a step or two behind her, she flicked the lights off without a thought.

Just then, Harry spoke. "Wait a minute Sarah, come back here."

She turned around and saw Harry standing by the windows that overlooked the heart of downtown

Manhattan. He was a silhouette against the city lights. "What is it, Harry?"

"Look out there, Sarah," and he made a gesture toward the window as if he were a king bestowing a knighthood. "I want you to think of every light as a person who ever had a dream of getting somewhere in New York City. You're one of those lights, Sarah, and in the years to come, I predict you'll shine as brightly as any of them."

She was silent. "Thank you, Harry," she said at last. "I don't know what else I can say."

"Good night will do," Harry said. "We're both dead tired."

They rode wordlessly in the limo driven by the faithful Charlie until they reached her apartment. Then Sarah muttered a simple, "'Night, Harry,'" and stepped onto the sidewalk. She stood there alone. Unable to face Allen with what had happened, she had to find a way to turn the situation around. Thanks to an all-night liquor store two blocks away, Sarah did.

"Wake up, Allen. Wake up."

Allen was a heavy sleeper, but when he opened his eyes, he saw a broad grin on his wife's face and a bottle of champagne held only inches in front of him.

"Sarah, what is it?" Then, he finally woke up. "Did the deal go through?"

"You bet," she said. "Goldsmith & Hammer is now a player in the New York real estate world. The deal closed right after you called, so you brought us luck. We've been wrapping up paperwork until just now. Harry is so pleased he gave everyone connected with the deal a week off with pay. Where shall we go?"

Now, Allen was wide-awake. Returning from the kitchen with two wine glasses, he offered a suggestion. "Can we go to Zueno again? We had such a great time there."

"Yes, I'd love it, and I love you."

When she went off on her honeymoon, Sarah spent days preparing for the time she'd be away from work. But she was not going off on an expedition of love and joy this time. Now, she was facing a crisis, the worst she had ever known. The day after the big deal closed, she came to the office and either postponed everything scheduled for the coming week or shunted it to other attorneys. Then, she made plane reservations and left the office at five. Sarah advised Natalie and Masaka she would check her e-mails once a day, but that was all. Natalie and Masaka were now far enough along to handle all but the biggest crises that might come their way.

At six o'clock the following morning, Allen and Sarah grabbed a cab for LaGuardia. They were in Miami at noon. After switching planes, they arrived in San Juan, Puerto Rico at three. Then, they chartered an amphibious plane to Zueno. Their pilot was a young man who wore a tan short-sleeved shirt with khaki pants. "Is this your first visit to Zueno?"

he asked.

"Our second," Allen said.

"Everyone makes a second trip to Zueno," the pilot replied.

They flew for fifty minutes in the lazy tropical afternoon. Then, as the sun started to set in the west, the plane landed in Half-Moon Bay and taxied up to the dock.

When she went on her honeymoon, Sarah packed two suitcases for herself, one of which contained nothing but legal papers she naively thought she would have time to work on. How times had changed. She headed to Zueno for the second time with two bathing suits and a few changes of casual clothing. The only thing in her suitcase that suggested civilization were her Sabbath candlesticks.

But Sarah did no work on this trip, and, despite Harry's admonition, very little thinking either. As if by unspoken agreement, she and Allen only talked about how they should enjoy seven days on a tropical island paradise. Weighty issues were being ignored, and they both knew it.

But, every night, after Allen went to bed early, Sarah would quietly go down to the computer in Ib's office and check her e-mails from work.

One night, as Sarah leaned close to the screen, she smelt the unmistakable scent of sweet chocolate. She turned and saw Ib standing in the doorway, holding a tray with two white mugs on it. "You look like you could use refreshment," he said.

"I could at that," Sarah replied, taking the cup he handed her. "But, where did you get this? I can't believe you got it at the local bodega."

Ib laughed. "No, it comes all the way from Denmark. Several times a year my family sends me a care package. They're still trying to lure me back."

Sarah took a sip. "Will you ever go home?"

Ib, who always had a perpetual smile, changed expressions. "I wanted to talk to you about that. I could use some legal advice."

Without realizing it, Sarah changed her expression as well. She adopted her business face. It had no laughter. "What's up?"

"Sarah," Ib said softly, "I think my time at the El Dorado has come to its end. Twenty years ago, I came to this island for a few months. I was young and on my way around the world. I never got there. You know why. Now, I want to see the rest of the world and then go home to Denmark. I've grown weary of paradise."

"I see," Sarah replied, trying to be professional. "What advice do you need?"

"You once told me your firm handled real estate. Could you handle a hotel sale here in Puerto Rico?"

Sarah grabbed paper and pen. "I don't know. Give me the details." And then, they talked business.

CHAPTER XVII

.

Sarah sat at her desk, doing no work, rolling a pencil back and forth with the flat of her hand. She looked at the clock: 6:10 p.m. Harry always went home at 6:30 p.m. That gave her 20 minutes to get up the courage to walk into his office and resign.

Today was her last day to do it without losing a great deal of money. It was January 28th. Sarah and Allen were the new owners of the El Dorado as of March 1st. Her partnership agreement required her to give 30 days-notice, or she'd lose her quarterly share of the profits. In her case that came to $125,000 before taxes.

She kept rolling the pencil, back and forth. The clock said 6: 15 p.m.

When Ib told her that he wanted to sell the hotel, Sarah knew she wanted to buy it. She and Allen would hire some retired couple to run the place, and they would be absentee landlords. They would fly down for long weekends in wintertime and, when their retirement years came, they could spend the cold months there and summers somewhere in the northern latitudes.

But, when Sarah told Allen, she got an unexpected reaction. Yes, they should buy the place, but why wait until retirement to live there? The place was paradise; it was a world of blue skies and tropical breezes. Besides, didn't thousands of lawyers leave the profession every year because of stress or simple disgust? Why not leave it right now?

Allen was transformed as he spoke. Suddenly, he became the man Sarah knew he could be: happy, enthusiastic and confident. Only in their intimate moments -- when they were a man and woman alone together -- did he ever seem this way. She was overwhelmed. For the time being, this was enough to persuade Sarah.

Ib was delighted when Allen and Sarah said they wanted to buy the place, but he cautioned them that it was not heaven-on-earth. There would be hard work to do once they moved in. In fact, he would not sell them the place unless they submitted to a three-day crash course in tropical hotel management, starting *mañana*.

The next morning, Sarah made beds while Allen fixed breakfast for the guests. Even though hired staff from the village normally did these tasks, the new owners had to know how they were done. Then, Sarah handled reservations and billing in the office, while Allen greeted guests at the dock. That afternoon, the water pump broke, and Ib wouldn't lift a finger to repair it; he only told Allen what to do.

At the end of the three-day indoctrination, Allen and Sarah found themselves on the honeymoon beach. Allen talked on and on about what a wonderful life they would have.

Sarah was beginning to feel doubt, real uncertainty at the same time Allen seemed more in love with the project than ever. But anything that could so transform her husband had to be given a fair chance. She owed him that. "We'll do it, Allen. I've made the calls, and, we'll have the closing over the Thanksgiving weekend."

What Sarah did not tell him was that she never sold her Washington home. She had kept it as a rental property, and she would do the same with their New York address. Sarah always had a practical side.

But now she was sitting in her office in New York. The papers for the hotel were now signed, and the movers had already come to give an estimate to put their furniture in storage. The clock said 6:20 p.m.

Sarah finally got a grip on herself and called Harry to tell him she'd like a few moments of his time. Then, she slowly rose from her desk and headed to his office.

CHAPTER XVIII

"In my end is my beginning...."

Sarah believed in symbolism. She had begun her career with Goldsmith & Hammer over lunch at the King's Grille, and now, she chose to eat lunch there on her last day. Officially, Natalie and Masaka were taking Sarah out to talk over old times, but she had her own agenda. Sarah did most of the talking while Natalie and Masaka took notes. At Sarah's recommendation, the two young associates had been given their own cases, most of which they inherited from Sarah. Now, Sarah was spending her last few hours with the firm making sure that her files would be well managed after she was gone.

As Sarah ate a mouthful of salad, the maître d' tapped her on the shoulder and whispered something in her ear. Sarah held up a finger as if to say 'pause' and then, got up and left the table without a word.

"What was that all about?" asked Masaka.

"I don't know," replied Natalie. "I think I made out the words, 'Call your office,' but I'm no lip-reader."

Within a minute, Sarah came back to the table running, looking as if she had been slapped across the face. "Listen," she said, "Max keeled over at his desk about five minutes ago. They've called the paramedics, and they're giving him CPR. They think it might be a stroke." She reached into her wallet and dropped several large bills on the table. "Whatever it comes to, pay it, and I'll see you back at the office. I've got to get back immediately." Then Sarah bolted.

It was five blocks back to the office. A taxi in mid-town at the height of the lunch hour would take forever, so Sarah ran all the way, and she was back at 500 Fifth Avenue within 15 minutes. The elevator ride seemed so slow she almost got out and took the stairs.

When Sarah finally walked through the front door of Goldsmith & Hammer, she found the recep-tion area deserted. Heading down the main corridor, Sarah found it full of people in random groups. They all looked stunned. Then, she saw Moses; for the first time, he neither held a law book nor seemed happy.

"What's going on?" she asked him.

"The ambulance crew is working on Max in his of-fice. Harry is in there with them, and he's been asking for you."

The door to Max's office was wide open; what she saw inside horrified her. Max lay on a stretcher, his eyes closed, his face drained of all color. An oxygen mask was fitted over his nose and mouth. Two EMT workers in green uniforms labored over him, trying desperately to stabilize his condition. With each slow, labored breath, Max's vast stomach rose and fell, reminding Sarah of a sow. Over in a corner sat Harry with a forlorn look that suggested a child, who feared he was about to become an orphan.

"Harry, what happened?" she asked, her anguish real.

"I don't know Sarah. Someone passing by his office happened to look inside and see Max on the floor. The phone had fallen off his desk, and it was on top of him, so Max was probably making a call when he had an attack."

"Will he be all right?"

A paramedic answered for Harry. "We can't say. It's not our job. We must get him stabilized and take him over to Lenox hospital. Ready, Jack?"

"Pulse is stable. Breathing on his own. But he's so heavy I wish we had a third man."

Brad pushed his way into the room. "Let me help. I'm a volunteer EMT in Jersey. I'm certified."

"Then you're drafted. Come on. Let's lift."

Together, they raised the stretcher a few inches off the ground. Then, one of the men kicked a switch that lowered a set of wheels. As they rolled Max out into the corridor, Harry followed, taking his hat and coat from Helen. "Cancel all of Max's appointments," he said.

"No!"

All eyes turned toward the stretcher. Max had somehow pulled off his oxygen mask and sat bolt upright on the stretcher. "Don't give any of those bastards a break. They're all a bunch of ...." But what they were would never be known. Max's eyes rolled up, and he fell back on the stretcher with a thud that frightened everyone.

"Keep going," said one of the paramedics.

"I'm coming with you," said Harry.

"Sorry sir, only next of kin."

Now, Harry recovered for a moment and spoke in his normal manner, the quiet voice that could move mountains. "I am his family, and I'm coming." There was no more argument.

As they headed toward the elevator, Harry motioned Helen and Sarah to follow him. "Sarah," he said in a pleading voice, "can you just stay a few days more and run things until I get back? I'm not leaving the hospital until I know Max is all right."

Sarah had never seen Harry in such a state, but the thing that frightened her most was his hands. Harry's hands were usually the most expressive thing about him. A well-aimed index finger could make a point better than anything else that Sarah knew. But now, Harry's hands moved aimlessly as if unconnected to his brain. She was frightened for him.

"Of course, Harry. I'm here until the crisis is over."

"God bless you, Sarah," Harry said. She had

never heard him invoke the Divine before. As Harry stepped into the elevator, he told Helen to move Sarah into his office, and as the elevator doors closed, he yelled out, "Call the bank. Tell them to give Sarah check signing powers. I'll sign whatever forms are necessary." Then, he was gone.

Max, Sarah thought, you never cease to amaze me with your ability to screw up my life. Then, Sarah turned around to find a good portion of the office standing behind her, waiting for commands. All eyes were fixed on Sarah. For a moment, she felt flustered. But then, she drew herself to her full height and issued her first orders as managing partner. "Everyone get back to work. It's the best thing we can do right now, both for Max and ourselves." The strength of her own voice came as a surprise. Then, Sarah walked into Harry's office and shut the door.

Sarah had been in Harry's office countless times; she typically went in three to four times a day. But, when Sarah sat behind Harry's desk, she felt different in some way, as if she had never seen the room before. There was the antique globe in the corner, and on the desk was Harry's collection of classic fountain pens. Now, for the time being at least, they were hers. Sarah slowly realized why it all seemed so unfamiliar; she had never sat at Harry's desk before, neither literally nor symbolically. Now, quite without warning, she had what she always thought she wanted -- power.

But then, she thought of Allen. They were

scheduled to leave for Zueno in three days. What on earth was she going to say? Sarah decided to wait until she got home to deal with the problem. Now she had work to do. Helen came in with Harry and Max's schedules for the rest of the day, and Sarah personally called up the clients and explained that their appointments would have to be postponed briefly. When that was attended to, she called in Brad to discuss a big trial that was due to start in a few days, and then, she called in Moses to review a brief that had to go out the next day.

When Sarah first sat down behind Harry's desk, she asked Helen for reports about Max every few minutes, but, within an hour, she felt at home at Harry's desk, and then she stopped inquiring so frequently. Besides, the news was always the same; Max was in intensive care, and they were running some tests. Finally, at the close of business, Helen came in to announce that she finally got some news from the hospital; it was a stroke, a very bad one. Harry was going to spend the night at the hospital, and he would call Sarah at home tonight.

"Should I go to the hospital?" Sarah asked.

"Harry specifically asked you to stay away. He doesn't want anything to distract you from running the firm."

"Tell Harry I will honor his wishes," Sarah said.

"Anyway, it's six o'clock now," Helen reminded her. "Do you need me to run late tonight?"

Sarah leaned back in Harry's chair. "No, go

home, and I'm leaving too. Have Charlie bring the limo around."

Allen did not take the news well. "I thought this was coming too easily," he said with an air of resignation. "Three days left until paradise, and Max manages to screw it up for us."

"Allen," Sarah insisted, "people don't have strokes just to inconvenience other people." Although with Max, you never know.

"I'll be a good soldier, Sarah," Allen said. "Do what you have to do. Meanwhile, I know someone who may want to give me a court appearance tomorrow. Let me make a few calls."

Max had his stroke on a cold, clear Tuesday afternoon in early February. On the following day, a freezing rain fell that turned into snow for a few hours after sunset. On Thursday morning, bundled up in her winter coat, Sarah walked through the front door of the firm at seven a.m. to find Harry Goldsmith sitting quietly in the reception area. But this was a Harry she had never seen before. He hadn't shaved and his hair was uncombed. Gone was his expression of critical intelligence. This Harry looked like an old man sitting in the park feeding pigeons.

"Harry, what are you doing here?"

He's looking at me like a kindly old man. That's not Harry.

"Oh hello, Sarah," he said. "I've been waiting for you."

She sat down beside him. "How long have you been here, Harry?"

"I really can't say," Harry began, looking off into space. "Let me think. Max died around three …."

"Max is dead?" Sarah was stunned.

"Yes, early this morning," Harry said quietly. "It was terrible watching him struggling to breathe with all those tubes coming out of him. Then, suddenly, he was still, and I could see he was at peace." Then, Harry pulled his gaze back from the void and looked directly at Sarah. "He was my best friend, Sarah." Tears welled up in Harry's blue eyes, and his voice began to break as if he were about to cry.

Sarah put her arm around him. "It'll all be okay, Harry. Come to your office." Then, she helped him to his feet. But, instead of sitting at his desk he sat down on the corner couch by the antique globe. She undid his scarf and unbuttoned his coat. "Can I get you some coffee, Harry?"

He nodded. Afterward, she sat down next to Harry for a wretched hour filled with a torrent of memory, tears and even a few stories that made Sarah laugh. Finally, the barest hint of the old Harry began to return.

Harry put down his coffee. "Listen, I haven't had more than two hours sleep in the past three days, but there's so much to do."

"Name it," Sarah said.

"That's my partner," Harry replied. "First, Max has two ex-wives. They both live in the city. He's got one son who lives in California. None of them were on speaking terms with Max. Call them and get them to come to his funeral. I don't care if you have to bribe them."

"Got it, next?"

Harry's strength seemed to return, but very slowly. He began to use his hands to make his points and that cheered Sarah. "Now about the funeral. Max had no use for religion, but he never denied being a Jew. That's the way he's going to be buried. Make the arrangements. Buy a plot out on Long Island; spare no expense. Charge it all to the firm."

"If you want a proper Jewish funeral, that means it will have to take place tomorrow."

"Do it," Harry said. "And another thing, no rabbi. Aside from your wedding, Max hadn't been in a synagogue in the last thirty years. I want you to conduct the ceremony."

"Are you sure you want it this way, Harry?"

"Yes I am. I cannot risk breaking down in tears in front of the office. You'll do it the right way, and you'll be fair."

"I'll do it, Harry."

He rubbed his cheeks. "I need a shave. Dear God, I must look a horror."

Sarah touched his arm to reassure him. "You look fine," she lied. "Listen, the Hilton has a salon that opens at six. I can have Charlie take you, and then, you can go home to sleep."

"How I wish I could fall asleep right here on the couch."

"You can't Harry," Sarah with a mild rebuke. "As you always say, your name is on the door."

Sarah called Charlie on her cell phone and asked him to come as quickly as possible. When he was in front of the building, Sarah helped Harry on with his coat and walked him to the waiting limo. The city was just waking up, and crowds of people marched through the slush, heading for their jobs in the canyons of New York. Sarah waved goodbye as the limo disappeared into traffic, only to suddenly realize she was re-enacting her first meeting with Harry six years earlier at Harvard. So much has changed, Sarah thought. I'm his equal now. She did not want to admit to herself that she might be even more.

The following morning, Goldsmith & Hammer was deserted except for one secretary and a single attorney standing by to handle emergencies. Helen had canceled everything. The entire office reported to a funeral home on the West Side of Manhattan. Both of Max's ex-wives came to the ceremony as did Max's son, but most of the attention seemed to focus on Harry; associates, clients and even a few judges came up to Harry to offer condolences.

Then, a polite, well-dressed young man came into the waiting area and invited everyone into the sanctuary. Inside the room were rows of wooden pews, a pulpit and a gurney on which Max's coffin rested; it was as big and outsized as the man himself. Sarah sat in the chair normally reserved for the rabbi. When the mourners had taken their seats, she stood up, walked to the podium, and began:

"Max Hammer. A blunt name for a blunt man, but, that bluntness was part of his achievement.

"Max was a man who was larger than life. I could spend an hour just talking about his love of food, his loyalty to his friends or the fervor with which he practiced law, and I would still be presenting only a small portion of him.

"We all have our stories about Max. In a few moments, I will open the floor to people who wish to share their recollections of him, but before I do that, let me share my own memories.

"Max practiced law the only way it should be practiced, with joy. He adored the law.

"In all my years of working with him, I never heard him say anything less than the blunt truth. I do not have his bluntness, but I like to think that I retain his honesty and his sense of honor.

"Whenever I stand my ground in a courtroom, or when I'm negotiating for a client, a part of Max always will be there with me. That is a fine legacy for anyone."

Sarah paused to catch her breath. "When someone dies, it simply means that he or she lives on in memory, so the appropriate thing to wish someone at a time like this is good memories. If someone wants to offer a story about Max, the floor is open."

Brad got up and said a few words about Max's loyalty and hard work. Then, Sarah looked at Harry. He seemed on the verge of tears. He started to get up, but Brad and Roy, sitting on either side of him, each put a hand on a shoulder and sat him down. At the sight of her mentor seemingly about to lose control of himself, Sarah wildly fantasized. She saw Harry as a soldier whose best friend had just been shot in front of his eyes and who now wanted to charge the machine gun that had fired the fatal bullet. But Harry sat down, and Sarah resumed command.

"Let us now recite the Kaddish prayer," she said with quiet dignity. Every mourner had been given a booklet entitled 'Memorial Service.' Sarah announced the appropriate page, and everyone read it aloud, the law firm of Goldsmith & Hammer becoming a congregation.

When it was over, Sarah smiled for the first time. "Now, what would Max say if he were here?" she asked. No one spoke. "Come on, wouldn't he say, 'Get back to work?'" Someone chuckled, and then a few people laughed. "See you back at the office," she said.

Everyone then headed back to the office except for Sarah, Harry, Brad and Roy. They got into a limousine and followed a hearse with Max's coffin out to Beth Abraham cemetery on Long Island for the internment. Not ten words were said on the trip out. Only a few moments were spent at the gravesite. The coffin was lowered, and Sarah recited the Kaddish prayer again. In keeping with Jewish custom, each mourner shoveled in a few spadefuls of earth on top of the coffin in the grave. Then, the mourners headed back to the city.

Once back in New York, Harry walked directly into his office, motioning for Sarah to follow him. He collapsed into his chair and stared up at the ceiling.

"I'm here to help you, Harry," she said.

When Harry wanted to overwhelm Sarah, he usually leaned forward and looked right at her with his blue eyes, but his body language was now that of a man who was defeated. He put both feet up on his desk and let his arms dangle at his sides. Anyone looking at him would have thought he was about to pass out.

"Sarah, this firm cannot survive the loss of you and Max. You're out of here now, but you've still committed to come back and argue Metcalf in April before the Supreme Court. I need you here on some basis until then, until we can transition."

"But, Harry, I...."

"Let me finish, Sarah. I'm about to offer you a great deal of money."

She went silent.

"Work as managing partner until Metcalf is argued, Monday morning through Thursday night. Spend the other three days of the week on Zueno, living in paradise. If you do this for me, I'll see you'll get your full partnership draw through the end of the year.

He was offering her about $450,000. "Harry, I can't say no." Who could?

Sarah didn't bother going home, even though she was dead tired. She went to her office and got to work.

CHAPTER XIX

From the journal of Harry Goldsmith ....
It took me a long time to recover from Max's death. That's what happens when you've worked side-by-side with someone for thirty-seven years. At first, I simply didn't want to go back to the office. I just stayed at home, wearing my bathrobe and slippers, and drinking tea. More than once, I asked Grace if it simply wasn't time to retire. We had plenty of money, and we had always talked about seeing the world.

But Grace would only shake her head. "You're not ready to retire," she said sadly. "We still have time to see the world. You just need something to get you back practicing law."

'Something' turned out to be Sarah. A week after Max's funeral, she appeared at our door wearing a black dress and a tan Burberry, briefcase in hand. She seemed to stand taller than ever, and when I saw her, I suddenly felt very old.

"Sarah, why are you here?" I asked. "Is something wrong at the office?"

"Yes, there is," she replied softly. "You're not there."

"She's come to take you to work, Harry," Grace said to me. "I called her. You can be ready in 30 minutes."

Before I knew what was happening, Grace had made me shave, and then, she put me in a suit. I rode down the elevator flanked by Sarah and Grace. As I got off the elevator, Grace kissed me and sent me off alone with Sarah. One crutch was gone.

The strong winter morning sun made me blink hard twice as we stepped out onto 72nd Street. It felt strange to hold a briefcase in my hand. Glancing at the ice on the sidewalk, I thought of the circle of events that began on a winter street like this one and ended with Sarah at my side as my partner. Charlie had parked the limo at the curb. Sarah helped me in.

When we walked through the doors of Goldsmith & Hammer, I felt tears welling up. Would the other partners want Max's name off the door now that he was gone? Would my name come off when my time came? Everyone greeted me politely as Sarah guided me to my office, her hand never leaving my shoulder, gently urging me forward.

Someone with extremely bad taste had put a 'Welcome Back, Harry!' sign over my desk. Sarah silently pulled it down, helped me off with my coat and then sat me down in my leather chair as she said, "Only you could ever fill it, Harry." Her words gave me comfort.

"Oh, Sarah," I gasped, and now, I did shed a few tears.

"It's okay," Sarah said. "Just stay in your office today and relax. I'll send in some mail for you to review and some papers to sign. Trust me, it'll all be routine stuff. You'll be back in command before you know it."

That's how I spent my first day back. But Sarah was right. Slowly I started to feel like myself again. Still, it took time. At the weekly partners meeting, I sat with regal bearing carefully designed to hide my fear that my mind was far away and would not be coming back. Sarah was the leader, and she wielded power as to the manor born. Yet, she never overshadowed me.

One Friday afternoon, a few weeks later, Sarah appeared in my office and handed me a few sheets of paper.

"This is a schedule of what's coming up next week and whom you will be seeing."

I looked it over quickly. "I don't see your name on it," I said.

"And you won't. You're all right now, Harry. You're back. I've got 30 days to get ready for the Metcalf argument, and it has got to have my full attention. If you have a specific problem, just call me."

Did I want to be back in charge, facing a hundred

decisions a day? Didn't I enjoy having Sarah watching over me? Part of me wanted Sarah to watch over me forever, but I knew that her respect for me was based on my strength, not my weakness.

I put the papers down on my desk, stood up and held out my hand to her. She shook it with a firm grip.

"Damn it, you're right, Sarah. I am back. You've got a date with the Supreme Court of the United States of America. Go study for it and knock 'em dead."

Sarah walked out of my office and, for all practical purposes, dropped out of the daily life of the firm. Her new routine ran something like this: she would arrive in a running suit after her morning jog. After a steam bath and shower in the health club, she'd be dressed to the hilt and seated at her desk, poring over thousands of pages of transcript. She was constantly on the phone with legal scholars throughout the country. If Sarah wasn't in her office, she'd be in the library reading cases -- and if you're arguing before the Supreme Court, you had better know every case ever written on your subject.

Goldsmith & Hammer always had a receptionist, even at midnight, and they told me Sarah was coming in at 6 a.m. and leaving at 8 p.m.

Once I stopped by the library and asked her to lunch, and she didn't even lift her head when she answered me.

"Can't Harry. It will ruin my concentration."

But Sarah would come to my office occasionally to run ideas by me. Yet, she was never obsessed by Metcalf. I have met attorneys who have been driven utterly mad by a case; Sarah wasn't like that, instead, she was as focused as a laser. I was starting to feel a sense of awe. Only later did I learn that Sarah was leading a kind of double life at the firm. While pretending to devote herself to Metcalf, she was still making many of the decisions that had to be made about the firm. She always wanted to make things as easy for me as she could.

And every Thursday night, ever the good wife, Sarah jetted off to the Caribbean with a laptop loaded with work. She would be on a 7:30 p.m. direct flight from New York to Puerto Rico. She traveled light, carrying only a large briefcase. (Lawyers call it a litigation bag.) Going to LaGuardia straight from Goldsmith & Hammer, she never changed out of her business suit, and her case held a lot of work that needed to get done. Sarah never slept on the flight.

After her plane arrived in San Juan shortly past midnight, she headed to a hotel near the airport and grabbed some sleep. When she checked out at eight the next morning, she was dressed for the climate. Gone was the woman who loved 'power suits.' In her place, was a woman wearing cut-off jeans, sandals, a brightly colored cotton shirt, sun glasses and a straw hat.

A quick flight to Ponce got her there in time for the morning ferry to Zueno. She always stood at the bow when Half Moon Bay came into view because Allen would be at the dock to greet her, his arms spread wide.

As soon as Allen grabbed the rope from the boat's skipper and tied it to the dock, he took her in his arms.

"I missed you," he'd say.

Sarah grabbed the bill of his baseball cap and swung it around to the back of his head. "Why don't you show me how much?" she asked, not at all like a lawyer.

Then, they would vanish for about an hour, emerging from their apartment on the top floor for an early lunch. Sarah would then throw herself into her strange world--hotelier, litigator and wife.

There was so much to do at the Hotel El Dorado. The rooms were cleaned by women from the village who worked as part-time maids. Sarah inspected their work and told them in broken Spanish how they could improve. The hotel was past its prime, and contractors from the mainland would have cost a fortune. So, Allen and Sarah did what they could. Then, there were the guests, constantly check-ing in and checking out, and they always wanted something.

While she was on the island, Sarah carried a smartphone clipped to her waist, and she was con-stantly getting e-mails from her life back in New York. The client in such-and-such a case wants to take an appeal. Moses thinks it's a bad idea. What to do?

Even 1,500 miles away, lightly clad for life in a hot tropical paradise, Sarah exerted a firm grip on what was happening back in chilly New York. Somehow, the control she exercised at long-distance seemed even more exciting than when she was on the scene.

Around five o'clock, Sarah relaxed and took a bit of time for herself. Switching from sandals to bare feet, she ran up and down the beach. But, somehow, it was different than circling the Central Park Reservoir.

Running in New York meant staying in condition for the extraordinary life she led. Everyday brought something new, something wonderful. Now, she was going to have a different kind of life, an infinite sameness in paradise. People from all over the world would come and go. But she and Allen would stay in this one place and grow old. Could she bear it?

Then there was Allen, her husband, who seemed to adore this place; and nothing gave her more pleasure than to know he was happy. Could there ever be an answer? She stopped thinking and just kept running.

Around sunset on Friday, she took a quick shower and changed into a dress. On the mantle over the fireplace, Sarah lit two candles. She drew no attention to the ritual, and any guest who happened to watch her light them would have assumed it was simply for atmosphere.

But Allen always stood by her side as she lit the candles, his arm around her shoulder. At no time was he ever more conscious of what she was giving up by moving to the island.

"Thank you, Sarah," he would whisper once they were lit.

"There's nothing to thank me for," she would answer. "We're together." She might have added, that is all I can say right now.

Sleep came early in Zueno. The days were so busy, and the nights were so quiet. Warm breezes from off shore brought peace, and the nights were filled with stars. Allen slept more easily than Sarah; he had left behind the cares of New York and was immersed in a new world while Sarah was managing a law firm and getting ready to argue before the Supreme Court. She got up often during the night. Once, when she woke up, she saw a look of such ease on Allen's face she asked him the next morning what he had dreamt.

"Funny you should ask. Last night, I had one of the few dreams I can recall. I was back at the University of Chicago. In the library. Miles and miles of books. I seemed to be floating past rows and rows of books filled with the most glorious knowledge in the world."

Sarah was silent.

Saturday was the busiest day on the island. Sarah had to get up extra-early for her morning run, and she would be busy straight through till about three o'clock. Then, she took time both to do paperwork she brought from New York and prepare for Metcalf.

That pushed her into the night, her last chance to be alone with Allen for a week, and she tried to make the most of it.

But Sarah had a funny experience every Saturday morning while she was on the island. At about ten o'clock, whatever she was doing, she would excuse herself and sit on the veranda for half an hour, staring at the sea, perhaps reading some mindless magazine left by a guest. It took her some time before she understood why.

Sarah caught the Sunday noon ferry back to Ponce, the first leg of the journey back to New York. Standing on the stern, she would wave good-bye to Allen until he disappeared in the distance.

It was late that night in a soothing bubble bath in her New York apartment that she solved one mystery and realized there was another.

When she stopped her exertions on Saturday morning and relaxed on the porch, she was repeating what she would have done in New York -- going to the Sephardic synagogue for reflection and the pleasures of family and friends. How would she feel when she had lived on the island for 20 years and these memories were long in her past? Sarah forced the thought out of her mind, but another one took its place. It was a question: why was it she never heard Allen quote a poem since he moved to the island?

From the journal of Harry Goldsmith....

With two weeks to go before the Metcalf argument, Sarah appeared in my office and handed me a thick law journal entitled <u>Proceedings of the North American Society of Appellate Attorneys</u>. I opened it and studied the table of contents.

"What's in this, Sarah? I've got lots to read."

"It's the first article," she said.

"The one entitled 'Reading the Supreme Court: Predicting How the Justices Will Vote'?"

"That's it. A scholar sat in on ten Supreme Court arguments and noted how many questions the judges asked each side and how tough they were. There was a definite correlation between the questioning and how the judges voted."

"I think I see what you're getting at...."

Sarah began to get excited.

"If we can predict in advance how the judges are going to vote, and, if they were leaning toward us, the other side will do anything to settle before a decision comes down."

"That would be terrific, Sarah."

Her manner changed from imperial to intimate. "Harry, I want you at the Supreme Court with me when I argue, both for moral support and to monitor the questioning."

"I was planning on going as a visitor, but it would be the peak of my career, (I stressed that word) if I could help you out, Sarah. Count on my being there."

The next Monday and Tuesday, Sarah had her

practice argument at Georgetown Law School Supreme Court Clinic, and so she spent two nights in Washington, D.C. When it was over, she called me up to say she wouldn't be back in New York until the morning. She was going to the theater that night to see *Romeo and Juliet*. She told me she'd seen the play at the same theater just before starting at the Supreme Court, and she expected it to bring back happy memories. I was glad Sarah was going; she certainly needed the rest.

CHAPTER XX

When Sarah came back to New York, she slowly began to taper off her preparation. Sarah skipped going to the island that weekend and stayed in the city.

But something had happened in Washington. After *Romeo and Juliet* was over, the audience began to put on their coats and move to the exits. Sarah stayed in her seat. It was as if she had heard a few notes of some distant, beautiful music and feared that if she moved from the spot, she would never hear it again. Then, a soft voice said, "Miss, are all right? The show is over."

Sarah turned to see an usher leaning over her shoulder with kind solicitation. "Oh, I'm sorry," Sarah said. As she stood up to go, a thought came to mind. "Would it be okay if I walked across the stage?" she asked. "I used to be an amateur actress."

"I'm sorry but that's impossible."

But Sarah thought fast. "How about if I gave the theater a $1,000 donation?"

The usher thought fast too. "Wait here. I'll get the manager."

A few moments later, the usher came back down the aisle. Following her was a bearded young man with a happy smile clad in a casual business suit. "Hi, can I help you?"

Sarah repeated her request.

The man rubbed his chin as if he were thinking, but Sarah sensed he had already made up his mind. "Are we talking $1,000 in cash?" he asked politely. Sarah opened her wallet and brandished two hundred dollars. "And I believe there's an ATM on the corner."

"You've got a deal," the man said. He took the money and turned to the usher. "James, would you go get my receipt book? Thanks." Then, the manger spoke into a walkie-talkie that he had clipped to his waist. "Moe, anyone from lighting still in the building? Good, we're going to need a spot-light in about a minute." Looking at Sarah, he said happily, "We might as well do this with a touch of class."

James came back, and the manager hurriedly wrote out a receipt. "You can give us the eight hundred when you're finished with the stage," he said.

"Thank you," Sarah said.

Silently, almost reverently, Sarah approached the stage. Once up the side steps, she walked across the center stage where a spotlight shone. She was going to get her money's worth. Standing in the spotlight, Sarah thought of all the great roles from her college days, each one was part of a world: Rosalind in *As You Like It*; Ophelia in *Hamlet*; Nora in *A Doll's House*. The hard work of learning her lines and attending rehearsals while living a second life as a top student all flooded back to her in that single moment, and for once, all her achievements in the law could not force her life on the stage back into the deep recesses of her memory where they could only return in dreams.

"Miss, Miss," asked the young manager. "Have you had your money's worth?" posing the question in the gentlest manner possible.

Sarah put on a conspiratorial smirk and walked up to the footlights. "How'd you like a $5,000 donation? I can have it in your bank by ten o'clock tomorrow?"

The young man smiled back and again pretended to take a moment to think. "I believe the question to ask at this point is, 'Whom do I have to murder?'"

"Nothing so drastic," Sarah said. "I need something in return. Listen . . . ."

From the journal of Harry Goldsmith ....

It was getting down to the wire. With Metcalf set for argument on Tuesday, Sarah showed up in my office that Monday afternoon, suitcase in one hand, brief case in the other.

"The court will hear Metcalf at ten o'clock sharp tomorrow, Harry. Be there at 9:30 a.m. Come to the side entrance on Massachusetts Avenue. Give your name to the guards. You're down as part of my team."

"I'll be there, Sarah. By the way, do you have any idea who's arguing for the other side?"

"Yes, I checked. It will be John Maynard Hastings. He's a partner at Stepman & Marston. He's good. He specializes in arguing before the Court. I must've seen him six times when I was a clerk."

"Will he be a problem?" I really wasn't worried, but I felt the need to show concern.

"No, he won't be."

I came out from behind my desk and shook her hand. "You know Sarah, this is scheduled to be your swan song. After the argument, you're out of here. You are gone from the firm, gone from the law, gone from all our lives."

"There are no good-byes for us, Harry."

Strange, I couldn't tell if she were happy or sad as she said that. I asked her where she'd be staying that night.

"With a friend in Georgetown. I haven't seen her since she got married, and she's due in a few weeks. She's a doctor. If you need to reach me, use my cell." Then, Sarah left for the airport.

I didn't get much work done for the rest of the day. Could anyone? I went home earlier than usual, got a good night's sleep and caught the 7:00 A.M.

shuttle to Washington.

As my plane landed in D.C., I realized that I was the one who had introduced Sarah to appellate work when I took her to the General Sound argument. Now, she was leading off an argument before the Supreme Court of the United States, and I would be there as her junior attorney. I felt old and young at the same time.

Like thousands of attorneys, I am admitted to argue before the Supreme Court. But, only a few hundred lawyers have ever had the chance to appear there. When I was admitted to the Supreme Court--and that was about thirty years ago-- I took the day off and went to Washington for the ceremony. Max ridiculed the whole thing, of course. "Why are you wasting a day of billable time just for a trophy to hang on your wall?" he asked. "I'll be happy to shoot you a moose." Max had a thing for shooting moose.

It was a quarter to nine when the taxi pulled up to the side entrance of the Supreme Court. The last traces of early morning sunshine--the kind that gives everything a special glow--shone on the Supreme Court building, making it seem like a large white palace of the law. With a clear blue sky above it, it seemed like the most beautiful place on earth, at least for that moment.

The guard walked me down a corridor toward a bank of elevators. "Normally we'd never do this. You'd have to go through the front entrance. However, sometimes we do favors for former clerks

-- and their friends." I just nodded.

I was trying to remember everything I saw because I knew I would never be there again. Finally, after making our way through those halls of power, the guard opened a door for me, revealing a purple curtain. "Here we are," he said. With a wave of his arm, he pulled it aside, and I found myself in the most magnificent courtroom I had ever seen. Standing alone, waiting for me, was Sarah.

I stood stock still. I had entered through the judges' entrance, and I suddenly realized I was actually standing behind the bench where the Supreme Court sat. Up until that moment, I had never felt true awe in a courtroom, but now I did.

Sarah spread her arms. "Welcome to my world, Harry," she laughed. "Come, we've got a few minutes. Let me give you the grand tour." She started to explain the symbolism behind the decor of that awesome chamber when someone came in.

"Here comes Hastings," Sarah whispered to me. Coming into the chamber was the very image of a super lawyer. My recollections are vivid: tall and ramrod straight, dark pinstripe suit and a full head of grey hair. He carried a slim leather briefcase, and his stride suggested he could walk through a brick wall. A step behind him was a similarly dressed young man with dark hair and glasses, carrying a big, heavy briefcase.

Hastings gave Sarah the briefest of nods. Then, he and the young man took seats on the other side of the aisle and began to go over notes written on yellow legal pads.

Now, the general public was let in, and the room quickly filled to capacity. There were only a few moments of murmuring when a court officer silenced everyone with two whacks of a gavel.

"Hear ye, hear ye," she said in a booming voice that belonged on the stage. "The Supreme Court of the United States is now in session. God save this Honorable Court."

After two more whacks, the nine justices of the court came out through an opening in the purple curtain behind their bench. The Chief Justice then banged his own gavel, and they took their seats.

They got right to business. "The first case is Metcalf v. Alcott Insurance."

With these words, Sarah and I moved out of the visitor's gallery and sat at a table in the well of the court, only a few feet in front of the justices. Hastings and his young associate did the same.

"Proceed," said the Chief Justice.

Without hesitation, Sarah stepped up to a podium with one white and one red light, cleared her throat and began. "May it please the Court, Mister Chief Justice, Justices of the Court, my name is Sarah Mendes for the appellant."

"You are still remembered in this Court, Ms. Mendes," said the Chief Justice. It was not spoken in a friendly tone.

"Counselor, aren't you asking this Court to

reverse a decision only four years old," Justice Miller shot out. "Have you no respect for legal precedent?"

"But your honor, this Court has reversed itself many times. In your ten years on the bench, you have authored seven opinions reversing the law. We are not so much asking the Court to reverse itself, but rather to revisit the case and rethink it."

"Why should we?" asked the judge.

"Let's start with the practical aspect. Since Sierra-Monarch was decided, more than two thousand punitive damage awards in state and federal courts have been cut. And of those cases, nearly half have sought to appeal to this Court to reverse Sierra. If nothing else, you've created a lot of extra work for the Court, reviewing all those applications."

"I'll say," the Chief Justice chuckled, and a few of the other justices joined in.

That set the tone for the rest of the argument. As it wore on, I sensed a kind of energy rise in Sarah, an aura of electric charisma that dared everyone in the room to try to take their eyes off her. Sarah was at the top of her game. Her voice was strong, her carriage erect, her mind sharp as a knife. The justices pelted her with questions -- questions I could barely follow -- and she fired off answers like a tennis pro volleying back serves.

When the white light finally came on, signaling her thirty-second warning, I felt a sense of relief. I could soon start breathing again. Sarah finished her last thought, and then said to the bench, "If there are no further questions from the bench, thank you for your kind attention."

She was already in her seat next to me when the red light flashed. It was her final masterstroke --not taking all her time. I leaned over to Sarah and whispered in her ear, "You were brilliant."

"Shh," she said, and she touched my arm to silence me. She was right. The other side had yet to be heard from.

Up to the lectern stepped John Maynard Hastings, Esquire. "Counsel for the respondent," he said, and then he began his argument. He had argued before the Court a dozen times, and it showed. He started out by calling Sarah a liar. Of course, he did so in polite, lawyerly terms. Then he called her a fool and a poor legal researcher. After that, he proceeded to explain that no rational person could possibly disagree with him.

However, then he pushed his luck too far. "There has got to be respect for legal precedent," he said.

"But counselor," Bradford jumped in, "the precedent your adversary is seeking to overturn is less than a dozen years old, it was a 5 to 4 decision by this court, and it has been furiously criticized from the day it was handed down. How much respect is a case like this entitled to?"

"Is it a second Brown v. Board of Education?" another justice asked, citing the famous case that de-segregated America's schools.

That opened a floodgate. The justices began

to fire questions at Hastings. He dealt with them smoothly, but he seemed like an actor who had performed a role many times and could do it in his sleep. There was no fire in his belly, no magic when he spoke. I just sat there keeping score, knowing my chance to argue before the Supreme Court had passed and would never come again. It belonged to the next generation, to Sarah.

As Hastings' argument wore on, I began to think the strangest thoughts about him. Again, he was the image of a super lawyer: the suit, the hair and a habit of gesturing with a long index finger pointed forward. In the seat next to him was a similarly dressed young man with glasses and dark hair. In thirty years, he would be another Hastings; that was obvious.

Finally, Hastings finished and sat down. I was forced to conclude that he was good, he was very good, but Sarah was the one with magic. The Chief Justice turned to Sarah. "Have you a rebuttal, counselor?"

Then, Sarah did the bravest thing I ever saw a lawyer do. She stood up and said, "No, your Honor." She seemed almost delighted. My position is so strong, she was saying in not so many words, that there was nothing more to add to it.

The Chief Justice picked up his gavel and rapped the bench. "This concludes the business of this Court," he said.

"Be upstanding in Court," boomed the sergeant-at-arms.

We all stood up silently as the justices rose from their chairs and filed out through the purple curtain.

When they were gone, Sarah turned to me. "Okay, now you can speak."

I felt as enthusiastic as when I had won my first trial. "Victory, Sarah, victory," I whispered softly. Then, I looked over at our adversary's table. I nodded to Sarah, and she looked too.

"Someone isn't happy," she said.

The young lawyer was holding up a pad to Hastings, who seemed very displeased. "They had your idea, Sarah," I said. "Pardon me, this is my job."

I then walked over to Hastings, shook his hand, congratulated him on a job well done and offered him my card.

"Call me next week," I said. "Perhaps we can resolve this thing before the court makes new law we might both regret."

Then I walked back to Sarah and got one hell of a shock.

CHAPTER XXI

There were also different memories about what happened next. When the white light flashed, Sarah stopped herself in the middle of a word, closed her notebook and gripped the edges of the podium. "If there are no further questions from the bench," she said, "my argument ends here."

"Thank you, counselor," said the Chief Justice. After Hastings finished his argument, the Chief Justice glanced at his watch, and then, rapped the bench with his gavel. "That concludes the business of this Court."

"Be upstanding in Court," boomed the voice of the court officer. Sarah remained standing, straight as an arrow, while the justices rose and quietly filed out of the chamber. Just before Bradford walked out, he turned and looked at Sarah. For just one moment, there seemed to be the barest hint of a smile on his lips. Then, he turned away and headed out of the chamber.

Sarah had no more worlds to conquer in the law. From now on, the bar could only offer her more and more cases or a judgeship or teaching position at some Ivy League university. She felt free, really free.

Hastings stepped over and shook her hand. "Great job," he said.

"You were excellent too," Sarah replied. In victory, magnanimity.

Then, she felt Harry's hand tapping on her shoulder. He was beaming as she turned around to face him. "Sarah, you were ... well, you know how good you were. I can only tell you that Max would've been proud, and that is saying something."

"Thanks Harry," Sarah said.

But then, with Sarah looking over Harry's shoulder, he heard her ask someone, "How did I do?" Harry was startled to realize she was not talking to him. Out of the corner of his eye, he saw a small clique coming toward them from the visitor's gallery. They were two men and a woman; somehow, they didn't look like lawyers. Taking the lead was an older man, impeccably dressed, with a strong smile and a shining pate. With one of the most confident manners Harry had ever seen, the man held out his hand to Sarah.

"Ms. Mendes, Ms. Mendes, you were brilliant. Shakespeare's Portia would have been no match for you." At these words Sarah left Harry and ran to greet this strange man with the enthusiasm of a youngster.

Harry was bewildered. He began to ask, "Sarah, what is this?" But she cut him off.

"Oh Harry, I'm sorry. Let me introduce you. This is Mr. Hilton Gould of the Georgetown Shakespeare Theater. He came here with some people to hear me argue. It was my audition. You always said arguing an appeal is like being on stage."

"Audition? For what?" Harry demanded.

"Permit me to explain, Mr. Goldsmith," Gould said with a commanding courtliness. "Back in her college days, I saw Ms. Mendes play Ophelia, and she so impressed me that I offered her a chance to apply to our graduate program in classical acting. She couldn't defer law school, so she declined to audition for us. But imagine my delight when she called me a few days ago and asked if the offer was still open and, if it were, would an argument before the Supreme Court take the place of a dramatic monologue? I agreed. And now, Ms. Mendes, I am pleased to say that you have passed the audition, and you are admitted to the program."

Sarah beamed. Harry did not. "I see," he said dryly. "Sarah, could I see you back in New York tomorrow?"

"I can't Harry," Sarah replied. "I've got to make a quick trip to Zueno. Just give me three days."

Part of Harry wanted to tell her to stay in Zueno and never come back, but he managed to control himself. "All right, I'll see you in three days."

Picking up his coat and briefcase, Harry nodded to the group and walked out of the courtroom. As he walked alone down the courthouse steps, Harry saw the sun shining squarely on the Capitol dome; a warm breeze in the air reminded the world that winter was over and spring had arrived, but Harry would have none of it. He hailed a cab, told the driver, "Airport, New York shuttle," and slammed the door.

Sarah typically walked into Harry's office after a quick knock on the door, but now, three days later, she meekly asked Helen to announce her as if she were a cautious jobseeker just out of law school. Harry, still smarting from the surprise he got at the Supreme Court, debated a variety of crude replies. "Tell her to get lost," leapt to mind. But that made no sense; there were too many places she could go. He finally admitted to himself that none of the rebuffs that came to mind would be appropriate. He was a gentleman; Max had been the street fighter. And it would take all of Harry's patience to make sense out of this strange situation.

"Ask her to come in," he said evenly.

Sarah came in and sat down, quiet and reserved. Is this contrition? Harry wondered.

"Sarah," Harry began in his calmest voice. "I know you would never set out to hurt me. We've been through too much together, but you gave me quite a shock at the Supreme Court, and I don't like surprises. What's going on?"

Sarah was quiet. Then she said, "I didn't sleep last night wondering how I could explain all of this to you."

"Perhaps, it would be easier if I asked the questions. What happened to your plans to open a hotel?"

She spoke quietly as if she feared losing control if she raised her voice. "Oh Harry, that was running away. I saw that after a few weeks, but I couldn't admit it. Allen and I would never have been happy there, and we would've turned on each other and probably broken up."

"Where does acting come from? You've never mentioned it." Silence.

Harry was still curious. "Tell me, just how did you talk Allen out of the island? It seemed to me that he was pretty settled in there."

Sometimes an eternity can pass in the time it takes to draw one's breath.

She had spent the night before the argument with Ellen Stein in Georgetown. But now, Ellen had a new last name, and her first child was a month away.

Ellen's neighborhood was composed of town houses and private homes on a cobblestone street out of the nineteenth century. There were gas lamps and little gardens with wrought iron fences. It reminded Sarah of her Harvard days.

After showing Sarah the nursery, Aaron headed off to his study to work at his computer while the women settled down in the living room. Ellen curled up on the couch, Buddha-like, with her large belly; Sarah sat opposite her in a reclining chair, nursing a cup of hot chocolate.

The room glowed with soft light. It was painted in antique yellow. One wall was dominated by a fireplace with a captain's clock on the mantle and a mirror behind it. Ellen had closed the shutters on the bay windows that opened on to the street. I feel like I'm back in college, Sarah thought. But, on to the business at hand. Sarah had come for professional advice, and that is what she got.

Ellen blew away the steam rising off her hot chocolate. "It is self-abnegation on Allen's part. That's pretty straight forward."

"What do you mean?" Sarah asked.

"Oh, you know what the words mean," Ellen replied with a hint of professional triumph. "You're just too close to the situation to see it for yourself."

"Tell me," Sarah asked her....

.

After the argument at the Supreme Court, Sarah had many hours to fill before starting her journey to Zueno. The first thing she did was telephone Ellen to let her know the case went well.

"I knew it would," Ellen chuckled. "And I'm sure it'll go well on the island when you talk to Allen."

Sarah had her doubts.

She walked the few blocks from the Supreme Court to Union Station where she grabbed a quick bite. Then, of all things, she took in a movie at the multiplex on the lower level. Finally, it was time for the cab ride to the airport for the flight to Florida. Allowing for flying time, delays between connections and the like, Zueno was at least ten hours away.

She did not sleep on the flight, nor did she do

paperwork. Indeed, there was none to do. Officially, her legal career was over. She just stared out the window, even after the sun set.

Sarah decided not to fly directly to Zueno from San Juan. Instead, she flew to Ponce just in time to catch the morning ferry. She arrived at Zueno just before eleven o'clock, coming in at the village dock a short drive from the hotel.

As she stepped down the gangplank of the boat, Sarah heard a honking horn that somehow seemed to say it was beeping just for her. It was Allen with a jeep. When they bought the hotel, Ib had thrown it in.

Bounding out of the jeep, Allen embraced her joyfully. "You finished up in a blaze of glory. I read about it on the internet. You're an islander now."

Under the guise of weariness, she picked her words carefully. "Allen, I love you. I've been living on adrenaline for three days. I need sleep. Can I grab a few hours?"

Sarah had avoided a direct response to Allen's pronouncement, but Allen was so happy to see her that he didn't notice. Sarah said very little on the short ride back to the El Dorado. Ten minutes later, with a cup of herbal tea on a night-table by her bed, Sarah laid down to sleep.

Hours later, after she woke up rested, Sarah asked Allen to join her for a walk on the beach. The morning sun was strong, but it was not yet at its peak. A warm breeze blew from over the sea. T No one was close enough to hear them.

"Allen," she said, gripping his hand for dear life, "I need to talk to you."

He grew apprehensive. "What about?"

"Your love of the island. How real is it?"

Now, Allen was upset, thinking aloud. "How can you question it now? We're building a life here. Are you going back to the law after all we've done to break away?"

She stopped walking and turned to face him. "Allen, it's not that. If you love this place, then, my home is here."

"Of course I love it! What's the problem?"

"Because there's nothing about you that suggests someone who can be happy on an island, living away from the world. There's everything that says you were meant to teach English somewhere or do something else with the words you love.

"Your entire background, your family, everyone demanded you become a lawyer. They all rejected you when you couldn't do it. And you punished yourself by taking menial jobs and then exiling yourself on an island. Maybe that's why you don't quote poetry anymore. It's not in you to be a lawyer, and it's not in you to be an innkeeper on an island. You're writing yourself out of life."

She paused to catch her breath. "You don't have to be a lawyer any more to please your family or anyone else. If you want to stay on the island, then so do I, but you don't have to."

Allen just stared at her. "Sarah, where is all this

coming from?"

Hot chocolate: somehow it brought Sarah back to when she was sitting in Ellen's living room. She took a sip and asked her next question: "How on earth do you get someone to accept the hard truth in one moment? I thought psychotherapy takes years."

"Sometimes it does," Ellen replied. "But I've noticed that at other times there is a shortcut into the human soul."

"What's that?"

"Love."

"Come off it," Sarah retorted.

"I'm not kidding," Ellen said. "If someone feels alone and isolated in the world that makes my job almost impossible. For a patient like that, his problems are his only companions. Then, my work is cut out for me. But, if someone has love in his life, then his problems are an impediment, and he'll do anything to shed them. I've never seen it fail."

"But, Sarah," Allen gasped, "I want to stay here, and I thought you did too."

Sarah replied with a kind of loving sternness. "I want what you want, what you honestly want."

Allen's mouth hung open, wordlessly. He turned his head from side to side in utter confusion. Finally, he stopped and looked directly at Sarah. "May I take a walk and think this over?"

"Take all the time in the world, Allen. I'll be here for you, always." Then, he turned and started walking down the beach. After he'd gone a few steps, he turned and waved at Sarah. She waved back. Sarah knew that it took three hours to walk around the island, assuming one was going at a fast clip, which Allen wasn't.

Back at the hotel, the computer screen in the office was blinking off-and-on.

There were e-mails asking for reservations. She took care of them. An hour later, the seaplane arrived with guests. Sarah checked them in and carried their bags herself. She just wanted to get her mind off things, and there was a lot to do at the El Dorado.

Finally, after a couple of hours of work, with everything under control, Sarah went out to the hammock on the porch, put a straw hat over her face and relaxed.

The gentle rocking of the hammock and the soft warmth of the early afternoon soothed her. Had she really argued before the Supreme Court less than 48 hours ago? Was she even a lawyer? What was real? The paradise she found herself in at the moment? The theater? The law? They seemed one and the same.

"Sarah, Sarah...."

She lifted her hat with thumb and forefinger. It was Allen, standing over her. "Well?" she asked.

"Just call me Dr. Wasserman, your over-worked, underpaid professor of English."

Sarah threw her hat high up in the air ....

Harry's heart began to soften. "But why didn't

you ever tell me this before?"

"And what would you have said if I had?"

Harry thought for a moment before he finally answered. "I probably would have suggested that you work harder to put these thoughts out of your mind. If that didn't work, I would have suggested therapy."

"Do you know what a *malach* is, Harry?"

"No, I don't."

She sighed. "It's a Hebrew word meaning angel, but its literal meaning is messenger. Allen is my angel, my messenger, he came into my life and reminded me of the other world that I gave up when I opted for law school. Now, I can't get it out of my head. Besides, I love him, and so, now I have to follow my heart."

Harry gently asked if this was the end of the law for Sarah.

She shook her head. "I just don't know. I'd like a year's leave of absence to take the acting degree. Let me have my dream. Then, let's see what the future holds. Maybe I'll make it as an actress. Maybe I'll come back to the law and never give acting a second thought. Perhaps, I'll find a way to combine both worlds. But I've got to do this."

"What about Allen?"

"His family pushed him into the law. He's going to get his doctorate in English. It's not too late for him to teach. That was always his dream. I'm renting my New York apartment and moving back into my old place in Washington. I never sold it, I just leased it out. I think we'll manage."

Harry got up, walked around his desk and stood in front of her. "Sarah, this firm was begun with a dream. How can I deny you your dreams? Follow your heart with our blessings." He held out his hands to Sarah. She grasped them and stood up, face-to-face with Harry. "There'll be no problem with a leave of absence. I'll see to that. Just know from the bottom of my heart that you're a wonderful lawyer and a magnificent woman, and, if I've played any part in shaping you, then my life has been well spent."

"Thank you, Harry." Then she let out a nervous laugh. "I could really use some of your brandy."

Without a word, Harry went to his private bar and poured two glasses. As he handed one to Sarah, he asked if she would keep working at the firm until her school began in the fall. Sarah said she'd like nothing better. "One more thing," Harry said. "I want you to run everyday activities, Max's old job, until you leave. That means I want you in his old office next to mine."

"Of course, Harry," Sarah responded with joy.

"Good, now get to work," Harry barked with mock sternness. Then, they clicked their glasses, Harry thinking of the past while Sarah thought of the future.

She turned and headed out of Harry's office, but, just as she reached the doorway, he called out her name. Sarah turned back. Harry was standing at his desk smiling, his arms folded across his chest. He had the look of a man who thought he had discovered a great secret.

"Sarah," he said, "I don't think you really want to

be an actress. This is just a year's diversion for you. I think you're really just doing this for the sake of Allen's conscience. You don't want him to feel guilty about leaving the law for literature."

There was silence between them for a brief moment. Sarah seemed about to speak, but then, she didn't. Instead, she held a finger up to her lips, turned away and walked off without a backward glance.

Suddenly, Harry felt no triumph at all. He sat down at his desk, grabbed at some papers that lay close at hand and started reading them even though the words meant nothing to him. He had to do something to get rid of the shame he felt. He had just seen the forbidden; he had just glimpsed the very heart of Sarah's love.

There comes a time--or should come a time -- in every life when all is at peace, the past is known and understood, and forgiven, and the future is bright with hope. Doubly blessed is one who knows such a moment when she is young.

On a bright sunny day in late June, Sarah found herself sharing tea with her mother in the Mendes apartment overlooking Central Park. The women were making small talk when Sarah suddenly questioned her.

"Mama, when I wanted to take a year off to study acting before law school and papa said no, you were silent. Why?"

Her mother laughed, it was a soft, simple chuckle,

seeming to come more from the wisdom of years than humor.

"Because, Sarah, you would not have been following a dream, you would have been running away from growing up. If it really were a dream back then, you would not have asked permission, you would have taken the scholarship and gone to acting school."

This left Sarah even more confused. "But you were willing to let me stay on in Israel when I met that boy on the army base."

"Sarah, the only way you would have stayed is if I had ordered you to come home."

Sarah was quiet.

"If you'll think back Sarah, we had this conversation some years ago. Your hair is still black. When it is the color of mine, and you have your own children, you'll understand." Somehow Sarah sensed that, in the course of time and years to come, she would.

EPILOGUE

It was the last days of August. Summer was still in the air at mid-day, but dusk brought cool breezes and long shadows down the canyons of Manhattan. Courts calendars began to get busier after slacking off in July. The seasons were changing and so were the lives of those at Goldsmith & Hammer.

Harry held up his hand and cleared his throat, asking for silence with his usual polite firmness. He stood in the firm library with the entire staff of more than forty-five lawyers present. The firm had grown so much that the library was the only room that could hold them all and then, only when most of the tables and chairs were removed. Sarah stood next to Harry on his right. To his left, standing by the door, were the four new associates who would be starting right after Labor Day. On the wall behind Harry was a framed picture covered by a velvet mantle.

"I've called everyone together because it seemed to be the best moment to honor the past, present and future of Goldsmith & Hammer. Let us proceed in that order."

He looked to his right. "Sarah, would you do the honors?"

With a solemn flourish, Sarah pulled the cover off the picture, revealing an exquisite oil portrait of Max. Chin proudly raised, his eyes stared off into the distance with the grandeur of a prophet, and his gray hair looked as if it had been carved out of marble. Under one arm was a law book. Behind Max was the federal courthouse in downtown Manhattan, the same one where he had been led out of a courtroom in handcuffs. It was someone's private joke.

Then, Harry remembered it was Sarah who arranged for the portrait.

There were a few gasps from those assembled; Max had never looked so good alive.

Harry waited until things calmed down; then, he nodded to Sarah. "A few words are in order," he said.

Sarah stood in front of the portrait. "You know," she began, "It is hard for me to picture a Goldsmith & Hammer without Max. But now, we have new attorneys coming in who will not have had the privilege of working with him. So, it is time to build his legend. Max founded this firm with Harry more than thirty years ago. They were just two young lawyers with a part-time secretary in a one room office. But they had brains and sweat. A lot of lawyers have those things, but they had dreams and a vision, and that is rare.

"When Max died last year, he left behind one of the powerhouse boutique law firms in New York. In our time, we've handled gigantic cases, we've gone head-to-head with the biggest firms in America and the federal government, and we've been victorious in the Supreme Court of the United States. This firm will live on after Max. It will continue to achieve great things, and no finer tribute can be paid to anyone practicing law."

There was a round of applause as Harry shook Sarah's hand. As he did, he whispered, "You really are a great actress." Sarah only smiled.

Harry spoke. "Now that we have honored the past, let us talk about the present and look to the future. Sarah Mendes has been with this firm for six years. She has been part of the team that helped Goldsmith & Hammer achieve its dreams. I predict, that in years to come, she will be as much of a legend in this firm as Max. But now, as you know, she is taking a year off to pursue her own dreams. Sarah will be studying acting. What she will do after her year is over is an open question, but she will always be welcome back here. And, if she chooses to take another path after her year of study is over, she will always have our best wishes."

There was more applause. Sarah stood her ground in front of those assembled before her. Suddenly, Harry put a bunch of roses in her arms.

"In anticipation of your first opening night."

Now, she began to shed a tear. "Thank you," she said. "I'll remember all of you."

Applause, and then, everyone broke ranks for the refreshments. In twenty minutes, the library was empty except for Sarah and Harry. They spoke with the ease of friends.

"Good-bye, Sarah," he said. "I want you to know that you've earned the right to be doing this. All I ask is that you drop me a line or give me a call from time to time."

"Count on it, Harry," she said. "I'll send you copies of all my notices."

"Charlie is waiting outside. You should be on your way." The last gift of the firm to Sarah was a limo ride to Washington.

Sarah knew what she had to do. She went to her office and changed from her business suit into jeans and a sweatshirt. She shut off her computer for the last time and put a greeting on her phone referring all her calls back to the main switch board. Carrying a small suitcase with personal effects from her office in one hand, and the roses in another, she locked her office door and headed for the exit. Walking down the corridor, she saw all the eager young lawyers hard at work. Sarah sensed that she would soon be forgotten, and somehow, it pleased her; it freed her for the future.

When she walked out of the building onto Fifth Avenue, the shadows were long and the street was filled with people, moving quickly. Ahead of her was the company limo, with Charlie opening the door for her. "Hello, Ms. Mendes," he said.

Inside the car was Allen. "Did you get through it okay?" he asked.

She kissed him. "It was rough. I shed a tear, and for a moment, I felt like calling everything off. But then, Harry gave me these." She held out the roses.

"What a nice touch," Allen said. "He's really a great guy."

He wasn't so nice when he let Max tear you apart. But, then again, he only wanted someone working for him who was a good, tough lawyer. Max was his proving ground.

The limo pulled out into traffic. "Where to, Ms. Mendes?" Charlie asked as a matter of habit.

"Washington," Sarah said.

Holding hands, they headed out of New York. They rode in silence as night fell. When they reached the lights of Philadelphia, Allen turned to look at Sarah. She was still, and her head rested against the door, her smooth face wreathed by her thick black hair. The bouquet of roses lay in her lap. As Allen looked closely at her, he saw that she had begun to sleep, and to dream.

CPSIA information can be obtained
at www.ICGtesting.com
Printed in the USA
BVHW081444150222
629077BV00010B/482

9 781977 245526